SOME

About the story

Greg, divorced, past middle age, having lost his family and purpose in life reckons drifting along the South Coast in his yacht is all that life has to offer.

Mary, who he meets in extraordinary circumstances, not only arouses his ardour but also a zest for life he thought he had lost.

Swift, passionate, and intense, their romance inspires Greg, whose propensity for adventure brings him into conflict with the person he loves, but whose morals are on a higher plain.

Despite covert activities at sea bringing them into conflict the bond grows stronger as they share action, mystery, and tragedy. New life restores their dulled faith.

For those not entirely familiar with boating and sailing a glossary of terminology is included.

About the author

Educated at Charterhouse, and the 'University of Life' as he puts it, he is the son of an advertising pioneer. He became a pioneer himself after the farce of board meetings in The Palace of Westminster under the chairmanship of Robert Maxwell MP. He set up his own filmsetting business when hot-metal was still the norm. He also helped Unilever pioneer ink-jet printing in Britain with the largest printing machine in the world at that time.

Racing motorcycles, flying for hundreds of hours around the country in sailplanes, and sailing at sea single-handed, gave him an appetite for "a touch of danger with adventure". Always a 'doer' but now physically handicapped, he writes for recreation and, hopefully, the enjoyment of others as well as himself.

© *Rex Garland, 2013*
First published in Great Britain, 2013
All rights reserved.
No part of this publication may be reproduced
or transmitted in any form or by any means,
electronic or mechanical, including photocopy,
recording, or any information storage and
retrieval system, without permission
in writing from the copyright holder.

British Library Cataloguing-in-Publication Data.
A catalogue record for this book is available
from the British Library.

*The characters in this story are fictitious and any
resemblance to real persons, living or dead is purely
coincidental. Actual persons named in this publication
are for the purpose of establishing historical facts as
known at the time of the action portrayed.*

ISBN 978-0-7223-4312-8
Printed in Great Britain by
Arthur H. Stockwell Ltd
Torrs Park   Ilfracombe
Devon   EX34 8BA

"If I have learned one thing in my fifty-four years, it is that it is very good for the character to engage in sports which put your life in danger from time to time. It breeds a saneness in dealing with day to day trivialities which probably cannot be got in any other way, and a habit of quick decisions."

From the Autobiography of an Engineer
Slide Rule, by Nevil Shute
(VINTAGE BOOKS, London).

ACKNOWLEDGMENTS

Thanks to AP Watt at United Agents LLP on behalf of the Trustees of the Estate of the late Nevil Shute Norway for permission to include the quotation from *Slide Rule*.

Many thanks also to my friend and mentor, Martin Corrick, for his help in putting this book together.

I am also grateful for the skills of Don Hickey (front cover) and Dennis Moore (back cover).

And finally, my apologies to the good people in towns and harbours along the South Coast of England, and in Cherbourg, France, for any inaccuracy of account due to my memory of twenty-five years ago.

GLOSSARY OF BOATING TERMINOLOGY USED

Aft — *Toward the stern.*

Bar — *A shallow at entrance to river caused by deposits of silt, sand or mud brought there by the ebb tide.*

Beam — *Overall width of boat. 'Wind on the beam' is at a right angle to hull (beam reach).*

Bollard — *A round fitting to which ropes are tied or looped.*

Boot-top — *Painted line on hull at waterline.*

Brightwork — *On deck metal fittings or varnished woodwork.*

Burgee — *Small flag or pennant. If flown from masthead, indicates wind direction.*

Cleat — *A "T"-shaped fitting around which warps are "cleated", tied, or looped.*

Close-hauled — *Point of sailing closest into wind.*

Cove-line — *Decorative painted line on hull just below deck level.*

Dodger	*Canvas or vinyl protection from bad weather.*
Forward	*Toward the bow. Vernacular: "for'ard".*
Freeboard	*Distance from deck level to waterline.*
Genoa	*Large headsail (or foresail).*
Go about	*Moving helm and sails to enable boat to sail on the other tack (tacking).*
Goose-winged	*See "**Run**".*
Halyard	*Rope for hauling sails or other gear up mast.*
Headsail	*Jib or genoa ahead of mast and hanked or rolled onto forestay.*
Hove-to	*Sails and helm set to allow boat to lie nearly stationary in water.*
Jib	*Smaller headsail.*
Leading light	*Sectional light, red, white, green, beamed seawards to indicate safe passage.*
Luff	*To point into wind to a position where sails no longer draw (i.e. they flap).*
Mainsail	*Large sail aft of mast (Bermuda rig).*
Marlin Spike	*Sharp instrument used mainly for ropework.*
Pulpit	*Railing around deck at bow.*
Pushpit	*Railing around deck at stern.*
Painter	*Rope attached to bow of small boat for purpose of tying it up.*

Race	Stretch of rough and confused water caused by the tidal flow over rocks, usually off headlands.
Reach	Point of sail when wind is more on the beam than "close-hauled"; from close-reach through to "beam-reach" then (aft of the beam) broad reach.
RIB	Acronym: rigid inflatable boat.
Run	When wind is dead astern. Headsail and mainsail can be deployed – one to starboard, one to port. This is called "goose-winged".
Sheet	Rope used to control sails.
Shrouds	Wires attached from mast to side deck. Together with forestay and backstay prevents mast from falling down.
Sponson	Inflated tube around RIB that keeps it afloat.
Springs	Mooring warps from boat to shore – taken from forward to aft and vice versa.
Square away	Tidy up.
Tack	Move helm to put wind on other side of sails. "Port tack" = wind from port side.
Warp	Any rope used for marine purposes: most commonly for tying boat to its berth.

To Jill

SOMETIMES

A Novel by

Rex Garland

ARTHUR H. STOCKWELL LTD
Torrs Park, Ilfracombe, Devon, EX34 8BA
Established 1898
www.ahstockwell.co.uk

CHAPTER ONE

Summer 1984

That summer of 1984 was warm, dry, and sunny in the south of England. This suited Greg Norfield as he sailed to harbours in the Solent and westwards, trying to forget his past, not caring much about the present or the future. The Cold War with the Soviet Union and the ever present threat of nuclear destruction were not on his mind. Right now the quiet berth in the Medina River marina would suffice.

The sudden lurch of the boat and the thud of footsteps on the side deck caused the coffee on the saloon table to spill. No request to come aboard, just footsteps on the deck and the ugly face of a stranger in the companionway; an uncouth and menacing face.

'You Greg?'

'Yep.'

'Fred sent me. Let's go.'

The stranger made his way down the steps into the saloon, a stocky, coarse-looking man in his fifties, hatless with long lank greasy dark hair, a dirty white shirt, no tie and a shabby grey suit. He looked as if he hadn't shaved or washed for several days. He carried a large battered old brown leather bag, and after thrusting a bundle of notes into Greg's hand he settled himself down in the corner to read *The Sporting Times*. Greg wrinkled his nose as it told him he'd be better off in the fresh air of the cockpit than in the company of his passenger.

As they cleared Cowes Harbour and set sail eastwards up the Solent, the swell made itself felt and Greg's shabby companion poked his head out into the cockpit. He looked around and then at Greg.

Without a smile he said, 'Oy don't feel so good. Need a bit o' fresh air.'

'The loo is up forward, beyond the curtain,' said Greg.

'Oy'm not that bad,' replied the stranger and retired below, once again to read his paper.

Greg settled the boat on a broad reach and relaxed in the cockpit. He contemplated his pocketful of cash and the easy task ahead to earn it.

His dreaming was shattered by the sudden arrival from astern, where he was not looking, of a powerful grey launch which came close alongside. It was a Customs launch. A man in uniform was shouting across to the yacht.

'Good morning, sir! Do you have any other persons on board?'

'Yes I do, and from the sound of the pumping of the loo he's being sick.'

Within seconds the Customs launch had moved close enough for three uniformed officers to climb aboard Greg's boat. Two of them hastened down into the saloon and the third stayed with Greg in the cockpit.

'What's up?' cried Greg, alarmed at the speed of events, and even more alarmed as the other two officers dragged his guest out into the cockpit and bundled him protesting on board their launch.

Without answering Greg's question the third officer told him to hold his course and went below to return with the leather bag, which he handed across the deck to his companion in the launch.

'Now,' said the officer, 'start your engine, take down your sails and I'll tell you what we do. You turn round and return to Cowes at your best speed.'

On the way back he made it clear to Greg that he was implicated in the possession of a class-A substance, which appeared to be cocaine. Greg gleaned the last piece of information when he overheard the officer talking via his portable with his companions on the launch ahead of them. Greg was directed to tie up at the Customs Quay pontoon. He was escorted to an office with bars on the only window, six plain chairs round a plain table. They even pulled one out for him to sit on. A trio of Customs officers from the launch waited standing and silent until an older man they addressed as "sir" entered the room and told them to be seated. He looked at Greg.

'I am the senior preventive officer here. Perhaps you would like to tell us how you came to have your passenger and his baggage on board?'

Gregory Norfield was fifty-four years old, just over six feet tall with short, curly greying hair. He was clean-shaven and often had a look on his face as if he was trying to suppress a smile. Women called him good-looking in a rugged sort of way.

'I was in the pub last night,' said Greg, 'I was approached by the only other man in the bar and we sat by the fire with our pints, chatting. He told me his name was Fred. I thought he was another yachtsman, until after a couple more jars he revealed that he was making a bob or two from shipping people over to the mainland. He told me that there was a seamen's strike affecting the ferries, and there were some who would pay silly money to keep important appointments. All the available aircraft were booked for days.'

As he warmed to his story, the four officers listened in silence.

'Being financially embarrassed at the moment, I agreed to take Fred's friend to Portsmouth and be handsomely rewarded. I can now see how stupid this was. I had no idea what was going on. It just sounded to me like money for old rope.'

There was a long silence.

They looked at Greg coldly, until eventually one

of the officers said to Greg, 'Do you really think we should believe that claptrap?'

'Yes, I do,' said Greg, 'because it really is true. I have never been in any sort of trouble. You have all my personal details and I've given you the names and phone numbers of several people who can vouch for me.'

The senior officer told him to wait where he was as he signalled the others to leave the room. He was alone in the cheerless small room. The barred window only afforded the view of a brick wall. It was nearly an hour before the earlier spokesman and another officer returned.

'My name is Don Carruthers,' said the older man. 'I am in charge of the Island station. I am inclined to believe your story, but I must warn you that you may be the subject of charges for what is an extremely serious crime. However, with your co-operation we will give you an opportunity to help us and clear yourself of any wrong-doing. It may take a day or two, during which time I require you to remain with your boat in the marina you used yesterday and follow our instructions. Do I have your consent?'

'You certainly do, sir,' replied Greg, much relieved that he wasn't going to be locked up.

'OK,' said the officer, 'you will be free to take your boat to the marina this evening at the time when you would have arrived back from Portsmouth – let's say about five o'clock. In the meanwhile you will remain tied up on our pontoon here until one of my officers comes to tell you that you may move. Is that clear?'

'It is,' said Greg.

He breathed a massive sigh of relief as he made his way back to his boat.

At about four o'clock Greg heard a knock on the coachroof and a female voice called out, 'Permission to come on board?'

'Of course,' he shouted from down in the saloon, and felt a small lurch as his visitor climbed from the pontoon to the side deck.

She was in the dark uniform of the customs service with just one gold ring on the cuff of her jacket. Her blond hair swept back into a short ponytail. He guessed she was around thirty years of age. She was lithe and had blue friendly eyes and a clear complexion. There was just a hint of dimples when she smiled and broke that otherwise serious and rather severe look she had when she first appeared at the top of the companionway.

Far more appealing than he imagined an official of Customs & Excise should look, she nimbly descended the steps into the saloon and introduced herself: 'My name is Mary Rowlinson.'

Greg held out his hand which was taken firmly.

'Please sit down,' he said.

'My job is to outline to you our plans for catching up with your man Fred. We have spent much time this afternoon checking on your story. If you don't like what we propose, you may say so, but after promising your co-operation this morning I assume you will agree. Is that the case?'

'Perfectly, Miss Rowlinson,' replied Greg.

His offer to make a cup of tea was accepted. He put the kettle on.

'Please don't interrupt me until I have finished,' she said.

Greg nodded agreement whilst he prepared the tea.

'At five o'clock I shall return here and accompany you to the East Cowes Marina. At all times until this exercise is over you and I are to behave as good friends who have not met for a long time. We will start now by me calling you Greg and you calling me Mary.'

Greg's expression of concentration turned into surprise.

'Now, that would be nice.'

As she prepared to speak the corners of her mouth turned up and Greg's eyes spotted those dimples again as she smiled.

'I can tell you that the greatest danger of failure in a surveillance operation such as this is that the one we are trying to observe suspects a trap. After tying up in the marina, we will go to the pub where you say you met this Fred character.'

'Excuse me,' interrupted Greg. 'It's a fact. I did meet him in the pub.'

Mary frowned.

'We believe that he, knowing you were to return to Cowes after dropping his man off in Portsmouth, will attempt to contact you again. He will want to know what happened. He won't know we have his friend locked up and likely to stay that way until he appears in court. You will tell Fred, whenever he turns up, that his friend had changed his mind and asked to be dropped off on the other side of Portsmouth Harbour at the Camper & Nicholsons marina in Gosport.'

'Why?' interrupted Greg.

Mary frowned yet again.

'You of course have no idea why. It was none of your business. It did not inconvenience you in any way, but you have done what was asked. Is that clearly understood? No more, no less.'

'I have a feeling that I am not in a position to argue.' Greg said with a wry smile. 'I'm beginning to see the plot, but what happens if he doesn't turn up at the pub tonight?'

'We will return to your boat and wait until he does,' she said with conviction. 'My colleagues will be watching us round the clock. We are very determined to identify these people, who we believe are known to the authorities.' She got up to leave. 'I am going now. On my return we will motor up to the marina.'

Half an hour later when she returned, Mary was dressed in navy-blue slacks, a pink and white sweater, blue deck shoes and a short navy woollen jacket with brass buttons. Greg started the engine. She released the warps from the mooring cleats, threw them back on the deck, and pushed the boat away from the pontoon as she climbed over the safety lines.

'I guess you've done a fair bit of boating in your job,' Greg said.

'Not just in the job. I sailed a lot with my dad when he was alive.'

They motored up the Medina river, past the ferry port and the floating bridge, until the marina was reached on the port hand.

'You find a berth,' Mary said, 'and I'll step off and tie her up. Don't forget to use my first name at all times. We're old friends, Greg, remember?'

'That I would like, Mary.'

'That's better,' she replied.

They made their way to the pub, Mary's arm linked with Greg's as they walked. She moved her head close to Greg's.

'This does not mean that I am giving you the come-on. We don't have to let everyone hear our conversation,' she continued, 'but acting as friends is vital to the success of this operation. Tell me what you've been up to these last few years.'

With the ice broken, Greg told her about his meanderings along the South Coast and about the articles he wrote for the yachting press, from which he scratched a living.

'Mary, if it were not that you have found out what an idiot I can be, if it were not that you are a preventive officer with Customs and me being effectively under arrest, I would be looking forward to this evening with you.'

'Relax, Greg. We have a job to do. If it comes out right it could go a long way to clearing your name.'

When they reached the pub he bought them beers and they settled at a corner table in the saloon bar, from where they could observe the only entrance from the street.

'Don't make it obvious,' she said as she leaned over to whisper in Greg's ear, 'but have a good look round to see if he's here.'

Greg began to wish he had met Mary earlier and under different circumstances.

'We'd better not get too sozzled,' she said, laughing and talking quietly again close to his ear. 'Despite the fact that I'm beginning to enjoy the evening, don't let's forget this is serious work.'

Greg ordered their food. Just ten minutes after they had started the meal Fred came in from the street and took a quick look round. When their eyes met Greg raised an arm and waved him over to join the two of them, but he turned on his heel as if he hadn't seen them.

Mary looked enquiringly at Greg.

'That was him,' he said.

'Are you certain?'

'Absolutely. I spent two hours with him in here only yesterday. No doubt.'

Mary jumped up and made for the door.

'I'm going to tell my colleague outside. My guess is that he won't go far. He'll be waiting for a chance to quiz you on your own, and he'll probably follow you back to the boat. You leave in ten minutes – you'll be followed by my colleague. Give me the keys. I'll be aboard your boat when you get back. Our guess is that Fred needs to know what happened to his friend, and one way or another we'll grab him tonight. Don't forget your story. No more, no less.'

There was no sign of anyone on the pontoon when Greg returned to the boat. He pushed back the hatch, and in the shadows below, lit only by the pontoon lights shining through the windows, was Mary. With her forefinger pressed firmly on to her lips she signalled him to come down into the saloon and whispered to him to put the coffee on while she waited in the darkened forecabin behind the curtain.

'Mary,' he said quietly, 'do you think he followed me?'

'Schssh' was all he got back. 'Be patient.'

Fred's arrival on the boat was, like that of his friend earlier in the day, without the conventional request to come aboard. A lurch as he clumsily clambered over the safety lines was quickly followed by his head peering over the washboard into the cabin.

'What 'appened to our friend?' he said angrily.

'What do you mean?' replied Greg.

''E never turn up in Pompey. What you do wiv 'im?'

'Keep your hair on, Fred. He changed his mind and told me he wanted to be put down on the other side of the harbour, so that's what I did.'

'Why?'

'I have no idea. It was none of my business. I did as he asked. It made no difference to me. What's your problem?'

Fred quickly departed, but there was only one way off the pontoon and it was blocked by two policemen. They quickly had him in handcuffs and bundled him away. Fred's curses on Greg could be heard as he was propelled up the gangway. Aboard the yacht, Mary emerged from behind the curtain.

'Well done, Greg,' she said. 'You did well there. We have enough evidence to get him locked away as well as his friend. I'm personally convinced of your story, but that's up to my boss. I'll put in a good word for you.' She was smiling as she said this, and he took her hand and thanked her.

'With a little more practice,' he said, 'I guess I could take up acting.'

'Greg, you mustn't leave this berth until you have our permission. I'll try to arrange that for tomorrow. Goodnight, and thank you for the evening.'

Next morning the Customs launch arrived at the pontoon and a uniformed officer came aboard Greg's boat.

'You are now free to sail, provided you do not leave the country.'

'I'll not be going further than Salcombe, as I told you.' Greg assured him. Later that day Greg sailed down the western approaches of the

Solent, headed for that attractive town and sheltered harbour. He sailed all night.

* * *

When daylight came, with visibility improved, he was able to go briefly below and grab some more food and a drink.

The waves were getting bigger as the morning progressed. The boat rose on each successive wave then crashed into the following trough behind it. His journey became a battle.

"Dover, Wight, Portland, Plymouth, west to south-west, five to six, backing south and increasing force seven, maybe force eight around headlands. Sea state moderate, becoming rough. That is the end of the local shipping forecast. There now follows our afternoon play, a story of love, life, and skulduggery."

He switched off the radio. The word 'skulduggery' brought a smile to his face, but the situation he'd got into the previous day was not funny. Now the worsening weather took all his attention. He was ten nautical miles south of Start Point. In normal conditions he would have been able to see his destination. He could not. A strong ebb tide was taking him to the west and the rising wind against that tide was producing waves of a height he had rarely seen or had to cope with. When the boat failed to crest a wave, which he estimated at over ten feet high, it ploughed straight into it. The sea swept along the deck and loosened the lashings that held the deflated dinghy in place. The boat was rolling wildly. The crests of the waves were foaming and spray was giving him a soaking. The sky darkened and the cloud base dropped as a line squall swept up from the southwest. Heavy rain now added to the misery and made visibility only half a mile or so.

Unable to see Salcombe Harbour entrance, on port tack Greg headed for the dramatic spiky Devon coastline at Bolt Head, where the sea was breaking on the rocks that mark the western limit of the harbour. With the wind backing to the south and the tide ebbing, the swell on the bar was increasing by the hour – this was a dangerous bar. He knew that soon the waves there would be steep and short, which meant that his boat would not rise from the trough of one wave to crest the next. A recipe for disaster: he knew that the book said that in these conditions he should not attempt the entrance.

Greg decided he had no choice. He had been swept west beyond the harbour entrance. The rocks in the shallowing water off Bolt Head made reading the depth from the echo sounder meaningless, and his normally clear thinking turned to fear, not knowing how much depth of water there was below the keels. The boat began pitching even more as it met the steepening waves head on, and water surged aft along the deck and into the cockpit before the bow rose again to meet the next sea with a crash that nearly brought them to a standstill. There was a foot or so of water in the cockpit as it drained only slowly after each soaking. He calculated (or was it prayed?) that there was enough water on the bar to avoid being smashed into it as the boat dropped some ten feet or so from the top of each wave into the trough.

Twenty anxious minutes of this and he knew that soon he would be in calmer water inshore of the bar. When he was finally able to alter course to the north-east in the shelter of the harbour he doused all sail. He was safe now, but he knew that he had stupidly risked his boat and his life.

He motored on past the deep-water moorings opposite the Marine Hotel, past the pretty village of Salcombe to port where the houses were interspersed with the woods high up on the hillside. He motored past the quay, the harbourmaster's office and the pontoon access to well-stocked shops and restaurants.

Further up the harbour, as the river narrowed towards Kingsbridge, Greg found there was still enough depth of water to enter his favourite creek and anchor between the reed beds. Tired from over twenty-four hours of hard sailing, mentally shattered by the risks he had taken and sheltered from the wind, he stretched himself out in the cockpit. The gentle murmur of the tide past the boat, the call of oystercatchers and the distant piping of a curlew added to the feeling that at last all was well with the world, and he drifted into a light, delicious doze, not quite oblivious but dimly aware of the gentle sounds and the warmth of the sun that had now come from behind the departing storm clouds.

The splashing sound came from somewhere close to the boat. Was that Old Sam? There were seals in this creek, and Greg always recognised one of them by a distinctive light-grey mark on its head. This seal had appeared one day, curious to find out who had invaded his private fishing ground.

'Is that you Sam?' called Greg. 'No fish today Sam.' Today had been too rough to put the line out for mackerel.

The splashing came again, but this time nearer, right under the stern, and the boat moved slightly. Greg sat up and looked out over the canvas dodgers surrounding the cockpit. There was another slight movement of the boat. He kneeled on the stern locker and peered down over the rail. There, holding on to his stern ladder, was a young girl.

'I'm sorry to disturb you, but I ran out of puff. I hope you don't mind if I rest for a couple of minutes?'

'Not a bit,' said Greg, looking around to see where she had come from – there was no sign of another boat.

'Are you all right?'

'I think so, but the tide is running very fast

and my things are over there.' She was pointing upstream.

'Are you saying you can't swim back to where you came from?'

'I guess that's about the sum of it,' she said, seeming to be in some distress.

'Right. I will launch my dinghy and with the outboard we should be able to get you to where you want to be. We'll have to hurry before we lose all the water. How far is it?'

'Oh, only a few minutes – couple of hundred yards or so.'

'Pull the ladder down. Climb aboard. You can give me a hand. And hurry.'

Greg was already untying the inflatable dinghy strapped to the deck. The girl was standing in a one-piece yellow bathing costume, shivering and dripping in the cockpit. He went below and returned with a towel and a sweater which she took gratefully.

As he was pumping up the dinghy she said, 'Here, let me do that. I'm very good at pumping dinghies.'

'Great. I'll get the engine sorted. We have little time to spare,' Greg said, as he lifted the outboard motor from the stern rail and checked the fuel.

His visitor completed the inflation, attached the oars, and between them they launched the dinghy over the side. She tied the painter to the stern cleat and Greg soon had the engine installed.

'You're no amateur at this sort of thing – I can

see that,' said Greg as they motored up the creek. 'Give me directions. And what's your name? I'm Greg.'

'I'm Julia. You'll see a gap in the reeds about fifty yards ahead on the left. There's a landing, quite steep-to. I don't think the engine will ground.'

She stepped ashore near a bundle of clothes.

'I can't thank you enough. It was stupid of me to go swimming on the ebb tide.'

'No need to thank me,' said Greg. 'But if I don't get out of here right away, it'll be me who is stranded. The water is going out as if someone has pulled the plug.'

He pushed the dinghy off and powered away downstream with a wave to the girl. It wasn't until he was back on board that he realised he'd given this young woman his best sweater.

An hour later the chops were sizzling gently in the pan and the aroma was drifting up from the galley into the cockpit, where Greg was contemplating the magical scene. The ebb had eased and the boat was about to take the ground on its twin keels. With the falling of the tide the mudbanks on either side were at eye level. The graceful curved bills of the curlews prodded deep, a grey heron stalked the water's edge, a turnstone sorted the weed and terns wheeled overhead, diving for the small fry that had been stranded in the drying pools.

'Sufficient unto the day,' muttered Greg, and

after the first proper meal for two days he was soon in his bunk and fast asleep.

* * *

He woke the next morning to find the day well advanced. He was refreshed, the sun was bright and the wind had dropped. He set about tidying up the boat, bringing the dinghy back on board and stowing the engine.

In the afternoon Greg tackled the monthly yachting article that brought him a small but regular fee. He was using his portable typewriter on the saloon table when he heard the sound of a powerful outboard coming up the creek. He climbed into the cockpit. Approaching was a dory driven by a ruddy-faced and tanned individual of about Greg's own age. He had a short grey beard and wore a well-worn Breton cap.

'A fisherman,' thought Greg.

He slowed down and as he came alongside he called to Greg in a distinct soft West Country burr: 'Evenin', I'm Robbie, and I've a present for you.' He waved a bottle at Greg.

'What have I done to deserve that?'

'It's a bottle of Calvados from Frank for helping me niece yesterday.'

The stranger explained that he was Robert, Julia's uncle and brother of Frank Trehairne, Julia's father.

'Well, that's thoughtful. I'm Greg. Come aboard. Reckon the sun's over the yardarm. Let's sample it together.'

In no time the dory was tied up to Greg's stern cleat and the stranger climbed aboard.

'I've also got your sweater. Mus'n' forget to give it 'ee before I leave.'

Greg produced glasses and a corkscrew, and opened the bottle. He poured two generous tots.

'I've seen 'ee anchored in my creek afore,' said Robbie.

'Your creek?'

'No, no, 'tain't mine, but those round yere do call it Robbie's creek. Used to have oysters, but they got poisoned some'ow long time past.'

As they lowered the level of the spirit in the bottle, swapping stories and getting acquainted, Greg warmed to Robert's friendliness and asked him if he would like to join him for an early tea of bangers in buns, the yachtsman's standby.

'Like a bit o' blotting paper, eh?' chuckled Robbie.

Greg soon had the bangers on the go, and the smell wafting up from the galley was almost as intoxicating as the Calvados. They tucked in.

'So what brings 'ee up this 'ere creek, then?'

'Peace and quiet,' said Greg, noticing that the ebb was beginning to run.

Greg's glance at the water was spotted by Robbie.

'My, I must be on me way. Oh, and I nearly forgot your invite. We'm having a beach picnic tomorrow – how about coming along? What do you say?'

'That's kind of you,' said Greg, 'but I'm sailing back east to the Solent early in the morning.'

'Just the job. The beach is east of here, on your way home. Me brother Frank and his wife, Joan, and Julia will be disappointed if you don't come.'

Greg was in no hurry to return to the Solent, and was intrigued.

'If you put it like that, I can't say no.'

Robbie smiled and held up his forefinger.

'A mile or so west o' Prawle Point you'm see the Ox and Chicken rocks, they'm marked on the chart 'bout half mile offshore. Afore 'ee get there, due west of them rocks you'm see my pot markers with red flags atop. Go to the north of them flags – they mark the passage inside the rocks. Once you'm due north of the rocks in plenty of water you'm see our little beach in a cove. Can't mistake it. See you there 'bout noon.'

Robbie shook Greg's hand firmly, climbed over the stern, untied the painter, and with a wave roared off downstream.

CHAPTER TWO

The Trehairnes

Soon after high water, with the sun barely up, Greg motored downstream and out into the open sea. Once outside the harbour the ebb tide was against him, and the northerly breeze was light. It was two hours before the Ox and Chicken rocks came into sight. The pot markers were easy to find in the calm sea, and as he conned the boat between the rocks and the shore a small cove was revealed, with a steep-to sandy beach. This was the place – a totally deserted spot. He dropped anchor some fifty yards off the beach in deep water.

It was ten in the morning and he was beginning to feel the warmth of the sun as he stepped from the dinghy and hauled it up on to clean, firm sand. The cove was surrounded by high, steep and ragged cliffs, and appeared inaccessible from above. The Ox and Chicken rocks offshore were fifty feet high or more, helping to hide the cove from seaward – only the inshore fishermen would notice its existence.

After an hour or so Robert's dory approached fast from the west with four people on board. Robert jumped ashore with an anchor and trod it into the sand. Greg strode to greet them. A man stepped out of the dory and firmly grasped Greg's outstretched hand as he introduced himself.

'I'm Julia's father, Frank. You've met Julia and my brother Robbie, of course. This is Joan, my wife.'

Greg's reaction was, and sounded, genuine: 'You just don't look old enough to be Julia's mum.'

Joan laughed and replied, 'I can see you and I are going to get along like a house on fire.'

The family likeness was obvious – fair hair, blue eyes and a slim figure. What surprised Greg was Julia's father, Frank. He seemed a lot older than Greg himself and although Frank was clean-shaven Greg could see the likeness to his brother: stockily built, ruddy cheeks, and piercing blue eyes.

'So this is Julia's knight in shining armour, eh?' His voice carried only the slightest hint of the regional accent that was so strong with his younger brother.

The five of them made their way up to the high-water mark carrying bags and two cool boxes. They set up camp beside a large rock which partly hid the entrance to a deep cave.

'We'll put the food in here. 'Twill keep it out of the sun,' Robert said, ducking into the cave with his brother.

'I'll bet this was used for smuggling in the old days,' said Greg, following them into the cave

'You're right there. You'd best ask Frank about that.'

They deposited the food and returned to the beach.

'Yes.' said Frank with a smile. 'The farmland on the top of the cliffs belonged to a distant cousin of ours, and has been with one family for as far back as we can trace – at least two hundred years. The cliffs have always been unclimbable, as they are today, but they say there was a way up from the back of the cave into a well outside the farmhouse. The booty would be hauled up at night, loaded onto a cart, covered in hay, and sent on its way. When the revenue men found out what had been going on they filled in the well and no other way down has ever been found.'

Greg laughed, and Robert, who was just behind him, said, 'You can laugh all right, but this yere smuggling used to be a serious business.'

Frank smiled and said, 'It's been going on for hundreds of years around here, Greg. Of course today it's harmless enough, and with laws on the import of booze now relaxed we take it as a bit of a game. Ask Robbie he does a bit o' trade with the odd French fisherman. Where do you think the Calvados came from, eh?' As he spoke he pointed across the water to the south-east. "Tis Calvados country just over the horizon. At the worst I guess it's on the fringe of the black market, like asking somebody to mend your fence for cash. We all do it to some extent – save a bob or two where you can.'

As they left the cave Robert took Greg by the arm.

'I tell 'ee what: how would 'ee like a couple of cases of that Calvados for twenty-five smackers cash?'

'If I were you,' said Julia, who had overheard, 'I should take him up on that. He's not usually so generous.'

Her mother nodded agreement.

'I'll have to think about that,' said Greg.

'I wouldn't think too long if I was you,' Frank said. 'And while you're thinking, we'll go for a swim. Coming?'

Greg excused himself on the basis that he had no swimming shorts.

With the exception of Robbie, the family changed in the cave and returned to the beach in their swimming gear. During the incident in Robbie's creek there had not been time for Greg to consider Julia's looks or figure. Now, in a white bikini, as she pinned up her long blond hair Greg's thoughts were that she could win Miss Universe. He followed them down to the water's edge. When they were in the water they laughed and joked, and Greg was included in the banter.

While returning to their clothes, Frank said to Julia, 'Take Greg round the headland now the tide has fallen. Show him that other little beach whilst we get the food ready. It'll help you to dry off.'

Julia darted off at a run with her blond hair streaming out behind her, and Greg followed at a leisurely pace. She had disappeared around the small rocky promontory and by the time he got there she was at the far end of another little beach. Greg sat down on a rock, and as she ran toward him this delightful girl slowed her pace and executed four or five graceful cartwheels. He was struck dumb by the beauty of this performance.

Then he said exactly what came into his mind as she stood in front of him a few feet away, scantily clad, her blue eyes looking at him enquiringly: 'That was clever. Lovely.'

She stuck her tongue out, he smiled, and they started back along the beach toward the others, who had changed into their dry clothes. Julia went into the cave to do likewise. She returned in a loose white cotton blouse and flowered skirt.

'Come and join the feast,' Julia said to Greg.

Joan had laid out the food on a large coloured tablecloth. Greg was mightily impressed.

'I've never seen such a spread. You must have spent hours preparing it.'

'We did,' said Julia. 'There's crab and cucumber sandwiches, and peeled prawns. I did the salad and Scotch eggs; Mum made the cheese; Robbie supplied the prawns. The spring onions, lettuce, tomatoes and farmhouse loaf are all home-produced. Even the ice cream. We've been up since dawn. Mind you, we only do this once a year.'

'Fantastic,' commented Greg as he sat down with the others.

'Tell us a bit about yourself, Greg,' said Frank as he poured the wine.

'I've been sailing along this coast for a few years – I scratch a living from writing for magazines. As I told Robbie yesterday, I often anchor up your creek for some peace and quiet.'

'You didn't exactly get peace and quiet a couple of days ago when you helped me,' said Julia, 'Or are you always rescuing damsels in distress?'

Greg smiled. 'All in a day's work. Tell me, Frank: do you live near the landing where I dropped Julia?'

It was Julia who answered: 'I live with Mummy and Daddy on their farm on the other side of the field where you put me ashore. I have no idea', she said with a mischievous grin, 'how they will manage without me when I go to university.'

Joan said, 'It's true that Julia has been a great help. It's a smallholding – we have goats, geese, turkeys and a few chickens. Most of the land is a cider-apple orchard and of course we grow our own veg. I milk the goats and make the cheese and Frank looks after the cider side of things. We all muck in really, and we'll miss Julia. She's the best daughter one could wish for.'

Julia blushed as she looked at Greg.

'I wasn't fishing for compliments, Mum.'

'Look, Greg' – it was Frank speaking now – 'Why don't you come over to see us when you're next in the creek? Jot down our number. Give us a bell when you next arrive and I'll show you over the place.'

Robert, who had said very little for some time, looked at Greg.

'It shouldn't take me to tell 'ee that tide has turned. Not that we want to get rid of 'ee but 'tis eastbound now and you'm got a way to go, eh?'

Greg was reluctant to leave these new friends and said so; but yes, it was time to set sail for the Solent, and he said his goodbyes. Robert and Julia walked with him to the dinghy and waved him off as he rowed out to his anchored boat. He was climbing aboard when Robbie came roaring up in the dory.

'You'm forgot the booze,' he called out, and before Greg could answer he heaved two cases on to the side deck.

'I'm not sure I've got enough cash on me.'

'No matter, my friend – next time. Take care.' And he sped back to the beach.

Greg stowed the cases in the forecabin, raised the anchor, motored out past the rocks and set sail eastwards. He was not only stocked up with Calvados at a bargain price, but also had a warm feeling that he had made lasting friends.

* * *

Back on his mooring in the Hamble river at Bursledon Greg tidied ship, rowed ashore and made the short walk to his caravan behind the garage. He phoned Customs and Excise, Southampton Office.

'May I speak to Mary Rowlinson, please?'

'Who shall I say is calling?'

'Please tell her it's Greg Norfield,' said Greg, not really expecting her to come to the phone. But she did.

'Have I got this right? Am I speaking to the man we arrested in Cowes?'

'Bang on,' replied Greg. 'Please don't hang up on me.'

'No, I won't do that, but you're talking to the wrong person. If you need to know anything about your case, you will have to talk to Don Carruthers.'

'Look, I didn't call to talk about that miserable affair. I rang to talk to you.'

'Why me?'

'Because I thought there might be half a chance, if I asked you nicely, that you would let me take you out to dinner.'

There was a pause, and then, 'My first reaction is to say that I don't think that would be at all proper.'

There was another pause so Greg said, 'How about your second reaction?'

'My second reaction is to say, why not?'

* * *

They met in a small Italian restaurant in Southampton the next evening. The friendship started a little on the chilly side. Greg wasn't sure if the attraction was mutual. He was acutely aware of their age difference. Having already spent a few hours with her as a suspected criminal, he was keen to show he wasn't a rogue. Mary was more cautious. She was aware that in a court of law this liaison could be interpreted at the very least as unwise.

They met many times. Tentative about their relationship at first, there were walks in the park. One day he rowed her out to his boat on the mooring at Bursledon.

Another day, as they left the cinema, she turned to him: 'I like your company, Greg, but I do wish you wouldn't appear to be frightened of me. I may be a vicar's daughter and a Customs officer, but I'm not an ogre.'

'That you are not. I think you are beautiful. What I'm frightened of is losing you. I behaved like an idiot that day in the Solent.'

They were in the street now. She turned to face him and placed her hands on his cheeks.

'We all make mistakes,' she said, 'even at your age.'

They both laughed aloud. And they kissed.

They were sitting in the park one day feeding the pigeons when she asked, 'Why don't you settle down to something more permanent? You've told me about your divorce, the loss of your business and that your children are abroad. I know you can't really afford to take me out, and you won't let me pay for anything. Where's your future, Greg?'

'If only I knew, Mary. Since meeting you I've been thinking the same thing. I don't seem to have a purpose in life. You are the first person I have met who cares. You are right. I must do something about it. Tomorrow I'm sailing down to the West Country. I have a good friend who runs a boatyard in Dartmouth. I haven't seen him for ages. Think I'll drop in and see how he's getting on.'

Greg's arrival in Salcombe – in far better weather than on the previous occasion – saw him anchored in his favourite creek. He planned to stay for a couple of days. He set about his supper to the sounds of Vivaldi from the radio.

After he had cleared away, the sun was setting and the boat was aground. In the slow, shallow trickle of the stream a pair of shelduck was paddling; dunlin rushed around along the low tide mark and gulls and terns wheeled to catch the scraps Greg threw them. Across the nearby fields, now in shadow as the sun dropped low, came the harsh croak of the roosting ravens and the soft cooing of pigeons.

Greg did not feel the chill as the sun set over the reeds: he was warmed by a glass or two of Calvados and thoughts of Mary. He believed she liked him despite the age difference.

Next morning Greg was on deck when he

recognised the sound of a powerful outboard motor. He helped Robbie to tie up and climb on board.

'Just in time for a cuppa,' said Greg.

'How did 'ee get on with the stuff, then?'

'Excellent. I've got your money below. I'll fetch it.'

'Aw, don't 'ee worry about that. Any time'll do. I got summat better than that for 'ee this time.'

Greg had gone below to make the coffee. He called out, 'Not sure about that, Robbie. I'm a bit short of a bob or two these days.'

'What you'm mean not sure? Don't 'ee want to do no more trade, then? I thought we'm doing 'ee a favour, I did.'

'Oh, you did, Robbie, you did.'

'Well, then, if you be short a bob or two here's an answer to your prayers. You'm make hundreds from what I can offer 'ee.'

Greg came up into the cockpit with the mugs, eyebrows raised enquiringly.

'Hundreds, Robbie? Is this on the up-and-up?'

Robbie's smile evaporated and his voice changed to one of concern. 'We'm not doing much trade together if we'm can't trust ourseln, eh?'

Greg could see this new friendship with the Trehairnes finishing right now.

'Nothing to do with trust, Robbie. Of course I trust you. I was only being a bit cautious. Wouldn't you?'

'Ain't nothing wrong wi' a bit o' caution. Look, I got some really good stuff coming. Could make 'ee a nice few bob. How long you'm goin to be 'ere?'

'Couple of days,' replied Greg. 'How are your brother and his wife, and Julia?'

'They'm busy today, but told me to tell 'ee to call them tomorrow. Any road, I'll be back in the morning on rise of tide. Talk to 'ee then. Got to go.'

He finished his coffee and Greg gave him the cash he owed. With the usual cheery wave he untied and was away down the creek. Greg got on with his writing and looked forward to the next day.

True to his word, Robbie was back in the morning.

'Morning, Greg,' he shouted as he tied up alongside and began to heave four boxes onto Greg's side deck. 'Twenty-five quid for the Calvados as before, and three hundred each for the caviar. You'm make a few hundred on this lot and you'm not be saying where 'tis from, eh? And give Frank a bell; they want you to go over this morning.'

And then Robbie was off again, in his usual hurry. Greg looked at the boxes. The Calvados was less than half price, and as for the caviar . . .

Joan answered his call, and seemed genuinely pleased to hear from him.

'Come and have a look at our place as soon as you're ready,' she said. 'We'll all be pleased to see you again. You've made a real hit with Julia.

Take your dinghy to the landing where you dropped Julia. She will come down to meet you and show you the way to our place – tide is OK for two or three hours. Have a look around and then something to eat with us at lunchtime if you like.'

'If I like?' said Greg. 'I'll say I like. That is most generous of you. I'll be on my way in twenty minutes or so.'

Julia was at the landing stage when Greg arrived in the dinghy.

'Daddy sent me to show you the way,' she said with an appealing smile and a nod of her head to show the direction.

'My guess is you're about the same age as my daughter,' he called out.

'How old is your daughter, then?'

'Eighteen.'

'Spot on,' she replied as they climbed a stile and turned into the lane.

The smallholding was only about half a mile from the creek. Frank and Joan greeted him warmly at the farm gate some distance from the house. Greg offered Joan the small china figurine of a little girl with a goose that he had bought for her in Bursledon.

'In appreciation for the other day,' he said, and she blushed.

'You shouldn't have. Frank and I were only saying yesterday how we looked forward to seeing you again.'

Greg found her slight and warm Devon accent as appealing as that of her daughter.

'Come and have a look around,' said Frank and led Greg off on a tour, firstly of the land and buildings that catered for the birds and animals; then the dairy, where he sampled the goats cheese; and finally to the russet brick farmhouse.

'Come in,' said Frank, taking Greg via the porch into the living room.

Then they went through the large stone-flagged kitchen and outside to what looked like stables. As they entered, the strong smell of apples was unmistakeable.

'This is the cider house. We import apple juice for about 75% of our production, but we use the fruit from our own orchard just once a year for the strong farmhouse "scrumpy", which commands a good premium. We don't employ anybody, so the family are kept pretty busy.'

Frank showed Greg the machine for turning the apples to pulp, the cider press he built himself, large wooden barrels (pipes) and glass carboys, for fermenting and maturing the juice. His enthusiasm for what, to Greg, appeared pure alchemy was a joy to share. He took an earthenware mug, filled it from a small barrel and handed it to Greg.

'We don't bottle anything; it all goes out in barrels like this one to local outlets – mostly pubs and clubs. The Excise people keep a close watch to check we're collecting their share. Mind you, their inspectors insist that, as well as seeing that the paperwork is in order, sampling is part of their duty!'

'That's good, that is really good,' said Greg.

Frank topped up their mugs and got technical about the art of pressing apples and fermentation. Some way through his description of the process Greg realised he'd better slow up as he was beginning to feel the effects.

'Bring your mug with you,' said Frank as he led the way back into their charming house.

Here indeed was an example of old England. As they came back through the kitchen Greg noticed that the stone sink seemed to be as large as a horse trough. Joan, Frank's wife, came out of a pantry as big as a small bedroom to tell them their lunch was ready on the table in the living room. Dark low beams, antique furniture, and a large open oak-framed fireplace bedecked with horse brasses. There was an old walnut upright piano in one corner.

Before they set about the homemade cheese and pickles Frank enquired, 'How did you get on with Robbie's bit of trade?'

'Fantastic. Your brother's a genius.'

'European free trade,' laughed Frank. 'If you can't beat 'em, join 'em, I say'.

When Joan came she was carrying a jug of cider. She topped up Greg's mug again and sat down. Frank got up and left the room, explaining something about an urgent filtering job he'd forgotten that required his attention in the cider house.

Greg asked Joan as he looked at the piano, 'Who's the musician, then?'

'When my mother was alive and living with us I used to give piano lessons, either here or in people's homes. Mum would look after Julia when I was out. I was eighteen when Frank and I married. Julia was born the following year. It wasn't until Julia was six years old that I went to college to train as a music teacher. Frank decided he ought to do what he used to preach at the agricultural college, so we built up this smallholding, which keeps us more than busy.'

At this point Julia joined them.

'Has she told you that it's me that's up at dawn cleaning out the water troughs in the chicken sheds and collecting the eggs? Going to Exeter to stay with my aunt while I'm at university will be like a holiday camp compared with this place.'

'It's true, Greg,' said Joan. 'Julia has more than pulled her weight here, and that's not the only reason we'll miss her. On the other hand she'll meet a lot of young people and maybe meet the man of her dreams!'

'I can't imagine she'll have much of a problem over that,' said Greg.

'Now look here, Mum, it sounds like you want to marry me off. And what makes you think I don't fancy older men like that good-looking fella sitting next to you? Dad's all of twenty years older than you,' she said mischievously.

They laughed.

Joan went to the kitchen. Julia picked up the

jug to fill Greg's mug. As she bent forward over the table he had time to study her face, her pale blue wide-apart eyes, no make-up, flawless complexion and her flaxen hair tied back with a red velvet bow.

'I know what you're thinking,' she whispered.

'No you don't,' he replied as he put his hand over the mug to signify he'd had enough.

She bent close to his ear, so close that he felt her lips brush his flesh as she said even more quietly, 'Bet I do.'

Frank and Joan came back into the living room, and round that well-worn oak table they enjoyed the fruits of the family's hard work.

'Don't ever get into this farming lark, Greg,' said Julia. 'It's much too much like hard work, and seven days a week. Stick to sailing and smuggling.'

At the word *smuggling* Frank frowned.

'Julia darling, I've told you before not to use that word.'

'The word is *trade*,' said Frank, looking at Greg. 'Not everything goes through the books in any business, does it? Old Arthur down the road puts his mower through the orchard couple of times a year, so I gives him a barrel – otherwise he'd be billing me for the service plus VAT, which I'd be claiming back. If I be charging him for the cider plus duty and VAT then he'd be claiming the VAT back and all we'd be doing is keeping that army of pen-pushing civil servants in fat pensions. Keeps them buggers in Brussels busy, that's all.

Ask Robbie. He and his French friends settle with a bit of trade, no fuss.'

Joan and her daughter nodded vigorously in agreement.

'Are you with us, Greg?' said Joan.

Greg responded by standing up, raising his mug and saying, 'Here's to the Trehairnes – long may you prosper.' Canting his head toward the two women, he added, 'Long may you be so charming.'

They clapped their hands in response to this short speech, and then Frank reminded him it was getting late and that the water at the head of the creek would be getting too shallow for his return.

Julia walked down to the dinghy with him. By the time they reached the gate Greg decided that he would remind Julia that he was old enough to be her grandfather. This he did when they arrived at the landing. She did not like it; turned around and ran back to the house.

Once back on board he wondered what she would say to her parents, his new-found friends.

He finished his typing in the late afternoon, and by supper-time he'd decided to sail to see Chris Curnow in Dartmouth early next day. It would mean a flog against the west-going tide, but with a bit of luck there would be a fair south-westerly to keep him on a broad reach or a run most of the way.

As Greg sailed he reminded himself of how he had first met Chris Curnow. Shortly after the break-up of his marriage and loss of his business some ten years previously, Greg had taken six months off to sail and try to forget. He found the Curnow Yard on the Dart just after Chris had bought it, and he spent six months living there on his boat.

Chris's mother had died two years before his father, a trawler owner, succumbed to cancer. He was an only child working as repair manager in a small shipyard in Plymouth. On his father's death he inherited a substantial sum and the parental house. He was happily married, but they could not have children. His inheritance enabled him to purchase the run-down boatyard on the river Dart. There was a good demand at the time for boat repairs in that part of the world, and there was also a surplus of skilled boatbuilding workers as the recession bit harder.

Chris had rebuilt the main shed and time had proved him right about the demand for traditional wooden yachts. The Curnow Yard had gone from strength to strength. Chris, fifteen years younger than Greg, had taken advice from him when they first met at a time when his own business experience was nil. They became friends. Greg had the business experience and Chris was a skilled boatbuilder. They had not met for several years.

As he sailed Greg wondered if there were any grey hairs in that wavy ginger mop that ended on Chris's forehead in a pronounced widow's peak. Perhaps Chris might not be pleased to see him. Perhaps he wasn't even there.

CHAPTER THREE

The Curnow Shipyard

Sailing from the west and clear of Start Point on a northerly course Greg saw the daymark on the top of the east cliffs marking the entrance to the Dart. The cliffs and rocks are steep and jagged either side, above as well as below water. He made for this landmark until, as if by magic, the vista of Dartmouth town became visible through the narrow entrance. He took down his mainsail and started the engine before reaching the Castle on the port side. Once through the narrows, past the ferry terminal on the Kingswear shore and the large marina to starboard, it was a short distance to the Curnow shipyard on the east side of the river.

Greg tied up at the visitors' pontoon and made his way along the gangway toward the offices.

'Well, well, well, what do I see coming toward me?' called out a voice from the top of the outside wooden staircase.

'Chris,' cried Greg. 'How the devil are you? Thought I'd give you a surprise.'

'You've done that all right. If you'd phoned

first, I'd have put out the red carpet.'

Chris came down the steps to meet his old pal with a bear hug.

'It's been a long time,' said Chris. 'Your ears must have been burning. 'Twas only the other day I said to John – he's our accountant, you remember – that I could do with somebody like you to handle the publicity and PR. It's getting too much for me, and I'm not really qualified. Come on up and tell me what you've been doing. Why have you left it so long?'

Chris introduced Flossie, his secretary, who promptly put the kettle on and commenced to make tea for them. She was a startling-looking girl in her twenties, with a big mop of fuzzy auburn hair and a red ribbon tied in a bow on top. She was dressed as if she was someone in showbiz, not a secretary.

'Is this private, Chris?' she enquired. 'I'll go and have my tea with John.'

'No, no. You carry on, Flossie. I haven't seen Greg for – how long? – three, four years?' he said, looking at Greg, who vigorously nodded assent. 'I've been struggling to get out a press release about an agency we've taken on. It took me more than a week to produce. It's a French company. We are to be the sole UK distributors for a range of their chandlery. You would have done a job like that in an hour or so,' he said to Greg, and then, turning to Flossie: 'Please carry on and type it, Flossie. I will get my old pal here to give it the once-over; he used to be in the advertising and publicity business.'

With Flossie clattering away at her typewriter the two of them reminisced about past times and Greg filled Chris in on his wanderings. Chris Curnow told Greg he now employed some thirty staff on boatbuilding and maintenance.

'Greg, why don't you stay where you are for the night?' said Chris. 'From what you tell me you don't have to go back to the Solent in a hurry. Flossie here will fax that article of yours. I've got a plan brewing in this grey matter of mine and a busy afternoon ahead. May I come on board this evening, say about five o'clock, and try you out on what I have in mind?'

'Sure, Chris. In the meanwhile I'll nip over on the ferry and top up my victuals. See you at five.'

Chris came on board that evening and explained what he had in mind: 'Firstly, some good news about the shipbuilding side of the business. I'm about to sign a contract with the state of Qatar to build a fast patrol boat. From what you told me earlier, Greg, I believe we can help each other. Here's what I propose. My workload has increased to breaking point over the last year. I'm a boatbuilder, not a publicity man or a writer like you. I have taken on more than I can chew. I told you about the agency for the French company. Six months ago we also went into the brokerage business and sales look promising, but it takes up far too much of my time. Why don't you move down here, lock, stock and barrel? I'll give you a pontoon berth and a site for your caravan, no charges. In return, you take over all my publicity work, including the new agency, and run the brokerage. What do you say?'

'I say that's fantastic, that's what I say.'

They shook hands and Chris said, 'Have you got any problems you haven't told me about?'

'Well, yes, just a small one. I'm a bit involved with a family who have become good friends in Salcombe. Before I could think what I was doing I found myself tempted by what they called "a bit of trade".'

Chris looked at Greg enquiringly with one eyebrow raised.

'Being a bit short of the readies, I was talked into accepting some cases of Calvados and caviar, which they told me would fetch a handsome profit. I can't think of a way of selling them. You wouldn't have any ideas, would you?'

'A bit of trade? That's a euphemism round these parts for smuggling. Well, let me think. I may have a contact – I'll let you know when you return. I must get back to Rosemary now – I promised her I'd be early tonight and take her out. She's had a rough time from me recently, and I haven't left here before six or seven o'clock for ages. Now that I've got something to celebrate, with you coming to help out, I know she'll be pleased. You don't want to change your mind?'

'My word is my bond, you know that, Chris.

It's the best thing I've heard for a very long time. I'll sail back to the Hamble in the morning. Give me a couple of days to sort things out. I'll tow the caravan down first, and then go back for the boat.'

* * *

Ashore in Bursledon, Greg's first thoughts were of Mary. He phoned her.

'I've missed you,' she said.

'And I've missed you too. I've got something to tell you, and I'd rather not do it on the phone.'

'Sounds serious. How would you like to come round to my flat? I'll rustle up some grub this evening. It so happens I have something to tell you too.'

Mary gave him directions, and he was round at her place at six thirty that evening. She'd just got back, shopping for their supper on the way from work. They greeted each other with a kiss and a hug and huge smiles.

Seated with glasses of wine in their hands, Mary spoke first: 'You've got something on your mind. I have a feeling what you have to say affects us.'

Greg put his glass down and took her hand in both of his.

'It does. Meeting you has made me think more positively than I have for years. I told you that I was going to visit my old pal in Dartmouth. Well, the result of that visit is that I've taken up a job offer from him based at his yard on the Dart.'

Mary pulled her hand from his and put it across her mouth as she raised her eyebrows in an expression of surprise.

'I knew it.' she exclaimed as her hand dropped back on his. 'Destiny has funny tricks to play,' she said wistfully. 'I've been putting off telling you that I have been offered a place on a management course in Aberdeen. This will last three months and could lead to a senior position in Scotland. I need to do this thing, Greg. An opportunity like this will not be offered to me again.'

There was a long pause.

'And why would you turn it down?'

'I seriously thought of turning it down, Greg, because of you. I thought we'd got something going between us. I know we are both strong-minded. Distance should not part us if what we have is strong.'

He wanted to say, 'Marry me and come to Devon,' but he held back, not only because he was afraid that her answer would be 'No,' but because he knew he too had put himself first with his decision to go to Dartmouth.

Mary went to the fridge and returned to top up their glasses.

'Mary, you are terribly important to me. I am going to miss you so very much.'

He watched the tears start to roll down her cheeks. He wiped them away with his thumbs, grasped her shoulders, and they rolled back onto the sofa. That kiss conveyed more passion and love than they had experienced together before.

After supper they extended the intensity of their feelings in the bedroom. Greg did not return to his caravan that night. They knew they had something special that was more than passing friendship.

Over breakfast they said much about writing and phoning. Contact numbers were exchanged. Mary went to work and Greg returned to Bursledon.

He hitched the caravan up to the old Consul and set off for Devon. When he arrived late in the evening Chris Curnow was still in his office. He directed Greg to a cleared concrete apron near No.1 Shed and personally helped him to jack up the caravan, lay a cable to a power point, and connect a hosepipe to a nearby tap.

'You go back to get the boat tomorrow, Greg, before we get down to business. See you in two or three days. Saturday or Sunday I'll have more time to hand things over to you.'

'Sounds about right,' said Greg. 'I'll sell the car when I get back to Bursledon – or, to put it more accurately, my pal with the garage where the caravan has been parked will sell it for me. It will help me to reimburse him for past favours.'

Once back in Bursledon, Greg resisted the

temptation to phone Mary. He sailed down the Hamble, out into Southampton Water and on westwards through the Solent into the English Channel. He sailed on toward his destination. Or was it his destiny?

What had he done? He was supremely happy in Mary's company. Had he found love again – and thrown it away? No. Their feelings for each other were mutual. They would last. Between them they would find a way. What was it she had said outside her flat when they had parted that morning? She had said, 'This was meant to be.'

Aground and tucked up in the south-west corner on the sand in The Cobb at Lyme Regis, he was safe for the night. He dropped off to sleep with positive thoughts for his future.

* * *

With the rise of the tide in the morning he set sail for Dartmouth.

Greg was no sooner tied up to the visitors' pontoon at the Curnow Yard on Friday afternoon than Chris came down to greet him. Greg invited him on board.

'I've got your "bit o' trade" sorted,' said Chris. 'I've a pal in London with a wine bar and restaurant, a man I can trust. He told me on the phone that he'll take them, but he first needs to know what he is buying. We'll ship the cases up to London to Antonio, who I know will offer you a good price if the goods are the real stuff. I assure you that, despite his name, Antonio, like me, is of good Cornish stock and not averse to *a bit of trade*.'

'I shall be glad to unload this lot,' said Greg.

'The staff will all be gone shortly, and I'll give you a hand to get those cases into the warehouse. I'll explain to the despatch manager on Monday morning that they are a gift for a business contact in London, and give him the address.'

When Greg entered Chris's office on Saturday morning he instinctively knew that the other man present was Chris's brother. He was tall, had the same dark complexion, and his ginger hair reached forward to a widow's peak.

'Meet my brother Harry,' said Chris.

Apart from Harry's short military-style haircut they could have been twins.

'I'll not beat about the bush,' said Chris. 'Harry's been in prison for the last three years. He's not proud of it, and he'll tell you his story in his own good time. He's out on licence. I'm helping the company as well as my brother by giving him a job. Old Seth, who runs the warehouse, is retiring at the end of the year, and I've given him another easier job in the yard without a drop in pay, so he's happy. With the new agency the warehouse work will become more exacting and, whilst Harry is overqualified for the job, we have agreed he will be able to do it well.'

Harry departed for the warehouse. Chris and Greg spent the morning covering what Chris wanted from Greg, from launching the new chandlery line to building up the brokerage business.

'One thing more,' said Chris: 'Flossie didn't think much of the press release I was doing when you were here last week. Do you think you could put it into some sort of order for me?'

Greg was in Chris's office with Flossie on Monday morning when a slightly built handsome man of about sixty, peering over the top of spectacles halfway down his aquiline nose, and with a mass of nearly white hair, came in from the adjacent office and looked enquiringly at Flossie.

'Oh, John, this is Mr Norfield, Chris's friend.'

They shook hands and the tall man said, 'We met many years ago, you may remember. I'm John Dalton, the company secretary and accountant. Welcome to our establishment. Chris has told me what you are going to be up to.' With raised eyebrows and a grin he added, 'Provided whatever you suggest doesn't cost us too much, you won't be seeing a lot of me.'

He returned to his office.

'I know Chris is away for a couple of days,' said Greg to Flossie. 'I have rewritten his press release, but I expect you'll want to retype it.'

'I'm not surprised at that; I nearly rewrote it myself!' she said.

The two of them had a chuckle.

'I've got another item of my own which I need to fax, if I may, and I'd like to phone a couple of people that Chris says may be interested to have us sell their boats for them.'

'Let me have your stuff for faxing, Mr Norfield. I'll do that, and you use Chris's desk there. Any numbers you need just ask me. Use the green phone, the black one is internal.'

'You're a gem, Flossie. I can see what Chris meant by you running the place. And please call me Greg.'

After a quick sandwich in the caravan Greg made his way to No. 1 Shed to reacquaint himself with Bill Fossett, the shipyard manager. He found him finishing his own lunch in the little office built for him high up overlooking the workspace.

At Greg's request he trotted out how he came to be there: 'A five-year apprenticeship at Mashfords in Plymouth. Ten years with a small builder in Looe, during which I obtained my HNC in shipbuilding by part-time study in Plymouth. I jumped at this job when I saw it advertised seven years ago.'

Greg explained why he was there and moved on to find Harry in his cubbyhole in the warehouse.

'I've got a list from the French of all the items we will be importing,' said Harry. 'They've marked the most popular items within the existing markets in Europe. I need to devise our own list for this country with reference numbers to make it easier for stocking. Got any ideas?'

Greg looked at the list.

'I need to study this more carefully. I'll get a copy for Bill Fossett. Three heads are better than two. What do you think?'

'Good idea,' replied Harry. 'By the way, I used to be an accountant.'

Greg did as he promised and went back to the caravan to see what he could make of his own copy.

On the Wednesday he had a further session with Chris. He cleared the air to be away until the following weekend, when prospective brokerage customers were more likely to want attention. Then he set sail for Salcombe.

* * *

Greg tied up at the town quay. It was convenient for shopping and there was The Victoria, a pub that sold proper draught beer and had first-class bar food at Greg's prices. The harbourmaster was on the quay to extract his dues.

'Good evening, sir. I've seen you here before, I believe?'

'That's right. May I tie up here for tonight?'

'That will cost you the princely sum of two pounds, please, sir.'

It was late in the afternoon by the time he had finished his shopping. He found a comfortable corner in The Victoria and settled with his pint. The only other occupant of the bar seated nearby was an old man with grey hair down to his shoulders, a long white beard, well-worn jeans, shorty gumboots and a white roll-neck. He looked every bit the ancient mariner, complete with a greasy Breton cap pulled down low.

'Good evening to you, sir,' he said, eyeing Greg over his pint mug. 'I'm be guessing you'm be a visitor to these parts.' He sounded like Robert Trehairne.

'And good evening to you. I'm guessing that you are local.'

Over the next hour or so Greg was regaled with the history of the area and was not surprised to hear from this character much about the smuggling of "the old days".

At this point the harbourmaster entered the bar. Greg, now well fortified, took a bold approach and invited him to join them for a beer on the basis that he might learn even more about the potential dangers of 'bits of trade'.

'I see you've already met Josh,' said the harbourmaster as he sat down. 'I'm Nick Wroughton, ex-merchant navy, paid by the council to keep an eye on you mariners and the suchlike. Good health to you.'

'Josh here has been telling me about smuggling and the local history.'

'Oh, he can do that all right. He's part of it himself – aren't you, Josh? He's been around these parts for ninety-odd years. Might have been smuggling in his early days – isn't that right, Josh?'

Josh mumbled something into his beer mug that sounded a bit like "Ooh ahrr" and Nick addressed Greg again.

'Don't you sometimes anchor in Robbie's Creek, upriver?'

'I have done,' said Greg cautiously, fearful that maybe he was about to be charged harbour dues for all the times he'd anchored there.

'It is beyond the jurisdiction of the harbour authorities up there,' continued Nick. 'Robert Trehairne owns the rights to the oyster beds. Not that there are any oysters any more. He used to have a noticeboard on the bank prohibiting anchoring or fishing, but it blew down in a gale.'

Greg decided that he'd had enough ale and was hungry. He thanked the two of them for their company and moved to the eating area. After his meal he returned to the boat. As he lay in his bunk he found comfort from what he had learned that evening in the pub. He was not under suspicion. He had not owned up to knowing the Trehairnes, and it didn't seem that present-day smuggling existed, at least in the mind of the harbourmaster. And he should know.

CHAPTER FOUR

More Skulduggery

The town quay is not the most peaceful place to be. In the early hours Greg was woken by fishermen as they unloaded tea chests full of live crabs to go by road for processing. As soon as he could, he departed upstream to the peace and quiet of Robbie's Creek, where he could work on Harry's chandlery list.

Later, Chris called him on the cellphone.

'Good news, Greg: Antonio is happy with the shipment. The fishy stuff will last him for months, but he could take more of the liquid stuff any time. Thought this info might help. However, Paul Partick, whom you spoke to the other day about selling his boat, is coming in to see you on Friday morning. I tried to put him off until you got back on Saturday, but he has to go abroad. I thought you'd rather see him yourself.'

Greg did a quick think.

'Thanks for the news, Chris. I'll be back later today. No problem. Bye now.'

A familiar sound got louder. Yes, it was Robbie. He tied up alongside.

'Got some stuff for 'ee. How did 'ee get on with them cases?'

'Morning, Robbie. Just got some good news. I can't take any more caviar for a bit, but I can dispose of the Calvados all right.'

'Well, fancy that,' said Robbie. 'Caviar has dried up a bit anyway, but it just so 'appens that we have a couple more of the hard stuff right yere.'

The two cases were quickly transferred to Greg's boat.

'Come aboard and I'll get the kettle on and bring you up to date.'

Greg told Robbie about his evening in The Victoria.

'Nick's one of us, but be careful with old Josh. 'E's a bit of a blabber.'

Greg explained to Robbie that there was a change to his plans. He had to get back as soon as tide permitted, so couldn't see Frank and Joan this visit.

With tide and wind against him, Greg made slow progress toward the Dart. He must get back to see Paul Partick – he was not going to let Chris have to deal with a matter that was now his responsibility.

A fair run soon took him to the Dart entrance. Approaching Dartmouth from the west on a fine day such as this presented no problems, but arriving at this harbour in rough weather can be tricky until the rocky shores and high cliffs either side are cleared. Once inside, the harbour is a safe haven.

The advantage of his berth at the yard was that it was secluded and just a few yards from his caravan. Boats on the pontoons were rarely occupied and shifting his 'bit of trade' from the boat to the caravan at night, with the yard closed, guaranteed secrecy. From caravan to warehouse was just a few paces.

He tied up at the pontoon, went below and was in the forecabin when he heard footsteps on the decking. Creaking, and movement of the boat, confirmed someone was approaching. He flung a spare headsail over the cases on the bunk. Panic was setting in as he quietly moved into the main saloon to see who it was.

A female voice called out, 'Permission to come aboard?'

For a moment recognition failed him. He poked his head out of the companion way – it was Mary! He managed a grin of pleasure.

'Darling,' he stuttered, 'what are you doing here?'

As she made to climb over the safety rail he was on the pontoon like a shot.

'I've missed you,' she said. 'It's as simple as that. They've given me some leave before I go to Scotland, so here I am. You don't look well' were her next words when the kissing had stopped.

All he could think of was to say that he'd been working hard and that the passage from Salcombe had been rough.

As they stood, arms about each other, Greg's thoughts began to settle. Physical contact with Mary, the look in her eyes, her words, reassured him of her feelings. A sense of enormous pleasure came over him as his guilty conscience about the loot on board subsided.

'You look better already,' she said.

'I feel it,' he replied truthfully, but the brain was still telling him to keep her off the boat at all costs.

'I'll give you the grand tour tomorrow,' was all he could think of as he explained he didn't want her to see the mess on board. He steered her along the pontoon, saying that the mess in the caravan was less than that on the boat. Her bag was at the top of the steps to the pontoon. Her little MG was outside his caravan. 'Are you staying?' he asked.

'Do you want me to?'

'What do you think?'

They had not been in the caravan for long before Greg realised how much he was going to miss her when she went to Scotland.

'How long have you got?' he enquired as she looked around.

'I've only just arrived, and now you're asking when I'm going.' She giggled and looked around. 'Long enough to clear up this shambles.'

'You'll do no such thing. I like it this way. There's nothing in the fridge, I'm afraid. How about I take you out to dinner?'

'Thought you were broke?'

'Not quite, and anyway this calls for a

celebration. I didn't expect to see you for months. When are you going to Aberdeen?'

'At the end of next week. Let me have my way. Tomorrow I'll do a bit of shopping if you're busy; meanwhile I'm starving – it's been a long drive, and I haven't had anything since I left Southampton this morning.'

'Mary, I think you're wonderful. And yes, I have to see a customer in the morning. I'm starving too. Let's go and refuel.'

Early the next morning Greg said to Mary, 'My guess is that Chris will be in the office shortly. I must get the gen on Group Captain Partick. He's bringing his boat in this morning. I think there's a problem with it.'

'Will you be back if I get some breakfast on the go?'

'Breakfast! You'll be lucky. I told you the cupboard was bare.'

Sure enough Chris was at work in his office.

'Did you enjoy your surprise when you got back yesterday?' enquired Chris.

'Surprise? I nearly had a heart attack. You've forgotten that Mary is an officer in Customs & Excise. Why didn't you warn me?'

'Hell,' said Chris, 'you haven't told her about your *bits of trade*, have you?'

'Not bloody likely. My concern is getting the stuff off the boat.' Greg explained that he hadn't decided whether to tell her or not. Now that Harry had moved in, Greg suggested, the warehouse didn't seem to be the place from where to ship it.

Chris went over and put his arm round Greg's shoulders.

'Fear not, my friend, Harry hasn't spent years in the nick without learning a thing or two.'

He reached for the yard Tannoy and called for Harry to come to the office. Harry listened to Chris explain the situation, and then he looked Greg straight in the eye.

'You had better make your mind up right now what you are going to do about your girlfriend. She told me she was a Customs officer. When you've decided that, I'll decide about myself. Personally, I'd dump her like a hot potato.'

For Greg, getting rid of the stuff on the boat was number one priority. As for dumping Mary, it didn't bear thinking about. He needed breathing space.

'OK, you're right. There's too much at stake for all of us. But I'll need time. I can't just push her out just like that – she might get suspicious. She's trained that way. Anyway, we must get the stuff off the boat and away before I have to show her around,' Greg continued. 'Mary's going shopping in Dartmouth later, Harry.'

Chris and Harry looked relieved.

'I'll give you a shout when the coast is clear. Chris will give you the address, won't you, Chris?'

Harry looked pensive and left them. Greg raised his arms in a gesture of helplessness and concern.

'Stop worrying, Greg. Let's talk about the Group

Captain. A few weeks ago he came in wanting to know if we'd sell his boat for him. You chased him up last week, so he's back again this morning. There's a history to this boat.'

'I'm all ears – go ahead,' said Greg.

'It's a Westerly thirty-six-footer by the name of *Amity*. She's been badly neglected even though only about eight years old. We quoted him something like seven or eight grand to repair the osmosis in the hull and replace the engine and propulsion. The rest of the boat was sound but needed a good bit of loving care and attention.'

'Sounds like a wreck to me,' said Greg.

'Not really. You should know that Westerly made them as strong as tanks. You were talking to me about wanting a bigger boat. I reckon this is your chance. I suggest you buy it yourself at the best price you can knock him down to. We'll repair the hull and put in a new engine etc., for which we'll charge you at cost. If we can find space for you in No.2 Shed, you can do the rest of the work yourself this winter. If you play your cards right, you'll end up with a boat worth twice what you paid for it.'

Back with Mary, and bubbling with enthusiasm, Greg told her about the plan to buy *Amity* and that with a bit of luck he'd have some news for her when she got back from the shopping. She left to do her shopping in Dartmouth, on the other side of the river. They kissed and hugged before she set off to walk to the ferry.

Greg nipped back up to the balcony outside

the offices. Here was a clear view up and down the river. With Chris's binoculars he could see Mary getting onto the ferry to cross the river. He went down to see Harry in the warehouse.

'There's nobody within sight of my boat at the moment.'

'OK, I'll give old Seth a job at the other end of the yard. Let's get the stuff into the warehouse, and I'll deal with it from there.'

Greg had never intended to move the cases in daylight, and his heart was pounding more from fright than exertion as they worked. It only took five minutes to have them safely on a shelf in the store, where, amongst so many other boxes of goods, they assumed an innocent look.

Greg was further reassured by Harry who whispered with a wink, 'You look more like someone who's nicked the Crown jewels than a couple of cases of booze – good thing you've got me around. I take it you'll make it worth my while next time.'

There had been no sign that this remark was a joke. Greg smelled blackmail.

'Harry, how about popping down to the boat in a minute, where we can't be overheard? I'd like a quick word.'

A little later, as Greg was refilling the freshwater tank on the boat, Harry arrived. They went below and Greg put the kettle on. Over coffee Greg gained the impression that it was not Harry's top priority to 'go straight', but more not to get caught.

'The next time doing what?' asked Greg.

'Acting not quite according to the law' was his reply, 'like you are doing now.'

Greg reckoned he was trapped. Trapped by his greed. Trapped into his deceit of Mary. And, looking at Harry across the cabin, trapped by this man to whom he was taking an increasing dislike by the minute.

Harry's parting shot was, 'Just this time, I'll do as Chris and you want and get the stuff off to London pronto.'

Greg made for the office, anger welling up. By the time he arrived in Chris's office he'd got up a fine head of steam.

He was glad Flossie was not there as he exclaimed, 'I know I'm on a fiddle with these 'bits of trade', and I thought you reckoned it was just a lark, but I'm not sure about your brother.'

Chris looked shocked.

'I thought I had reassured you,' he replied. 'And Harry needs my help.'

'I admire you for that,' said Greg, 'but at the risk of losing our friendship, can you expect me to have faith after the conversation I've just had with him?'

Greg repeated all that had been said between him and Harry on the boat and elsewhere earlier. 'Chris, it's not just me at risk here. You and I are more than just pals. Whether he's your brother or not, talk like that doesn't fill me with confidence. A few days after meeting me he's trying to blackmail me. It's not just a question of the pot calling the kettle black. I've always trusted you, and you me. If either of us did not like something the other had done, we would have it out, so that's why I'm here now.'

Chris was clearly disturbed. He said nothing for a few seconds. Then: 'Look, Greg, I value what you are doing for me a lot. Sure the *trade* is a bit of a lark and I'll tell you when it must stop going through here. I don't like what I hear, but I must trust him until events prove I can't. Leave it with me.'

'OK,' replied Greg, 'I am going to ask Mary to stay for a few days whilst I think about our future together. I am more than very fond of her. What I would really like is for us to be married.' He asked Chris if there was anything at the yard he shouldn't show Mary, as he knew she'd be interested in it all.

Chris's humour returned, and he said with a smile, 'Don't go into the warehouse until your stuff has gone!'

Greg was on the boat when Mary returned, empty-handed.

'You don't look very pleased to see me,' she said as she climbed aboard. She then explained that she had promised a couple of quid to a boatman to bring the shopping across to the pontoon as there was too much for her to carry.

Just then an old boy in a dinghy cut his outboard and tied up to the pontoon as Mary waved to him. They unloaded from the dinghy what looked like half the contents of the supermarket, and Mary paid him off.

'I must settle with you for all this,' said Greg.

Mary shook her head. 'Forget it. It'll be my contribution.'

'You're a lovely, lovely person. What am I going to do without you?'

'Well, not starve, I hope!'

The Group Captain arrived in *Amity* at the pontoon astern of them. Greg helped him to tie up.

'My guess is that you are Paul,' called out Greg.

'Indeed,' was the reply. 'And you are Greg Norfield?'

When the boat was secure Greg was invited on board. They shook hands.

'I won't beat about the bush, Greg. Your firm has a good reputation around these parts. I want the best deal you can offer me – or if not a deal, the best advice. I've been posted abroad. Your boss, Mr Curnow, knows the boat from my visit here last year.'

'I won't waste your time either. I have checked our records. You have our quote for repairs. We understood last winter that you didn't wish to go ahead with these repairs. Mr Curnow and I agree that we cannot sell the craft in its present condition. We think our suggestion for repairs, which includes a new engine, is the minimum required to make the boat saleable. We would be happy if you sought another opinion. However, I have a proposition.'

'Please say what's on your mind.'

Greg had a good look around the boat, started the engine, listened carefully, and pointed out to the owner the black smoke from the exhaust.

'I wish to upgrade to a larger boat myself and am prepared to spend my own time and money on yours. To this end I will buy her from you and personally attend to all the suggestions in the Curnow recommendations of last year, but the maximum I can offer you as she stands is six thousand pounds.'

'I'll have to think about that. I'll let you know.'

Greg helped him to cast off and walked back to his boat.

'Well?' queried Mary.

'He's going to think about what I offered him. It was a bit low – but fair, I think. We'll just have to sweat it out.'

'Come on – positive thinking,' she said. 'I've seen a big change in you. You've got a wonderful opportunity down here. You have a real purpose to your life now. I'll keep my fingers crossed for you.'

'Do you know, Mary, I don't think I would have done that had it not been for you. You are such a positive person.' He put his arms round her. 'You make me so happy, and then you push off and leave me for God knows how long!'

'Firstly,' she replied, 'I don't like to hear you use God's name in that way. Secondly, what makes you think this happiness business is one-sided? We both have our lives to live. I shall miss you, you know that. But it doesn't have to be for ever.'

'No, indeed. Come on – we'll go up and tell Chris about *Amity* then I'll give you the grand tour.'

They saw Chris after their lunch in the caravan. He said nothing about Harry as Greg told him of the outcome of the Group Captain's visit. Chris had already met Mary the previous day. Greg announced he was now going to take Mary on a tour of the yard.

As they were going out of the door, Chris called, 'Don't forget to see Harry in the warehouse,' which Greg took to mean that his stuff was out of the way.

When they got there Harry was all smiles, and shook Mary's hand.

'We're new boys together, Greg and I. Expect Greg has told you,' he said, addressing Mary. 'This new chandlery agency my brother has taken on is going to mean quite a lot of work for both of us.'

'Yes, indeed,' Greg responded, 'especially for you at the start-up, Harry. Good luck.'

When they got outside Mary said, 'You didn't tell me Chris had a brother.'

'I didn't know until I got here' was the most Greg felt he could tell her about Harry.

They set off on their tour of the rest of the yard.

They returned to the caravan arm in arm.

'That was fascinating,' said Mary.

Greg gave her a hug.

'There's food here to last both of us a month,' he said laughing. 'You didn't actually say when you had to go back?'

'Must get back on Wednesday, I'm afraid. Have to see my letting agent about the flat, move my personal gear into the spare bedroom, and pack in time to set off for Aberdeen.'

Next day, Sunday, Paul Partick brought *Amity* round again and tied up at the pontoon. He agreed to Greg's offer, and they used Chris's office to draw up the bill of sale. Greg handed over his cheque. Within a few days, after clearance of the cheque, he would legally be the owner of *Amity*. Greg left a note on the office door to say he was around for business. He could keep an eye on the office from the pontoon. Now he and Mary could inspect his new purchase.

'That'll keep you busy whilst I'm away,' was Mary's wry comment.

Mary clearly was close to tears when they said goodbye on Wednesday. Greg walked slowly back to the caravan. Why hadn't he asked her to marry him?

The knock on the caravan door was Harry.

'I'm sorry, Greg, for what I said the other day. I've given it a fair bit of thought. My experience of the last three years has left me a bit edgy.'

'I really am trying to understand, Harry. Please

sit down and perhaps we can talk it through.'

'I think I was a bit harsh about your girlfriend and about dumping her,' continued Harry. 'After all, if you're going to run a scam, a bit of inside knowledge is invaluable. You could pick up a lot of tips about how not to be caught, eh? I also think I have a way of leaving Chris out of the equation altogether using a pal's courier business.' And with that he left.

Greg's moral indignation at Harry could hardly be reconciled with his own avarice. Over two thousand pounds was on its way from Antonio, Chris's London pal, in cash. Leaving Chris out of it all should safeguard the yard, and private road transport organised by Harry, who had everything to lose, like his freedom, ought to be fairly safe and reliable.

He went over to the office. Chris and Flossie were there.

'I've sorted things out satisfactorily with your brother this morning, Chris. I would like to go back to Salcombe if you don't need me.' Before Chris could comment Greg went on to explain that he had a prospective customer for the forty-five-foot ketch. After he completed the demonstration sail that morning he would speak to other boat owners who were on their brokerage list and that would tie things up for a few days whilst he was away.

Chris went along with this plan and spoke to Greg at the top of the steps, out of Flossie's hearing.

'I'm glad you've made it up with Harry. I don't think he means a lot of what he says. I guess three years in the nick makes you like that. Did you know his wife divorced him while he was in prison?'

Greg said he hadn't really talked on a personal basis with Harry, but he would make an effort to get to know him better.

'By the way,' said Greg, 'where is he living?'

'Oh, he's sharing a cottage a few miles away with an old friend who has a courier business running goods between Torquay, Exeter and London. We might use him ourselves if he's competitive.'

Doubts returned to Greg's mind.

'Who is the old friend, then?'

'He's Harry's old cell mate from Dartmoor, by the name of Selby. Apparently they got on so well together in the nick that when Selby's mother died just before they were released Selby invited Harry to share the cottage he'd just inherited.'

The trial sail of the ketch went well. The couple he took out were pleased enough to leave a substantial deposit, saying they would be back in a week or so to pay the balance. He went up to Chris's office to tell him.

'I've decided to take *Amity* to Salcombe. A short trip like that will help me sort out things that require attention.'

'I just hope the engine doesn't conk out on you,' said Chris, pursing his lips and looking dubious. 'I seem to remember we thought it was shot.'

'Well, I will just have to sail, won't I? The sails are in good condition – they look as if they've hardly been used. Perhaps that's the problem. Previous owners have used the engine all the time and flogged it to death. It's only an underpowered auxiliary.'

With that Greg took his leave of Chris and set about getting *Amity* ready for sea. He could tell from the sound of the engine that it was 'tired', and the black smoke from the exhaust confirmed the yard's notes (that it had reached the end of its life), but he thought the sailing performance would be better than his old boat, and he was not wrong. He made good time under sail to Salcombe.

That evening at his usual anchorage in Robbie's Creek he called the Trehairnes on his cellphone. It was Frank who answered.

'Thanks for responding to my call yesterday. This is really important. Can you come over for supper? I've something we need to talk about urgently.'

'Sounds mysterious to me,' Greg answered. 'Ouch – just remembered. I haven't got a dinghy with me. I have bought a new boat and am trying her out. I forgot to bring the dinghy. Boat's name is *Amity*, by the way.'

'Hang on a minute, Greg,' said Frank, and Greg heard him put the handset down. He came back a minute later. 'Julia says she's going to row down to fetch you – needs the exercise or something. Says she will be there at five o'clock if that's all right.'

'Five o'clock is fine,' said Greg. 'See you later.'

Julia was on time. She came alongside in her dinghy and climbed aboard.

'Hi, you lovely creature,' said Greg. 'I'm flattered to have you come to greet me personally.'

'You know how I feel about you,' was her reply. Julia moved close to Greg.

'Now is the moment of truth,' he thought. He had come here partly to sort out his priorities. Julia was attracted to him. He was naturally flattered to have the attention of a pretty young girl. But wasn't he in love with Mary?

'Julia, I think you are a lovely girl, but . . .' he started to say as she moved closer.

She put her fingers to his lips to stop him.

'Don't you realise I love you,' she said.

The ring of his cellphone installed in the main saloon intervened. He went below to answer.

'What are you two doing down there?' said Frank with a chuckle. 'I sent Julia to bring you up for a very important meeting.'

'Leaving now,' said Greg and switched off the phone. He knew what he had to say next. 'Julia, you are not in love with me. Yes, I think you are terrific, but I am older than your father. I am also very fond of your family. You have all become good friends. Can we leave it like that?'

She replied with a brief look of real annoyance, 'OK, have it your way – let's go.' And leading the way down the stern ladder they boarded her dinghy. She grabbed the oars and pulled for the landing a little further up the creek. If she had been hurt by Greg's remarks, she certainly wasn't showing it any more.

As she rowed she said, 'You know, you really shouldn't rattle on about your age. It doesn't sound like you at all, so utterly negative. I took you as such a positive person. Are you saying you don't want to see me again?'

'I'm saying no such thing,' he replied, mindful that he wanted to keep his friendship with the Trehairnes. 'What I am saying is that you are barely eighteen. You have your whole life before you – just take it easy.'

Greg was glad that they had arrived at the landing and as they clambered ashore and hauled the dinghy up the slope he had time to think. He did not want to be discussing their relationship as they arrived at the house.

'Look, let's put this on hold for another time,' he said. 'You have all said that there's something important to discuss and your father called and seemed anxious that we should be home as soon as possible.'

Her reply was as disarming as usual: 'OK – another time. I suppose you are carrying those oars so that you can keep me at a distance!'

'You know perfectly well that nobody leaves a dinghy on the foreshore with the oars. That's like leaving your bike in the high street unlocked.'

She turned, and with her engaging smile, laughed, and said, 'Sorry, sir – I won't do it again.'

CHAPTER FIVE

Covert

Up at the house Joan greeted Greg with a hug and Frank's firm handshake was welcoming. Joan and Julia left them in the living room with a full jug of cider and a couple of mugs.

'Look, I'll get straight to the point. Do you trust me, Greg?'

'Well, if I didn't, I wouldn't be here.'

'This is going to push our trust to the limit,' said Frank. 'What I am about to tell you is highly confidential. Not even Joan and Julia know the details. If you don't want to have anything to do with it, just say so and we'll forget the matter altogether and never mention it again.'

'Well, I've gone this far. In for a penny in for a pound.'

'Thousands of pounds, more like it,' said Frank.

Greg looked amazed and thought of his pension fund.

Frank topped up the mugs and proceeded to outline an incredible plan: 'You have met Nick Wroughton, the harbourmaster. He has approached me to put this proposition to you. Nick has contacts in Whitehall. He will not identify who they are or which department they work for. I trust him absolutely.'

Greg remembered Frank had implied that Nick knew about the 'trade' and that he was *'one of us'*.

'You have been singled out for a secret operation under the code name of Troag. It is in the interests of the country, and you will be safe from any interference from the authorities. It is to do with transporting certain goods to Dartmouth which you have to collect from another boat a few miles offshore.'

'And the goods?' questioned Greg.

Frank looked him straight in the eye. 'I am not party to that information, nor am I permitted to give you any more details until you have agreed to participate in this clearly covert operation. However, because it has to take place tonight and we need your answer right now, I am permitted to tell you that the fee is such that you are unlikely to refuse! Your fee is ten thousand pounds. Yes or no?'

Greg looked astounded. 'Say that again, Frank.'

'I said ten thousand pounds. Yes or no?'

'Of course the answer is yes, but why tonight? I'm going back to Dartmouth tomorrow anyway.'

'For ten grand Greg, I don't think I personally would argue. There are very good reasons for the timing.'

Greg felt guilty for questioning his trusted and trusting friend and quickly apologised.

'Now that you have agreed, I have to make a phone call. After that I will tell you what you do.' Frank reached for the phone, dialled a number and said 'Troag – yes, and, note, new boat's name is *Amity* – Alpha Mike India Tango Yankee.' He turned to Greg. 'Now listen carefully and do not make notes.'

The supper provided by Joan was subdued that evening as they could not discuss what was foremost in their minds. Greg was glad when the time came to suggest that he should be away to catch the ebb tide. The prospect of more money in the bank in the next twenty-four hours than he'd accumulated in years was the driving force.

Julia walked down to the landing with him and again took the oars.

'When will you be back?' she said as they approached *Amity*.

'I'm not sure,' he replied as he reached for his stern ladder and climbed on board, deliberately avoiding any possible contact between them, 'but I *will* be back – I promise.'

She pulled hard against the ebb to return to the landing.

He raised anchor and motored downstream to the quay, where he was directed by Nick to a berth alongside. The adventure had begun and Greg rested in the main saloon as he went through in his mind his instructions: time and time again.

The forecast was favourable – west to south-west, force three to four. Now dark, his alarm had sounded but he had not slept. He cast off and motored his way slowly down the harbour. There was a neap tide with just sufficient water to clear the bar. He cleared the Poundstone to starboard, then Wolf Rock to port and found no swell on the bar as he made his way out to the rendezvous, eight miles offshore.

It was a clear night. He could see the flashing light at Start Point to reassure him of his position. He altered course eastwards for Dartmouth as instructed. Above the sound of his own noisy engine he heard powerful motors. Out of the east he saw the rapidly approaching navigation lights of whatever it was he could hear. The approaching craft moved around to his stern, shone a powerful light on the name of his boat on the transom and then drew alongside. In the dark Greg could just see it was a very large fast rigid inflatable (RIB) launch.

'Ahoy there, *Amity*,' a voice called out. 'Hold your course. This is Troag.'

'Come aboard,' cried Greg.

Two, out of what appeared to be five or six men, stepped from the RIB onto his side deck, climbed over the safety lines and made their way into the cockpit. The other craft, with a roar from twin outboard engines, powered away at speed.

They were dressed identically – white woolly hats, red sailing jackets, dark blue trousers and leather deck shoes. The taller of the two had a flight case in his hand, the other a backpack.

'I am your crew,' said the man with the flight case. 'I would like first to take our guest down below and make him comfortable.'

The second man did not speak. Although there was little light, Greg noted that he was dark-skinned with a neat goatee beard, and as the two strangers went below they were speaking in English. Greg's noisy engine excluded him from hearing more than a word or two. Within a couple of minutes his 'crew' returned to the cockpit and offered Greg a firm handshake.

'Call me Troag,' he said. 'I understand you are a single-hander; so if you don't want my help, just say so.'

'No, no,' said Greg. 'I've been told that you are a keen yachtsman – take the helm if you wish, whilst I go below and make us some coffee.'

'Not a good idea,' said the other man. 'I'll go below. Tell me where the stuff is and I will make the coffee. We'll easily make our landfall on time, so why not turn off the engine and unfurl your headsail?'

'It would be helpful,' said Greg, 'if I knew exactly where you want to go.'

'Dartmouth,' came the reply. 'I will tell you where to come alongside when we have entered the river. I understand you know these waters well.'

Greg knew he was going to get on fine with this man and guessed why he should not go down below. He set about unfurling the headsail and switching off the engine. With mugs of hot coffee they sat in the cockpit and discussed their position and distance to run.

This man was not giving much away about his present or past occupations, although it seemed likely from his conversation that he had been a professional sailor. Two or three times during the passage he went below to talk to his charge. He emerged into the cockpit to join Greg at about 2 a.m. and asked him if he had noticed the flashing light to port. Greg sensed that he was checking up on his navigation.

'Yes,' he said. 'That was Start Point. I've cleared it by a couple of miles to keep outside the race. In an hour or so we should be in the sector leading lights at the entrance to Dartmouth. We've a good flood tide helping us all the way now.'

Troag spoke: 'I can see you know what you are doing and I've enjoyed your company. Let's hope one day we can meet again under different circumstances, over a pint perhaps, and have a natter about it all. Don't forget that neither of us can ever talk to anyone else about this – ever.'

Greg felt that it was the moment to mention his payment and as if the other man had guessed his thoughts he spoke: 'The case that I brought aboard contains your money as agreed. You are going to have to trust me. I assure you it is all there. The case is weighted so as to sink should it fall overboard. I would have chucked it and still will chuck it over the side should we encounter anyone attempting to question our mission. It is yours, and neither I nor anyone else will have the slightest idea how it came into your possession. The reason why you were chosen was so that should this boat be seen entering the Dart it can be identified as being a local craft on legitimate business. Also you have a reputation as a person of integrity and can be trusted.'

Greg nodded his understanding and they both concentrated on identifying the leading lights on the Dart river entrance. They passed through the red sector and were into the white sector, where they altered course to stay in it and steer safely into harbour. Greg started the engine, cleared all sail and asked the other man where he'd be going ashore. The answer, much to Greg's surprise, was the Naval College pontoon on the west side of the river.

At that moment the engine stuttered and fell silent. Greg reached for the key. He turned it back to *OFF* and forward again to *START* – just a groan from the starter motor to indicate the batteries were flat.

It was a dark night. The moderate westerly breeze combined with the flood tide was taking the boat rapidly toward the rocks on the east side of the entrance. Whilst deep, the channel into Dartmouth becomes narrow, with jagged rocks on either side. Greg quickly unfurled the genoa to gain some control.

He said to his companion, 'What do you know about engines?'

'A bit' was the reply. 'Where's the access?'

'Behind the companionway steps. They lift out. Here, take my torch. Think I've got enough steerage with the headsail but the wind gets fluky in the narrows.'

By the time Greg had said his piece his companion had shot below and was peering into the engine compartment.'

'Stinks of diesel down here,' he shouted, and, a moment later, 'You've got a fractured fuel pipe. I need some tape.'

'Too bad,' Greg shouted back. 'This is the first time I've sailed this boat. I haven't a clue where anything is.'

By now Greg was peering into the darkness, trying to identify the Castle Ledge buoy. They were in the green sector of the light, which meant the danger was to starboard. There was no way he could leave the helm to raise the mainsail. He judged it better to give his companion a moment or two longer in case he could get the engine to start. He heard the sound of the engine being turned by hand.

'We're bloody close to the rocks.' The anxiety in Greg's shout was evident.

The steep shore of Kettle Point loomed into sight.

'Lean over here,' his companion gasped, 'and

drop the decompression levers whilst I use two hands to turn this beast.'

Greg switched the ignition key to *START*, left the helm to its own devices and hung forward over the step to feel for the levers on top of the engine.

As Troag reached maximum effort to turn the engine with the starter handle he yelled, 'Now!'

Greg dropped down first one lever, and, as the engine fired, the second. He reached back for the tiller, pushed it hard to starboard, put her into forward gear, and opened the throttle. His companion, now back in the cockpit, said, 'I'll take care of the headsail. We'll leave it out just in case. I can't be sure my repair will last long.'

'What did you do?' said Greg.

Their breathing returned to normal as they steered out of the green sector of the light and back into the white.

'Surgical tape' came the answer. 'Grabbed your first-aid box and bound the pipe with a sticky dressing, so keep your fingers crossed. Good thing you know this harbour entrance well. How close to the rocks were we?'

'Very close. At one point the echo sounder showed only five feet and there's a bit of a swell on at the moment. I was waiting for the crunch.'

'Well done, Greg. We chose you for a reason.'

'Joint effort, I think,' replied Greg.

They recognised the relief in their own voices. With the shore lights of Kingswear to starboard and the lights on Dartmouth's ferry pontoon straight ahead to guide them through the narrows they made their way upstream.

'It shouldn't need me to tell you', said his temporary crew, 'that, whatever you do, don't stop that stinking heap of metal you've got in the bilges down below until after you've dumped us and finally tied up wherever it is you're going!'

Well before sunrise they approached the designated pontoon. Greg brought *Amity* alongside. Several men he had not noticed in the shadows held her firmly just off the pontoon.

'No need for warps,' said his temporary crew and with a firm handshake and 'Good luck' he helped his passenger to disembark.

Before he stepped over the rail this gentleman offered his hand to Greg.

'I am grateful – thank you. May your God go with you.'

Greg detected a slight foreign accent. Then he felt the boat being pushed out into the river. The whole landing operation had taken less than a minute.

Moments later he reached the pontoon at the Curnow Yard and safely tied up. He was burning to look inside his suitcase down below. With halyards frapped, and deck tidied, he turned off the engine. There was still some time to go before dawn. He descended the companionway steps, closed the hatch and bolted it. In the forecabin on the bunk was the flight case. He checked that all the curtains remained drawn closed as they had been throughout the passage and turned on the bunk light, now dim from the depleted batteries.

The case had two combination locks, each with three wheels. For a moment he caught his breath as he wondered what the combinations could be and cursed himself for not having asked. The wheels had letters of the alphabet, not numerals. He did not dare touch the wheels until he had noted their positions and tried the opening levers. Nothing happened. He had three choices: work out the combination (normally thousands to one against), break the case open (it had an aluminium body and stainless steel locks and latches), or phone Frank. He began to tremble with anger and frustration.

'THINK,' he called out to himself. 'Eureka!' he cried as he aligned TRO on the left-hand wheels, flipped the lever, and the latch flew open. On the right-hand latch wheels he entered A and then G. Holding his breath, he tried each of the remaining letters in turn on the third wheel. At S it flew open. He raised the lid.

On top of neatly bundled banknotes was an ordinary sheet of A4 paper in the middle of which was written, "Ha, ha! Knew you'd get it. We'll meet one day. Now burn this note."

Ten thousand pounds – all there. He instinctively knew the used banknotes could not be forgeries. If they had wanted to cheat him, there need not have been anything in the case except the two bricks. He burned the note and flushed the ashes down the sea toilet. He celebrated with a large tot of Calvados.

No sooner had he got his head down than he was asleep.

When he woke, Greg's face creased into a smile. The under-bunk locker would do for a while but a safer place must be sought for his "pension fund". Over breakfast he decided on a deed box in the bank. Nowhere could be safer. Where else does one keep money? The smile was soon wiped out. Through the window he saw a stranger approaching the gangway.

This man had binoculars hanging round his neck. He was wearing a dark blue Breton cap, a heavy fisherman's navy-blue roll-necked sweater and smartly creased navy trousers. His shoes were of the cheap blue plimsoll variety. As he came nearer, Greg noticed he was short and slight of build with a thin black moustache. Greg moved up into the cockpit to investigate.

'I say, old boy, are you Gregory Norfield?' said the stranger from the pontoon.

Greg nodded.

'Hope you don't mind my intrusion but I thought it about time that we met. I'm Selby Somerfield-Smythe – Smythe with an 'e', you know. Harry's mate, so to speak.'

He struck Greg as a cross between an upper-class twit and a rogue. Terry Thomas came to mind.

'Tell me,' said Greg: 'how did you get into the yard?'

The man put his hand into his pocket and pulled out a bunch of keys, which he waggled in front of Greg's face.

'How did you get those?'

'Harry. Look, old boy,' said Selby, 'don't you think it might be a good idea if you were a little more friendly? For one thing I've been handling your stuff and for another you owe me seventy quid. Also I am here to take your latest loot.'

'There isn't any,' said Greg.

He smelled trouble.

'How about a friendly cup of tea,' said Selby, 'and we can have a nice little chat. It's been bloody cold around here for the last few hours.'

Greg was horrified. What had this man been doing in the yard for several hours?

'Come aboard,' said Greg, and told him to sit in the cockpit whilst he went below to get the tea.

When Greg emerged back into the cockpit Selby was scanning the other side of the river with his binoculars.

'Is that the Naval College on top of the hill over there?' he said.

Greg answered with a nod.

'Is there a landing or somewhere there where we could offload your stuff in future, so that we might avoid this place altogether?'

Greg suggested that would add some twenty or thirty miles to the journey.

'You're wrong there, matey,' said Selby. 'Harry and I share a cottage near Buckfastleigh. Distance is the same. I figured, old boy, having watched you coming and going, that you might know of somewhere convenient over there.'

Had Selby spotted his very brief stop at the College pontoon in the early hours? Unlikely. He had decided to turn off his navigation lights before crossing the river, as there was not much movement of other boats at that time.

'It's just that I was wondering, old bean,' continued Selby, 'that if your little bit of trade were to expand, Harry and I would like to think that we were your sole distributors, so to speak – if you get my drift.'

Greg got his drift all right. He smelled blackmail, just as he had done the first time he met Harry.

'There is nothing more at the moment,' said Greg. 'As far as money is concerned the arrangement was and still is that I only deal with Harry. I will let Harry have the money owing to you. Sorry to push you off but I have a lot to do this morning.'

Selby delivered a parting shot as he climbed off the boat.

'Well, old boy, we're all in this together, I reckon. Don't worry, I'll lock up behind me and let Harry have his keys back.'

Early next morning saw Greg in Chris's office. He told him about the meeting with Selby.

'I'm not happy about that one little bit,' said Chris. 'Firstly Harry should not have handed over his keys. That is something I can deal with, but, secondly, this bit of trade of yours is proving to be a complication. Look, Greg, I don't want to spoil things for you. Let me have a quiet word with Harry and then I will decide what we are going to do.'

With misgivings about the future for his pension fund, and whether he had been seen by Selby crossing the river in the early hours, Greg took the ferry over to Dartmouth. With his loot in a small holdall, and a deed box purchased from the locksmith off the High Street, he entered his bank. He had phoned them earlier to arrange a locker for his deed box. He was shown a small office where in total privacy he could transfer his goods into the box and then was given a receipt before it was taken to the vault. There was no evidence left except the flight case covered up in a forecabin locker, which he decided he would dump the next time he went to sea.

Chris came round to the caravan that Monday afternoon.

'How did *Amity* behave, then, Greg?'

'How right you were! The engine was big trouble.'

How could he possibly tell him about the drama with Troag, how he was lucky to have survived or why he got into such danger in the first place?

'When can I have her out, Chris? The sooner

the yard can get on with the repairs and replace the engine and batteries the better as far as I am concerned.'

'Right, I'll have words with Bill. My guess is that it would suit us if we had her out right away, before the crane gets busy with end-of-season work and probably the same applies to the workshop. I've had a talk with Harry. I want to support him and I want to support you as well. Harry desperately wants to keep both his job here and his nose clean. No way will he contemplate ending up inside again. He has admitted it was a serious mistake letting Selby have the keys. Selby had persuaded him that he would cut a deal with you that eliminated the Curnow Yard from risk. Harry's certain that if Selby's transport business is successful, your little scam will be safe with the two of them. Let's give it a go and see how we get on,' continued Chris.

'Agreed,' said Greg. 'Anyway, if my plans for the winter come about with your help, there won't be any 'trade' for some time. What I'd like to do is get the old boat sold. That will bring me some cash and some for the yard. This raises a point. It would be far more convenient both for you and for me if I conducted the brokerage and chandlery business from the caravan. Do you think we could get the telephone people to put an extension from your office to here?'

'Good idea,' said Chris. 'I'll get back to the office now; and I know you won't abuse it, but if you make the odd phone call to Aberdeen I'll keep

John Dalton off your back when he checks the bill!'

'I'll have room for her in the other shed at the end of the week.' said Bill, when Greg went to enquire about the hauling out of *Amity*. 'Depending on what we find when we start cutting out the osmosis-affected bits, we should need a week to repair the hull and another couple of days to install the new machinery.'

* * *

Many weeks later, during which time Greg had worked on *Amity* every spare hour at evenings and at weekends, Bill came to him.

'You are in luck,' he said. 'I know the managing director of a firm called 'X' Spars. They have designed self-furling mainsail gear for yachts. I mentioned to him that you were a writer for the yachting press. He wants to talk to you about fitting their new gear to your mast as a trial.'

After discussions with Bill's contact Greg ended up with a deal that effectively gave him furling gear for nothing, provided he could tell the yachting press that it worked well. This would greatly increase the value of the boat.

* * *

Those winter months flew by for Greg. There was the promotion of the new French chandlery agency and also Curnow's growing brokerage business, his own writing for two yachting magazines, plus the work on *Amity*.

The phone calls to Mary in Scotland became less frequent as the months went by, although he missed her more and more. She was busy. He was busy.

When Christmas came round Greg suffered the disappointment of Mary being unable to come down from Scotland. She was on duty over the holiday but thought she might get two weeks' leave at Easter. He applied himself to more work on the boat over the holiday.

He had another unwelcome visit from Selby, who wanted to know why 'trade' had dried up. Greg's relationship with Harry improved as they worked together on the parts listing and catalogue.

Amity was craned back into the water at the beginning of April. Greg was looking forward to Mary's visit, in a couple of weeks' time, for Easter. He was on *Amity* when he heard Chris call from the pontoon for permission to come aboard.

'Put the kettle on, Greg,' he said as he looked around. 'I don't wish to say I told you so, but you've got some boat here, you know.'

'Don't worry, I do know that only too well. I've got one hell of a lot to thank you for.'

'I'm not looking for thanks, Greg, but I have been doing some thinking. I've not asked you for anything in return for the use of the yard for transit of your stuff. Everybody is on a fiddle of some sort,' said Chris, 'but just how big is this fiddle of yours going to be?'

'Chris, you know I've been trying to build up a bit of a pension fund, that's all. I also realise this lark is becoming a liability for all of us.'

Chris replied, 'Your contribution has been every bit as good as I asked of you and more. Why can't you settle for what I have on offer here and that nice Miss Rowlinson? In fact, I've decided that, given 'a fair wind', so to speak, at the end of the year I'd make you a director of the firm. I've been speaking to John Dalton and we reckon we could split the takings from the brokerage with you by way of payment. How does that grab you?'

Greg was overcome with shame. Putting them at risk from his dubious activities had been bothering him for some time. What Chris had said made sense, and the thought of getting rid of a web of deceit was a relief.

'You are right, yet again,' said Greg, thinking of the tidy sum he had in the bank from the Troag episode, about which, of course, Chris knew nothing, as well as the other transactions. 'The "bit o' trade" lark ceases as from now. I'll take an early opportunity to tell the Trehairnes. Mary is coming down at Easter. She tells me that she thinks she will have some important news for me. Wouldn't say what it was. Your offer is accepted.

'OK,' said Chris. 'I'll tell John and he'll confirm it to you in writing.'

CHAPTER SIX

Mary

A week before Easter, Mary rang to tell Greg that she had procured a better job back with her old boss in Southampton. It started at the end of her Easter leave. Greg asked her to come down for Easter by train and then, if she wanted, they'd sail back together to Southampton.

'What do you mean, if I wanted?' she almost shouted down the phone.

'Oh, Mary, my love, you've no idea how I've missed you.'

Two days before Easter Mary phoned Greg to ask him to collect her from Newton Abbot. Nobody, observing them outside the railway station where they met, could have been left in any doubt about their fondness for each other.

'Oh, Mary,' he said as they hugged, 'you are beautiful.'

'Not so dusty yourself,' she replied

'Not very romantic meeting you in this,' he said, as he steered her towards the Curnow van.'

'Oh, I completely forgot you don't have a car.

I shouldn't have asked.'

On the drive back to Kingswear she told him about the choice she'd had to make between Aberdeen and Southampton. 'To say nothing of being nearer to you,' she said with a grin. 'I will effectively be understudying my old boss, Don Carruthers.'

As they drove, Greg told her about the new brokerage arrangement with Chris.

Back at the caravan Mary looked around.

'Glad to see the place tidier than the last time I was here,' she said with a chuckle. 'Now, what's the plan?'

'Firstly we open a bottle to celebrate your arrival. Then I cook you dinner. Tomorrow I show you the new *Amity*. I shall be working over Easter, I'm afraid. It's a good time for people wanting to buy boats, and we have a few which I've been advertising widely for sale. Got to be here for business over the holiday, but from Tuesday we are free, weather permitting, to set sail for Southampton. I don't have to be back until the weekend. Flossie will hold the fort.'

The next morning Mary went with Greg down to the pontoon.

'My word,' she said, admiring *Amity*, 'she really looks something now. You must have been working your socks off.'

He told her all about being under cover in the boatshed for the winter, Chris's generosity, and the massive help from Bill Fossett.

'You've got good friends there. Look, I don't suppose you've had time to stock up for our trip. When the shops are open again on Saturday, you are going to be busy. How about I take charge of the victualling for our sail to the Solent?'

'You're a gem' was his reply, accompanied by a hug.

Greg went around with a permanent smile on his face.

When Chris noticed he called out, 'What did I tell you, Greg? You look like the cat that's stolen the cream when that girl is around. By the way, Rosemary has talked me into spending more time at home this Easter. The shipyard is closed for four days. Will I be seeing you before you set sail to take Mary back?'

'Yep. Not planning to cast off until ten o'clock on Tuesday morning. I'll look in first thing.'

It was a busy weekend for Greg. The high point was that he sealed the deal on his old boat. It meant eleven thousand for him and seven hundred for Curnow. He took a deposit on the forty-five-foot ketch and dealt with three other enquiries that looked promising. Now he could sail with a clear conscience.

Mary never ceased to amaze Greg. While he'd been busy with the customers, in addition to the shopping she had checked everything on *Amity* – fuel, batteries, VHF radio, Calor gas, life jackets, flares – and topped up the freshwater tank.

It was the Tuesday after Easter. Chris arrived at his office at eight that morning. Greg was waiting for him.

'How did the weekend go, Chris?'

'Excellent. Rosemary and I have not spent so much time together for years. Our trip to Torquay, crowded though it was, seemed fun. Shops were fantastic. Rosemary was in her element. What about yours?'

'That was good too.' Greg gave Chris the news. He told him that the cellphone worked well on *Amity* and that they should be in range during the whole trip to Cowes. 'First stop Lyme Regis this evening. We should make Cowes on Wednesday. The forecast is good – a bit cold maybe, but I've got Mary to keep me warm!'

They sailed to catch the east-going tide. As they cleared the Mew Stone they set course for the thirty-odd miles to Lyme Regis. They huddled together in the cockpit – not just for warmth, but for the intense affection they shared.

'Oh, how I have missed you, my darling Mary! This is how I have dreamed our days would be: the cliffs, the sun, the sea, and you by my side.'

She smiled and drew closer. She closed her hand over his on the tiller.

'You do not have a monopoly on those feelings, my love. I have dreamed of this day for all those months I have been away.'

Never more than a few miles from the shore, they followed the big sweep of Lyme Bay along the Jurassic Coast. The coastline rises to high cliffs one moment, then stretches of low land. With the afternoon sun shining on the yellow sandstone at the top of Golden Cap, the highest cliff on the South Coast, they steered straight for this unmistakeable landmark that would lead them to the outer arm of The Cobb, the attractive little harbour at Lyme Regis.

Mary called the harbourmaster on the marine VHF to find out if they would be welcome for the night. A couple of hours later, running close enough to the shore to see the crumbling shale cliffs west of the harbour, they cleared the outer wall and turned back to the west, motoring through the narrow entrance of the harbour. They tied up at the old stone quay outside the Museum where *Amity* would take the ground safely.

Arm in arm they made their way along the granite Cobb wall.

'I tied up here,' said Greg, 'when I sailed from the Solent to start my new life in Devon. I was sad then, not knowing when I would see you again. Now I am blissfully happy.'

Mary whispered in his ear. 'Me too.'

On Wednesday evening, they reached Cowes.

As they furled all sail and started the engine to enter the river Mary said, 'Wouldn't it be fun to see my old colleagues?'

Greg had misgivings about that and said so.

'Don't be a spoilsport. I'll only be a few minutes. We can tie up on the Customs pontoon. When I've seen my old pals I'll pop next door and check on the ferry times to Southampton in the morning.'

They had agreed that Greg should sail from Cowes the next morning so as to be back in Dartmouth by the weekend. One stop in Weymouth should do it. He did not have pleasant memories of the last time he was tied up on the Customs pontoon.

She returned in half an hour.

'That was great to see them again. For old times' sake, can we go back to the pub where we had our first date?'

So up the river they motored to the marina in East Cowes.

Seven o'clock saw them in the pub. Nothing seemed to have changed, and after they were well into their drinks, and laughing at the incident that led to their first meeting, Mary leaped up.

'Got a surprise for you, Greg,' she said, and a tall man who seemed familiar walked over to them and held out his hand as he spoke.

'Our intrepid dope smuggler, I believe?'

Greg looked to Mary.

'You obviously don't remember my boss, Don Carruthers?'

'I'll put you out of your misery,' said Don. 'I

was in uniform then. You had a passenger on your yacht who tried to flush his dope down your heads.'

'Ahh,' said Greg, 'not something of which I am proud.'

'Let us talk about more pleasant things,' said Don. 'I think congratulations are in order, don't you, Greg?'

Before Greg could answer – in fact, he didn't understand the question – Mary intervened: 'I asked Don to join us. I haven't told you Greg; I wanted it to be a surprise for the evening. When I saw Don earlier he told me it was no longer confidential information that I am to take over his job one day.'

She went on to explain that her appointment was largely due to his recommendation and that it would mean a hike-up in grade from assistant preventive officer to a full PO – another ring on the sleeve.

'I have to tell you', said Don, 'that I am pleased to meet again the man who has so much influence on Mary. I really should have left you two alone this evening but I wanted to wish you both well for the future.'

There was an embarrassed silence for a few seconds as Mary and Greg looked at each other.

'Oh dear,' said Mary, 'I didn't realise that it showed that much.'

At that moment Greg's happiness was absolute. His face turned into a tender smile as put his arm around Mary's shoulders. As Mary coloured up, Don could see he'd said something out of turn. He thought Greg knew how fond Mary was of him. He felt embarrassed himself, and as he rose to leave he leaned toward them.

'Well, I'm glad we didn't lock you up, or Mary would have been visiting you in Dartmoor.'

'I wouldn't have minded if she'd had me in handcuffs the first night we met on the boat!' said Greg laughing, at which Mary coloured up again.

Don smiled, and said, as he turned to walk out of the pub, 'At the time, I advised Mary not to rely too much on intuition. I warned her that her intuition would get her into trouble one day. In the event she was right about you.'

Greg realised that he had been very lucky indeed not to have been prosecuted at that time and he now suffered stabs of conscience knowing that Mary's intuition about him being an innocent party had played a large part in him getting away with it, and an even larger part in their getting together.

The next morning he put Mary ashore on the Southampton fast-ferry pontoon and made his way out into the Solent. As soon as the diminishing figure of Mary blowing kisses to him disappeared from view as he sailed out of the river, he knew what he really wanted: a home with Mary. He could still turn back and tell her.

Why didn't he? Perhaps it was because he was reminded of his father's words shortly before his marriage over thirty years ago: *"Young men forsake all common sense when faced with the love of a woman."*

He turned westwards for Dartmouth. He decided to sail overnight non-stop for the Dart. The wind was south of west, which meant he could complete the passage with only a few long tacks during the night and make his landfall in daylight early next morning. A twelve-hour sail effectively cancels out the east/west tidal changes. His starboard tack took him well outside the Portland Race.

'There's one thing about night sailing,' he said to himself: 'it gives you plenty of time to think.'

As he sailed through the night he thought of his future. As he looked at the stars he thought of Mary – what life would be like with her by his side. Clear of the shore lights, the stars were bright – near enough for him to reach out and grab one. Was he mad not to have grabbed at the chance for happiness? All he need have said was 'Will you marry me?'

At first light the next morning he was some twelve miles south-east of Berry Head. He had been watching its flashing light for half an hour.

'Two short tacks and I'll be home in a couple of hours. No drama. Get your head down until lunchtime. And it's only Friday. Good 'un Greg,' he said out loud to himself. And so it was.

A voice calling out if it might come aboard woke him. It was Chris.

'Saw your arrival. Guessed you'd be tired, so left you alone.'

'What time is it?' said Greg sleepily.

He hadn't even bothered to take off his sailing clothes, just his boots.

'Four in the afternoon,' said Chris. 'I assume you sailed all night?'

'Yes indeed. And, ye gods, I'm hungry!'

'Well, before you attend to that I've some good news – lots of news actually, but this bit will do for now. The guy came back with his wife for the ketch, paid the balance with a building-society cheque. John called the bank to find his deposit had cleared so I let him sail away.'

'That's great. What's the other news?'

'I'll leave that until tomorrow, Greg. It's a bit complicated and will take time to explain. I assure you there's nothing for you to worry about. In fact I'm confident you will approve of my little plan for the future, and it involves you.'

'Well, sounds mighty mysterious to me, but as it so happens I too have plans to tell you about *my* future.'

'We'll swap plans in the morning, then, if you're free?' said Chris.

Greg was finishing his breakfast in the caravan when Chris banged on the door.

'Give us a cuppa and I'll get to the point,' he said. 'This is going to take a minute or two. During the three days you have been away things have moved fast. I didn't want to interrupt your time with Mary.'

'Great,' said Greg, 'but where do I come in?'

Chris continued: 'When I handed over the brokerage to you what I didn't tell you was that I had been approached a couple of years ago by a large international firm of yacht brokers to provide them with a branch office here on the premises. At that time I turned them down. They phoned again on Tuesday just after you left. John Dalton has, quite rightly, urged me to reconsider their improved offer. It would make a considerable contribution to our cash flow.'

Chris went on to tell Greg that he had agreed to their offer subject to Greg being the manager of the branch and wanting the job.

'What do you mean, wanting the job?'

'They proposed putting in a salaried manager. After talking to their managing director, Brian Hope, he said he had no objection to yourself, but the best way, if you wanted the job, would be for you to put forward to them a three-year plan showing costs, turnover and potential profit. We keep your services. You have a salaried job and still become a director of Curnow Ltd. Happiness all round!'

'You're a bloody genius, Chris. Now for my news. Thought you should be the first to know – I'm going to ask Mary to marry me.'

'That's great, Greg. What have I been telling you all along?' Chris answered with a laugh. 'I am so happy for you. Is it all right if I call Rosemary to tell her?'

Greg nodded his head vigorously.

'As far as the new job is concerned, you can go to Lymington, where they are based, and negotiate your own contract. They obviously need to talk to you before entering a deal with us, which they are keen to pursue. As well as the lump sum they will pay us for exclusive brokerage on this site; they will pay the Curnow Yard Ltd rent for the sales office, which Curnow will have to build and you manage.'

Greg thought for a moment.

'Why should I be so favoured?'

'Because you have done good work for me over the last eight months and barely been paid. You've been an asset to the company and I need an assistant. I trust you. You have proved your worth – will that do?'

Greg reminded him that he'd had free berthing, parking for the caravan and many other benefits.

'Sure,' said Chris, 'and now I want it on a formal basis. John and I have discussed every aspect of this plan. There is a place for you here. It's up to you.'

'What about your brother?' asked Greg.

'Harry is happy doing what he does, and I'm extremely glad he's doing it. Sure, he's overqualified, but the efficiency of the warehouse operation is more important now than it ever was. I have noticed a vast improvement there since Harry has been in charge. I'll be straight with you, Greg. You know that blood is thicker than water, but I know that given the right encouragement Harry will keep his nose clean. He is not anywhere near as experienced as you, either in business or to do with boats. He knows he could not do the job I'm asking you to do.'

'When do you want me to contact these people in Lymington?'

'As soon as possible' was the reply. 'Phone Brian Hope on Monday morning. Flossie will give you the details. The company name is QC Ltd. It stands for Quality Craft. You can use one of our vans to drive there if it's available – have a word with John first.'

Chris got up to leave but before he got to the door Greg grasped his hand.

'I don't know what to say, Chris.'

Back came the reply: 'Don't say anything until you return from Lymington. You might blow the interview! If you don't like their terms, I'm confident they'll still want to go ahead with their own manager; but Brian has promised to give me a full explanation if you turn it down or they turn you down.'

'Oh, come on, Chris,' said Greg. 'You know that's just not going to happen.'

Chris was beaming as he left the caravan.

Greg had much to think about and foremost was Mary. He knew she had moved back into her flat in Southampton. He phoned her there. She answered.

'There's a man here', he said in a disguised voice, 'who wants to marry you.'

The silence was agonising for Greg. He waited.

'That's Greg,' she blurted out. 'What did you say?'

'Will you marry me? I said.'

'I thought you'd never ask.'

'You still haven't answered me,' said Greg.

'Of course I will, you old fool,' she cried, 'but where are we going to live?'

'I admit', he said, 'there are one or two thorny problems to be worked out, but sailors are faced with such problems all the time, my darling lovely Mary. Let's work on it. Love will find a way, you said. You haven't told me you love me yet.'

'Now, listen, Greg, this isn't funny. Of course I love you, but I'm just about to start a new job and I'm a hundred and fifty miles away.'

'That's another thing we have in common' was his reply. 'I am about to start a new job and I also am a hundred and fifty miles away. Guess we need to talk about it.'

'Greg, my love, what are you on about?'

He told her about the QC offer. More important to him was the fact that he would probably be on his way to Lymington in the next few days, 'for my job interview', as he put it. 'Then I will only be about fifteen miles away. So how about giving me a bed for the night?'

'Put that way, and seeing as how you want my hand in marriage, I don't see how I can refuse,' she replied, laughing.

'I'll call you tomorrow when I know more,' he said, and they signed off with kisses blown down the phone.

Greg was waiting in the office when John Dalton came in on Monday morning.

'I know what you want, I think. Chris phoned me over the weekend. One of the vans will be available for you to take to Lymington any day this week.'

'Thanks, John. However, I've got another favour to ask. I'd like to see Mary in Southampton whilst I'm up there. Would it be OK to go up one day and come back the next? I'll make sure the tank is full when I return.'

John indicated his approval, as Flossie arrived for work, bright and breezy as usual.

'I know what you want,' she said to Greg.

'You lot must be mind-readers. You're the second one to say that in the last five minutes.'

'Use Chris's desk,' said Flossie. 'He won't be in for an hour or so. I'll try to get Mr Hope's secretary.

Flossie put the call through. Mr Hope could see him after lunch at two on Thursday. He was to bring his plan with him. Mr Hope and his financial director would go through it with him.

There followed two days of feverish activity, preparing the proposal for Greg to take to QC. On Wednesday morning Chris, John and Greg went through the plan they had all been working on. John Dalton emphasised that the sum QC were to pay up front was the main issue. In the short term it was important for their cash flow. They had taken delivery from the moulding company of the hull and deck for the patrol boat. Fitting out had commenced. The expenses were rising. John reminded Greg that Curnow had to bear the cost of the new office building.

Armed with all this information he phoned Mary, put on his one and only suit, and set off for Lymington on Thursday morning.

Brian Hope greeted Greg with a firm handshake. He was a man of about sixty, medium height, with plenty of well-groomed short grey hair. He introduced him to Tom Sinclair, the company secretary and financial director, who was sat next to him in a spacious office with a large mahogany table, at which Greg was signalled to sit. The panelled walls of this room were liberally decorated with Beken photographs of all types of pleasure craft. Greg didn't reckon any of these craft were worth less than quarter of a million.

'I like the principles agreed with Chris Curnow,' said Brian Hope. 'Tom here will check as to whether the sums add up. Tell me about yourself. I want to know why Chris has such a high opinion of you that he has practically made our agreement conditional upon our employment of you as branch manager.'

Greg gave Brian Hope a résumé of his business and boating experience and what he'd been doing for the Curnow Yard over the last seven or eight months. Thus, just half an hour after Greg had entered that office, Brian answered, 'Mr Norfield, I am satisfied you can do the job as manager. It remains for my financial director to comment on your figures.'

At that moment Tom Sinclair re-entered the room. He had a question.

'Mr Norfield, whilst it is commendable to link your salary to performance, rising as you suggest over the years as the sales volume increases, I am a little unsure how you will be able to do the job without assistance.'

'Mr Sinclair,' replied Greg, 'either our typist has made a mistake or I haven't put it down correctly but "salary" is meant to cover more than one person, when it becomes affordable. I'd like to think that employment of assistance is at the branch manager's discretion. Curnow will provide every assistance possible to make this plan profitable for both companies.'

'Does that satisfy you, Tom?' said Brian.

'It certainly does. I will amend the document to say "salaries", if I may.'

Greg nodded his assent, and Tom continued.

'My initial reaction from looking through the figures is that they will satisfy the board.'

Brian Hope rose from his chair.

'All that remains, Greg, is for us to chew this over. I don't have any more questions. If any arise, I'll give Chris or yourself a call. We have a board meeting next Monday. Tom will put this matter on the agenda and let you know our decision the moment we have made it.'

Greg shook hands with the two men and Brian's secretary showed him out.

The little MG was not in its reserved space outside Mary's place when Greg arrived. He parked the van nearby, from where he could see the entrance to the flat. He did not have long to wait. She parked, got out with an armful of packages, turned and saw him walking along the pavement toward her.

His arms went round her in an instant. She dropped her goods as they clung together. There is a closeness, a warmth, a fragrance, that is unique to lovers. They were oblivious to the obstruction they caused to passers-by on the pavement, who stepped round them and smiled – memories for some and hope for others.

'Now look what you've done!' was all she could utter as she dabbed at her eyes with the handkerchief she took from Greg's top pocket.

'Sorry, miss. Perhaps I ought to go?'

'You dare! And anyway, I could do with the money for the bed and breakfast!'

He helped her to pick up the dropped goods and they went up to the flat on the first floor. The table in the living room was already laid for supper.

'I'm so happy you are early, but I wanted to have the meal on the go before you arrived. I wanted it to be a surprise,' she said.

'I'll help you. I'm not going to let you out of my

sight, my lovely – not even for one minute. Got any wine? I want to hear all your news.'

'Never mind about my news. What's this new job you were talking about?'

Over their glasses of wine, sat on the sofa with their arms around each other, Greg explained the deal he discussed with Brian Hope that afternoon. Mary was clearly excited about it all and yet Greg detected a hint of disappointment when she talked about the new job that she had been in only for a few days. There was not the enthusiasm she had shown back in the pub in Cowes.

As they prepared the supper together they discussed every way open to them to be together as much as possible. Mary seemed the least happy about being so far apart, even if she drove down to Dartmouth every weekend. Her job looked like being a Monday-to-Friday affair whereas his made working at the weekends essential. Greg was more upbeat about it.

'Look, my love, although I was only ten years old at the beginning of World War Two I can remember that people got married during a few days' leave and didn't see each other again for years. It's only a hundred and fifty miles. Who knows, I might do so well with QC that I become managing director, and then I'll be based in Lymington. We can have a house halfway between our two jobs – say, at Lyndhurst – and live happily ever after!'

For the first time Greg saw Mary was cross.

'Greg, please, there you go again being facetious.'

'Oh dear,' he said as he pulled her closer, 'our first tiff. I'm truly sorry, but I refuse to put obstacles in the way. We will find that way together. Promise me?'

'I promise,' she said, smiling again. 'You were a drifter when I met you. Now you have a purpose. You have changed, and I love you the more for it.'

They ended the evening agreeing that Mary would drive down on Saturday and then Greg would take her into Dartmouth to buy an engagement ring. He had to be away early in the morning to report to Chris. That night happiness had returned for both of them.

Driving back to Kingswear in the morning Greg had time to reflect. His lovely Mary was part of his future. He was confident the QC plan would be agreed. He had good friends to help make it a success. He had a new boat even if the time to sail it was much diminished. He had a job: a regular income for the first time in years. He would throw everything into it. He would make it work. He'd find a way to include Mary. They would be together again tomorrow.

He was back by midday. He climbed the stairs to the offices. Chris was all smiles.

'I had Brian on the phone an hour ago. He was impressed with you and your presentation. He's going to recommend the board accepts the plan, with minor adjustments, on Monday. Well done, Greg.'

'I popped the question,' said Greg with a grin.

'What question?' queried John Dalton, who walked in at that moment.

'We're getting married. Mary is coming down tomorrow. We are going in to Dartmouth to buy the engagement ring.'

Flossie spontaneously gave Greg a hug.

'She's a lovely person. I'm so glad for you, Greg.'

Chris offered him a handshake and John voiced his approval.

CHAPTER SEVEN

Deceit

At seven next morning Greg was woken by the sound of a car pulling up outside the caravan. It was Mary. This early? He tumbled out of bed, through the front door, jumped down the two steps, and grabbed her in a bear hug.

'You lovely, lovely thing, you,' he cried, and they kissed. 'What are you doing here at this time?'

'I couldn't sleep so I just got up and drove. Do you realise you are barefoot and in your pyjamas?'

'Oh, I am so glad to see you,' he replied, and he guided her up the steps. 'I'll get the kettle on. What's the latest?'

She sat down on the bed.

'What would you say if I told you I was pregnant?'

Greg nearly dropped the kettle. He spun round, a huge smile spread across his face. He made straight for where she was sitting, sat down beside her and drew her towards him.

'Wonderful, wonderful,' he said as he nuzzled into her neck.

By now the tears were rolling down her cheeks.

He took her face in his hands and they shared a long and intimate kiss.

'Why are you crying?' he said.

'Tears of happiness,' she replied, 'but I am so ashamed. Will you ever forgive me, my darling?'

'Forgive you? What am I to forgive you for?'

She dropped her head, her eyes downcast.

'I'm not actually pregnant. I only said to you, "What would you say if I *told you* I was pregnant?" but you gave me more than the answer I was longing for. Greg darling, I can't live without you. I love you so much.'

'But why did you have to tell me you were pregnant?'

'I did not say that,' she cried as she flung her arms around him.

'God, how I love you!' is all he could get out as they both dissolved in tears.

'Darling, what have you got for our engagement breakfast? I'm starving,' she said with a grin.

Greg started to rustle up the perennial bacon butty.

All he could think to say as they tucked in was 'True love makes one hungry.'

'Now can I tell you the news I've been keeping back from you?' she said. 'I'm going to give up my job, come down here, and be your assistant. So will you please start the job interview now?'

'Good grief, woman, you can't give up your career just like that. Firstly the agreement with QC isn't signed yet. Secondly the job here is only going to pay barely a living wage for one person for months, maybe years.'

'Greg, it's not "just like that". I've thought this through since you told me about the new brokerage. I've done my homework on QC of Lymington. They are a big, well-established company. You told me that sooner or later you would have to have an assistant because you couldn't be in two places at once.'

Greg started to point out that they could only share the meagre salary he'd budgeted for.

'What's the point of getting married if we don't share everything?' she said.

'But what about your promotion and pension prospects?'

She put her fingers on his lips. 'Stop talking for once,' she said, 'and listen. Please don't take me for a fool. You really don't know everything about me. I can let my flat in Southampton like I did when I went to Aberdeen. It's right in the centre of town and very desirable. It will bring in a good regular income. I own it. No mortgage. You seem to have forgotten that two can live cheaper than one. Not literally, of course, but you're not paying your friend Chris to have this caravan here, you told me. My income from the flat will pay the extra cost of having me live here with you. I am arrogant enough to believe that you will do your job better with me by your side.'

'You can say that again,' he replied.

'Quiet, and let me carry on. I'm not going to marry you unless I live with you. Besides, I want the job anyway. I don't have to wait until you, the boss, decide you're going to advertise for someone and then apply with all the rest – do I?' Not waiting for an answer, she continued: 'This new job of mine is not quite what I thought it was going to be. I've been frank with Don. He's given me Monday off to sort myself out. As it is, I shall have to work for a month after handing in my notice before I can move down here. In that time I'll find a tenant for my flat. Please, Greg, we've got a couple of days to talk this through – OK?'

'I don't know what to say' was his reply.

'Then don't say anything. We'll make a wonderful team, I just know it. I'll even get used to steam trains rumbling through the cutting behind the caravan!'

'They don't do it at night,' replied Greg, mischievously with a grin. 'I surrender. As soon as I'm dressed, if you're not too tired, we are going into Dartmouth to buy that ring.'

'We can't afford it, can we?' she replied.

'You may run the office if you like, but you're not going to make *all* the decisions.'

Half an hour later saw them hand in hand walking through the yard. They went into No.1 Shed, where Bill Fossett, despite it being Saturday, was in his little cubbyhole poring over some paperwork to do with the patrol boat.

'You've met Mary once before if my memory serves me right,' Greg said. 'We're on our way into Dartmouth to buy the engagement ring. Soon Mary is going join me down here.'

Bill smiled. 'That'll be nice,' he said. 'This place is too much of a man's world.'

In the jeweller's Mary chose her ring after they had looked at several trays. It was a simple gold band with a single large brown topaz. Greg noted it was nearly the least expensive that they had been shown, but the look of delight on her face when she put it on and it proved to be her size stopped him saying that there were better. She turned to Greg, admiring her left hand.

'It's fabulous.'

Before they caught the ferry she insisted on shopping for something special for their supper – and paying for it with her own credit card.

'Now it's my turn,' she said, and all the way home she kept looking at the third finger of her left hand.

'I want to talk about a wedding,' said Mary as they enjoyed their sandwich lunch. 'Would it bother you very much if I told you that I would be happiest with a simple registry office marriage?'

'Nothing you say bothers me, my lovely Mary.'

'Doesn't it surprise you that a vicar's daughter wishes to be married in a registry office?'

'I don't see the connection really. You are your own person. I am happy about that if you are.'

'Good. Settled then,' she said as she leaned over to give him a kiss.

Greg had learned something about Mary by now: she always meant what she said. All he had to do now was to open his mouth when she wanted to know the date. She'd probably organise the whole thing. Without appearing to boss him, she most likely had it all planned.

She actually said, 'I need to sort out the details of my resignation with Don when I get back. Don't you think it would be nicer if we got hitched down here *after* I'd moved in?'

Greg looked at her in amazement.

'I may be old-fashioned, I may want to marry you because I love you so very much, but I didn't realise that I'd be getting a manager as well!'

Mary looked a little quizzical.

'Is that a compliment or a complaint?'

'Mary, Mary, in my eyes you can do no wrong. We'll do whatever you say.'

Mary produced pencil and paper and together they prepared a list of guests and things to do.

'Mary, my love, you've had a long day. You were driving before dawn. How would you like to rest here this afternoon whilst I go up to the offices and attend to the brokerage customers? Although I have the phone here now it's better to be in the office. Saturday can be one of our better days. On the other hand, maybe I won't have a single enquiry, but I have to be available.'

'I'm coming with you,' said Mary. 'My apprenticeship starts today.'

The notice at the bottom of the outside staircase to the offices now said "Brokerage" as well as "Office". They climbed up together.

'Would you like to know more about the girl you are going to marry?' she said, waggling her left hand in front of his face.

'Yes, I would' was his reply as he sat down behind Chris's desk. 'Make yourself comfortable in the client's armchair. You don't have to confess all to me – everyone should be allowed to have their secrets.'

She laughed. 'No secrets, really. My father used to say confession is good for the soul. I was engaged ten years ago to someone I met at university. We had a great future mapped out. We even talked about raising a family and looked seriously at buying a property together. One day I arrived unexpectedly at his parents' house. The front door was open. I found him in bed with another girl. Not just any other girl – my best friend. At twenty-five this taught me more in one minute than I had learned in four years studying sociology, among other things, at university. I thought that sort of thing only happened in novels. My parents died soon after. So I concentrated on building a career.'

At this point Greg could see she looked sad.

'You needn't continue, you know,' he said.

'I'll tell you about my parents another time,' she said.

A car pulled up outside.

'I'll just see if that's a customer,' said Greg as he moved across the room and out onto the balcony. He heard the phone ring when he was outside and returned to find Mary had got up from her chair and was answering it.

'Mr Norfield is coming right now – may I have your name, please?'

As he took the phone from her she said quite loudly, 'It's a Mr John Evett, Mr Norfield.'

When Greg had finished with the call he looked at Mary.

'Now you know it was a compliment when I said you were a manager.'

'The only thing that's been missing in my life has been a man. Now I've got you my cup is full.' She took his face in her hands and kissed him. 'Oops,' she said, 'I've never kissed my boss before!' – and they laughed.

The rest of the weekend together was dominated by Mary taking a close interest in how the new brokerage would be run if the QC plan came to fruition. Greg was impressed with her many suggestions, from the physical building of the office alongside No.1 Shed, to details of the equipment needed within.

Don Carruthers had given Mary the Monday off from her duties. She had told him the purpose of her trip to Dartmouth. She had not told him she was about to resign. She had something else on her mind as she drove back to Southampton that morning. Why was she going to need even more time off?

No call came from QC that afternoon. When Mary phoned Greg that evening to say she had arrived safe and sound he had no news for her. He spent the evening writing up his favourable report for 'X' Spars about the mainsail-furling gear. He also wrote his suggestion for a press release which they could use as they wished. It was late before he turned in, and he slept fitfully as he realised how much depended on the QC decision.

Chris got the call from Brian Hope at nine the next morning. He summoned Greg to hear the good news.

'All systems go. Opening day will be the first of July. Your employment with QC starts on the first of June. I've told them that you will be in charge as from now of building the new office and that you will liaise with them regarding the fitting-out and contents etc. John will deal with the builders, so work with him on that.'

Greg went into the next office, where John Dalton was waiting to talk to him. As he returned through Chris's office he asked Flossie to put a line through to the caravan. The next thing was to call Mary. He phoned her office in Southampton. They told him that she was out and not expected back that day. He phoned the flat and left a message on the answerphone.

* * *

Mary waited in the dingy wood-panelled office furnished with just one long oak table and nine dark leather-covered chairs, there was one ornate version with arms at one end and four either side without arms. There was a portrait of the Queen on one end wall and a small high window in the other that gave a view only of the sky. She sat down. The train to Waterloo had been crowded, also the Underground, and the side entrance to the building in Waterloo Bridge Road had been difficult to find.

The man who came into the room was tall and lean, with smooth grey hair. He was clean-shaven and aged about mid-fifties. He was wearing a light grey suit and sombre tie against a white shirt. She was reminded of her English master at school some twenty years earlier.

'Miss Rowlinson – is that right?' he said, as he held out his hand, 'I am Commander Williamson. I take it you have something important to tell me.'

'That is for you to judge,' she said. 'I think it is.'

'Before we go any further I am obliged to remind you that both you and I are bound by the Official Secrets Act,' said the Commander. With that he sat down in a chair opposite her on the other side of the table. He placed a file he had brought with him on the table. 'What is on your mind?'

Mary took a deep breath. 'When I was invited to join the organisation some two years ago I understood the aims and objects and why secrecy was demanded. I have maintained those criteria. Now I am faced with a moral dilemma.' She looked at the man on the opposite side of the table for some response.

He raised an eyebrow. 'Please continue, Miss Rowlinson.'

'I have passed on information to you and not known if it has been of value. The last time I responded was when I was asked to recommend somebody with specific attributes. I gave you the name of a person I thought fitted the bill and who might be of use to the department. You wanted an adventurer, someone who could be trusted but at the same time motivated by cash. You wanted someone with a boat based on the South Devon coast – a good seaman and navigator. Nobody has told me, nor do I expect to be told, the outcome of my referral.' Again she looked at the Commander for some response.

There was a long pause.

'And. . . ?' he finally said.

She continued: 'I have to tell you that since I gave you the name of that man I have become personally involved with him. He is terribly important to me. We are to be married. My idea of marriage is that there should be no secrets between husband and wife. What should I do? If necessary, I would resign.'

'Miss Rowlinson,' said the Commander, peering at the file in front of him, 'you would not be the first of our operatives to be so involved. However, we specialise here in the choosing of persons to work for us who have outstanding attributes and character. Because of the way human beings behave we are well aware that friendships, alliances, marriages, intimacies – call it what you will are forming all the time. You have sworn never to reveal the nature or details of the work of this department. You are never released from that, whether you resign or not. It is something we all have to live with. Is that all?'

Mary nodded her assent. She had dealt with men of few words in high places before.

He closed the file in front of him, picked it up, walked round the table, offered his hand and gave a slight bow, which was followed by 'Miss Kershaw will show you out.'

He left the room.

* * *

Greg did not get a reply from Mary's flat when he phoned in the evening. He phoned her at home again at seven next morning, Wednesday.

She answered and cut him short: 'Darling, I have to be early this morning, it's no good asking me why I wasn't around yesterday. You know I cannot discuss confidential matters with you. Ring me tonight after six. Bye.' And she hung up.

Greg seized the moment. He had promised Chris some time ago that he would tell the Trehairnes, and Robbie in particular, why there would be no more "trade". He phoned Frank and told him he was hoping to come over that morning.

John Dalton was in his office when Greg went in to ask if he could borrow a van. 'For the last time,' he said. 'I'm going to take Chris's advice and get myself some wheels. The Rover dealers in Totnes ought to have something decent.'

At nine thirty he was on his way. There was a

tidy white second-hand Rover 2000 in the showroom that he thought would look right for a brokerage manager. A deal "for cash" was agreed.

Now he would drive the short distance to Salcombe, to see the Trehairnes, to bring closure to the "bits of trade".

Frank and Joan ushered him into the living room, looking very concerned and muttering about how long it had been since they had heard from him.

'You sounded anxious on the phone, Greg. What's on your mind?'

'I know you guys are busy. Quite simply, you have been good friends to me. I owe it to you to tell you all that's been going on. He brought them up to date with his plans.

'More importantly, Frank, please tell your brother I will simply not have any time for his excellent "bits of trade". I doubt if there will be any sailing at all for some time.'

'Don't you worry about Robbie. No problem there. We'll explain. Last we heard concerning your new boat was something about engine trouble. Nick Wroughton was enquiring.'

Back at the yard Greg felt more at ease as he went to see John Dalton about the proposed office. He phoned Mary that evening to tell her all the news.

'Oh, Greg,' she said. I just knew it would come right for us. Don Carruthers is a lovely man. I am allowed to work two months instead of one, but I only have to work a four-day week.'

'So where does that leave us?' said Greg.

'You must have been working too hard,' she replied with a measure of sarcasm. 'It means that I can have a three-day weekend, *every* weekend, with my fiancé! I will be free to join you at the end of June. How's that for planning?'

'Oh, Mary, my love, that's fine for me but you've got to do all that driving.'

'Well, there's a fine thing. If you don't want me around we'd better call the whole thing off.' She was laughing as she heard him spluttering his apologies. 'You told me love would find a way. Perhaps you've got a better idea?'

'Can't think of one, but weekends are going to be busy here. It won't be much of a break for you was what I was thinking.'

'Greg, my dearest,' she nearly shouted, 'I don't want a break; I want to be with you. I want to share in this great new adventure. It's our future. I want to share it with you – right from the beginning. I know I can help to make it a success, even if it is only three days a week to start with. You won't get a better offer!'

'Indeed I won't, my lovely.'

Both of them were happy when they signed off, and even more happy at the thought that they would be together again in a couple of days.

Early on Friday morning Flossie called Greg in the caravan.

'I have had a call from QC – a Captain David Worthy. He says he needs a private word with you as soon as you can call him back. He's given me a special number to call him on. It's not very private over here at the moment – shall I give you a direct line?'

'Yes, Flossie. Thanks,' said Greg thoughtfully.

He dialled the number. A voice that sounded familiar answered.

'David Worthy speaking.'

'Greg Norfield here. You asked me to call you.'

'Yes indeed. I am the QC sales manager. I imagine that Brian Hope has told you about me. I have been overseas for the company for the last three weeks. Got back yesterday. I missed your visit here. Brian has only just filled me in on the details of the new brokerage. I rang by way of an introduction.'

'Captain Worthy. I do not recall Mr Hope mentioning your name but the voice sounds familiar.'

'So it should, Mr Norfield, but we will not discuss that now. I am about to jump into my car and drive down to see you if that's all right.'

'Why yes, of course,' replied Greg, and he furrowed his brow as he tried hard to recall when and where he had heard that voice before.

'We have a lot to discuss, Mr Norfield. Best we get acquainted as soon as possible. I reckon I should be there by lunchtime. Oh, I hope you've got that engine fixed!'

The line went dead. Where had he heard that voice before? What engine was he talking about?

Mary arrived about twelve thirty. Their greeting

was uninhibited and noticed by Chris from the top of the office stairs. He gave a smile and a wave to Mary.

'Makes me feel young again,' he called out.

'Me too,' shouted Greg, all smiles.

They made off to the caravan. As they were catching up with each other's latest news the phone rang. It was Flossie.

'I have a Captain David Worthy in the office to see you. He's having a chat with Chris and John at the moment. He says you are not to rush. He would like to wander along the pontoons and have a look around if you would meet him down there in quarter of an hour or so.'

'Tell him that's fine, Flossie. Thank you. I'll find him.'

Greg explained to Mary about the unexpected visit from the sales manager.

'It sounds like he wants to talk to you in private. Must be important. How about I get some sandwiches from the van and bring them down to *Amity*? You won't be disturbed there and you can make him a cup of tea. I'll take any calls or messages in the caravan.'

'You're a gem, my lovely. I'll be back as soon as possible.'

'You won't. This man is your future boss. He hasn't driven all the way down here to be fobbed off so that you can see your girlfriend!'

'Fiancée, please. Of course you are right as usual. That looks like it might be him going down the visitors' gangway now.'

Greg gave Mary a hug and left to meet his new boss. As he approached, the man was looking closely at *Amity* and had his back to him. Greg had a strange feeling of recognition. Hearing Greg approach, Captain David Worthy turned to face him with a grin.

'Told you we would meet again one day,' said Troag.

They exchanged a firm handshake and broad smiles, both shaking their heads from side to side.

'Call me David, please, Greg. I can tell you it was only yesterday that I learned of your involvement here. I had a job to control myself in Brian Hope's office when he mentioned your name. My boss, of course, knows nothing of our previous meeting. Where can we talk in private?'

'Right here on *Amity*. My fiancée, Mary, will bring us sandwiches. We will not be interrupted. Come aboard.'

'First things first, Greg. I suggest our cover is that we met briefly many years ago as visitors to the Royal Yacht Club in Lymington. I am here on official QC business, but before we get into that what did you do with the flight case?'

'Aha! Funny you should mention that. I've been meaning to sink it when I got out into deep water again but the opportunity has not arisen. Sailing back from Cowes recently I thought about it, but there are too many divers to the wrecks in those waters. I have it here in a forward bunk locker.'

'I imagine it is empty?'

'Nearly, all but a couple of bricks.' Greg grinned.

'And I burned your note.'

'Well, I can save you the trouble. That was a brand-new and very expensive case. I will have it back before I leave. I must get away about three. We will talk another time on those matters.'

Mary arrived with the food and Greg introduced her to David.

After she had left them David spoke: 'Charming. You must tell me all about her when we have more time together, and that may be sooner than you think. I have a prospective buyer in Cornwall for a rather nice Dutch steel cruiser, which is with our people in Amsterdam. I am getting it skippered to Cherbourg in the next couple of days. I would like you to crew with me to get it back to Dartmouth. My buyer will find it more convenient to have the boat here rather than in Lymington.'

'I will look forward to doing that trip with you. I'll reserve space on this pontoon to berth her.'

'This delivery exercise,' said David, may be required at very short notice. The way of these things is not always to our convenience. I have discussed everything I need to know here with Chris Curnow and seen the site for the office.'

After another firm handshake, Captain Worthy made for his car and was away. Mary came round the corner as Greg was walking back to the caravan.

'You two looked as if you knew each other,' she said.

'I don't know what makes you say that. But yes, long time ago. When I was given the name Captain David Worthy this morning it just didn't ring a bell. He reminded me that we met in Lymington at the yacht club years ago. I'm not sure I even knew the name.'

Mary gave him a funny look and he hated himself for lying to her yet again.

Later, she helped him move a couple of boats to make space for the Dutch cruiser. Then, after hugs and kisses, she left him standing there forlornly, to return to Southampton early Sunday afternoon.

When she got back to her flat there were two messages on her answer machine. The first was Greg to say how much he was already missing her. The second was the voice of Commander Williamson.

'Now that you have completed a few days with your boyfriend I would like to be updated about your resolve.' After a pause it finished with 'The terms of your service require you to erase this message immediately.'

This she did.

Tired from the long car journey Mary sat down with a cup of tea to think. Just how had the Commander known about her trip to Dartmouth?

It had been a long day. She was about to go to bed early. The phone rang.

'Yes, darling,' she said automatically, thinking it was Greg.

'I don't get called that very often,' said the Commander.

Mary felt a complete idiot and told him so.

'Well, don't,' he said. 'It confirms what you told

me last week. I'm sorry to have disturbed you so late. I'll make this short. I simply require affirmation that you are still prepared to serve.'

'Absolutely,' she replied. 'Nothing has occurred since our meeting to make me change my mind. Should you ask something of me that my conscience would not permit, I will tell you at the time. I will never betray that to which I have sworn. Will that do?'

'It certainly will' came the answer.

'Just one thing,' she continued: 'how did you know I've been in Dartmouth?'

'Really, Miss Rowlinson – we are the ones who ask the questions. Goodnight.'

Greg completed his business at the bank in Dartmouth. As he walked back to the ferry he had no way of avoiding Selby Somerfield-Smythe. This horrible little man seemed to pop up in front of him out of the pavement like a jack-in-the-box. The meeting was clearly intentional.

'I say, old boy, fancy meeting you,' said Selby. 'How very fortunate! I've been wanting to parley.'

Greg drew him to a quiet bench on the waterfront, where they would not be overheard.

'Look, Selby,' he said, barely suppressing his irritation, 'tell me what's on your mind. I'm in a bit of a hurry.'

'I hear you've gone straight. Just wanted to tell you that your secrets are safe with me.'

Greg smelled blackmail again. What was he to do about Selby?

'Exactly,' said Greg as he got up 'I'm off now – my ferry is due.'

He shot down the street as close to a sprint as he could disguise. Over on the Kingswear side of the river, as he walked back to the yard he asked himself several times, 'What to do about Selby?'

Back at the yard he went straight to the warehouse.

'Harry,' he said, 'would you like to pop into the caravan for a natter tonight on your way home?'

'Great' came the reply. 'How did it go at the weekend? I hear you had a high-powered visitor?'

'I'll fill you in when you come round tonight.'

There was a clatter at the door of the caravan. It was Harry.

'This is the last bottle of loot,' said Greg. He poured Harry a good tot of Calvados. 'I had an unwelcome meeting with your friend Selby this morning. You shared a room at Her Majesty's pleasure with him and you now share a cottage with him. What's he all about?'

'He was in for larceny. He's now going straight. He gets up most people's noses, I know that. I also know you think he's a problem. Well, he isn't.'

'Harry,' said Greg, 'we're going to make a go of all this. I want you to know that despite our differences in the past we can work together. We both owe it to Chris and we owe it to ourselves. I accept Selby is your business, and I must get on with mine. Please let me know how I can help at any time.'

'Thanks, Greg,' said Harry. 'The helping bit is

mutual. I think Selby feels isolated. There is one thing I learned inside – we all need help, and sometimes it comes from surprising quarters.'

They shook hands and Harry left for home.

The next morning Greg's Rover was delivered. John Dalton peered down from the top of the steps.

'Very nice. What did you do, then – rob a bank?'

'Something like that,' replied Greg with a grin.

Little did John know how close to the bone he'd come.

* * *

Next weekend when Mary arrived early on the Friday it was bright and sunny.

'I've got a plan for part of our day today,' said Greg after they had extricated themselves from their overt tender and warm greetings. 'I have no appointments today but it looks like being another busy weekend. I've put *Amity* on a mooring to make more space on the pontoon. How about rowing out there with our lunch to watch the world go by on the river – just you and me?'

'Yes, please.'

Mary went off to the caravan to get the lunch and Greg climbed the stairs to have a word with Flossie. He told her the plan.

'That's nice. I'll tell any callers that you are out with a boat and won't be back until later this afternoon. How about that? There's the cellphone if it's urgent.'

'The truth is always best,' Greg said with a wink.

And so before lunchtime they rowed out to *Amity* on her mooring. As they watched the boats plying up and down the river they snuggled up in one corner of the cockpit with their lunch.

'You really don't know very much about me, do you, Gregory Norfield?'

'You once said you would tell me about your parents,' Greg replied. 'You looked so sad when the subject came up.'

'Actually,' she said, 'it's a subject that I still find painful to talk about.'

'Then don't,' said Greg.

Mary was quiet for a moment.

'No, I want to tell you. This feels like the time. My father was ordained into the Anglican Church just at the beginning of the war and chose to serve his country by joining the RN Chaplaincy. He actually did his Royal Navy service training on top of the hill over there at the College. That's why I'd like to go there one day. Mum and Dad spoke little about the war. They didn't meet until it was nearly over. Mum was in the Wrens and Dad was for some reason or other a patient at Haslar Naval Hospital, Gosport, when they met in 1945. They married in 1947 and I was born in 1950. Shall I go on?' she said, and as he pulled her tighter to him she knew the answer. 'When I was a little girl, five or six maybe, I remember on more than one occasion when we had visitors at home, always men, I was pushed upstairs or out into the garden while they talked. One day I crept back and listened outside the living-room door and heard mention of *"men lost"* and the word *"tragedy"*. I thought for ages, childlike, that *"men lost"* meant that they had wandered off and couldn't find their way home. It was years before Daddy considered me old enough to be told of one horrendous event when his ship was sunk, and of the significance of the silver model of a battleship on our mantelpiece.'

Mary went on to tell Greg that the men who used to call had brought it as a gift for her father. He told her that he was on a battleship in the Pacific when it was sunk by the Japanese towards the end of the war. Hundreds of men were "lost". Her father was one of a small number that were rescued after many days clinging to a raft in shark-infested waters.

'He rarely spoke to anyone of his wartime experiences. The men that called at our house were survivors who had come to thank Daddy for helping them.'

It was a long time before either of them spoke as they contemplated the peaceful waters of the river and thought about what she had said.

'Would you like to hear more?' Mary asked. She looked pensive.

Greg smiled, and nodded his head.

'It all came to an end whilst I was away at Southampton University. Daddy was based in Portsmouth. One day they decided to drive up to Yorkshire to visit some distant relatives of Mum's. I didn't even know they existed.'

At this point Mary's eyes started to fill.

'You needn't go on,' said Greg as he kissed her gently on the cheek.'

'I must, I must. I have to get this out. They were driving north up the M1. A lorry from the southbound carriageway careered through the central barrier and hit them head-on. Somehow Daddy survived the horrific pile-up. Mummy was killed outright. Just a few minutes after the impact witnesses found the bodies of Daddy and the lorry driver in the crumpled cab of his vehicle. In Daddy's hand they found the crucifix that he always carried on a chain around his neck.'

Greg wiped away the tears that had started down her cheeks.

'Please go on,' he said kindly.

'At the inquest that followed, a verdict of death by misadventure on all three was passed. The lorry had a blow-out on a front tyre, causing the vehicle to swerve to the right and through the barrier. The coroner wished it to be noted that there could be no other reason for finding Daddy's body in the lorry cab other than that, after the crash, having ascertained that he could do nothing for his wife, he had managed to crawl to the lorry – there was a trail of blood to prove it – where he was ministering to the driver when they both died from their injuries. Mummy and Daddy were only fifty-two years old,' she sobbed, 'and right at the end Daddy was doing what he always did – comforting other people.'

Greg pulled her closer to him. Her head rested on his shoulder, and, with the gentle movement of the boat on the tide, Mary, totally exhausted, drifted off to sleep in his arms.

When she woke, she said, 'Thanks, I haven't spoken about that to anyone since it happened.'

'What are you thanking me for?'

'For helping me to lay a ghost,' she said.

Greg now remembered seeing the little silver battleship, and next to it a wood-and-silver inlaid crucifix, on the mantelpiece in her flat in Southampton.

'I was an only child, you see. I inherited the whole estate. I sold the house and was able to buy my flat in Southampton outright. This has enabled me to stand on my own two feet from the day I started work. Now I have someone to share it all with it doesn't seem such a burden any more. I know my Mum and Dad would have approved of you. Daddy used to say, "I do hope you'll meet someone *mature* at university." Well, it's taken rather longer to meet someone mature. But now I am supremely happy.'

Mary returned to Southampton. Her story gave Greg much to think about – mostly matters of morality. Could he meet up to her standards? He was a smuggler – of people as well as goods; she was dedicated to catching men like him. How could he make vows of marriage to the woman he loved, knowing that he would continue to deceive her about covert operations? Was he really prepared to work on illegal exercises because they were "in the interests of the country"? Or was it simply greed? Does the end justify the means?

CHAPTER EIGHT

L'Enterprise

Greg took a call from David in the afternoon. Greg was to meet him at the ferry terminal in Poole the next day. David would confirm the time later in the day.

'I hate to say this,' said Greg, 'but tomorrow is not very convenient. There's a lot going on here –'

David interrupted: 'My dear Greg, in my book it is the client who dictates what is convenient and what is not. We will cast off from Cherbourg after dark tomorrow. We should be back in Dartmouth in the early hours of Thursday. Make sure we have sufficient room to come alongside at the yard. As you know, the boat is forty-five feet overall. Will that be all right?'

Greg knew an order when he heard one. He also had his suspicions.

'Troag?' questioned Greg.

'Sorry – didn't hear what you said' came the reply.

Greg did a double-take.

'I said how long will the boat be berthed here?'

'Until it's sold, I expect. I will phone Alan Lucas

– he's our prospect in Fowey, as soon as I can tell him she's in Dartmouth. We discussed this last weekend, remember? Cheer up – it's our first bit of business.'

'Yes, of course,' said Greg. 'I'll look forward to hearing from you later.'

Within the hour David phoned again.

'The trip is on. The ferry leaves Poole at 2 p.m. tomorrow. We'll have time to have a meal in Cherbourg before getting under way to return.'

'I've made sure of our berth on the visitors pontoon,' said Greg. 'Plenty of room. I have to say I'm really looking forward to this trip and the forecast is OK.'

When David muttered something about it wouldn't have made any difference even if the forecast hadn't been any good Greg's suspicions were confirmed.

David was waiting for him at the Poole ferry terminal, and at 6 p.m. the ship pulled into the dock at Cherbourg. They made their way to where the yacht was berthed. The Dutch steel cruiser was built to the high specification that justified its price – luxury on water. They stowed their kit.

'I'll give you your skipper's tuition when we are under way later,' said David. 'Let's go ashore and find our dinner. We might as well enjoy some French cuisine whilst we're here.'

That cuisine was good indeed. It was getting dark

when they returned to the yacht, ready for the all-night passage. David had sorted their clearance and paid the berthing fees and harbour dues when they first arrived.

They cast off. Outside the harbour wall they could feel the swell and settled down on course for Dartmouth at a steady fifteen knots. Up on the bridge deck the engines were barely a rumble.

'Now we can enjoy ourselves,' said David as he tutored Greg in the use of the navigation aids. This boat was equipped with the latest. When David was satisfied that Greg could be safely left at the helm he said with a smile, 'Greg, we've been here before. I'm going below to make the coffee and check on our two passengers.'

This was the most expensive boat Greg had skippered. He was enjoying it so much that full realisation of what David had said about two passengers only hit him after David had gone below. So it was another Troag.

David was back within ten minutes. Greg waited for the explanation.

'Rather like the proverbial bus for which you can wait for ages, Greg, two come along at once: so it is with operations like this one. You might not be asked to participate again for months, maybe years, so don't expect to supplement your income this way on a regular basis. The two below are friends of the West. You need know no more.'

'Tell me about our first encounter. Who was he?' said Greg.

'That last gentleman we helped came for an

important government-sponsored conference. I am not at liberty to tell you his name. However, he is now back in his own country – safe and sound, as far as I know. These two below have knowledge that is of inestimable value to our government. They will become British citizens, albeit with new identities. They have enormous courage to flee their country and families because they believe that in doing so they are contributing to world peace. Be assured of one thing, Greg: we are not Mossad. We do not do torture, murder, or kidnap. We are the transport department. Those we transport come of their own free will. When we tie up at the yard pontoon we will put our crew ashore, just like any other visitors.'

They ploughed on. Occasionally they saw the navigation lights of ships that crossed their path. They hoped that none of those lights belonged to various authorities who had the right to board their craft should they be suspected of carrying illegal immigrants. The sea was kind that night and the visibility good. They spoke little as they checked their course and position. The screen in front of them on the open bridge deck above the main saloon shielded them from the wind. The boat rose and fell as they met the swell head-on. With only a half-moon, the bow wave, curling back and outwards, produced a sparkling luminescence in the otherwise black blanket of the sea.

Greg was first to identify the flashing light on Berry Head off the starboard bow. David agreed with Greg's distance estimate of fifteen miles. In an hour they would be guided by the Kingswear sectional light – the light that had been so important to their safety on that first mission together.

'Yet again, Greg, your navigation is spot on.' And then, as an afterthought: 'If one engine breaks down this time, we do have another!'

There was just sufficient light to see David's wry smile as he spoke. They slowed down to a sedate eight knots as the town lights came into view.

They tied up *L'Enterprise* in her berth at the Curnow Yard about an hour before dawn. As planned their "passengers" departed via the berth-holders' entrance, where the "taxi" was waiting, and Greg all but fell into his bed in the caravan.

Greg's alarm woke him at nine o'clock. He scrambled into his clothes and staggered hastily down to the pontoon. David was already on the deck of *L'Enterprise*, tidying up.

'Had your breakfast yet?' Greg called out.

'Not yet. There's not much to eat on board.'

'Come on up and join me in the caravan. How do you feel?'

'Fine,' said David. 'We'll wash down the decks and hull and clean up any sign of our recent voyage, but I'll take up that invitation to breakfast first. Then we'll contact Alan Lucas in the hopes that I can persuade him to come and view the boat today. I think he has a Ferrari or something exotic and it should not take him long to get here. Come to think of it, I'll phone him now. If he says he can come over today, we'll know he's keen.'

David phoned Alan Lucas from the caravan whilst Greg prepared a proper English breakfast that he reckoned they deserved.

'He's keen all right. Mr Lucas will be here at lunchtime. He wants us to take him out for a demo. When we've demolished the source of that enticing smell coming from the galley we'll get down there, square away any signs of our voyage, and hose her down. Oh, by the way, you left a bag on board. I suggest you dispose of it as soon as possible!'

Later, down in the main saloon, David handed him a small blue sailing bag.

'First thing you do', he said, 'is take it off the boat. On this occasion we've shared the "fee". The powers that be, being ignorant about these things, expected me to be single-handed. I thought otherwise. Where's the hose?'

Greg connected a hose on his way back from depositing the bag in the caravan and together they set about the washdown. After an hour or so David said that he had to go into Dartmouth. Greg borrowed the yard launch. He too had business – at the bank – so they crossed the river together and tied up at the steps on the quay the other side. David opted to return on his own later by ferry.

Mr Lucas was on time. The red Ferrari caused quite a stir among the men who were enjoying their lunch break in the sun outside No.1 Shed. David and Greg went to greet him as he extricated himself from this car, whose total height from the ground seemed only about four feet or so, and the driving position was more like lying down than being seated.

David introduced himself and then Greg.

'Let's go,' said Alan Lucas, a man of few words and fortunately, as a Ferrari owner, short of stature.

Greg thought it a bit over the top for him to be wearing a pale blue blazer with brass buttons, white slacks and fancy blue-and-white deck shoes. Never mind – he was the man with the money.

The demonstration went without a hitch. Once outside the river speed limit David opened the throttle and they were round Berry Head, into Torbay and back again within the hour. Alan had the helm all the time they were outside the river limits but he clearly knew little about seamanship and Greg wondered what he was going to do with this powerful craft if he bought it. Maybe have a paid crew?

Mr Lucas said he'd think about it.

David whispered to Greg as Alan Lucas walked to his car, 'I think he's hooked,' and the Ferrari departed with a subdued roar.

A van from QC, arranged by David to bring equipment for the new office, turned up after lunch and conveniently took him back to Lymington.

The next morning Mr Lucas phoned Greg to say yes, subject to his wife having a look. He added that he understood that the work could be done at the Curnow Yard should there be anything she'd like to "*personalise*".

'I wouldn't bank on any extra work if I were you,' said David when Greg phoned him with the good news. 'If I know anything about it, she'll probably want a bunch of flowers in the main saloon and some lavender water in the owner's cabin – something you'll be doing yourself at no extra cost.'

Mary arrived at midday. The whole yard knew about this love affair by now. It was no surprise for anyone to see the couple with their arms around each other.

'How did the Cherbourg trip go, then?' she asked Greg.

'The trip went fine. I am about to phone Mrs Lucas, the client's wife, who will give the final approval apparently.'

'Good for her!' was Mary's reply. 'Well, go and do it, then.'

Mrs Lucas answered the phone, and after Greg had explained the purpose of his call she said, 'You don't know my husband, obviously. He's going to buy that boat no matter what I say, but for the sake of peace and quiet I guess I'd better come along and give it the once-over. I'll be there after lunch, if that's OK by you.'

Greg said that it was very much all right and gave her directions how to find the yard.

Mary asked if there was anything she could do to help. Greg gave her the keys to *L'Enterprise*, pointing out where the boat was tied up.

'Have a look at that beauty. Mrs Lucas is coming over after lunch. See if you can spot anything amiss.'

Back at the caravan for their lunch, Mary explained that she had guessed he'd been busy so she had done a shop on the way down. She dished him up a crusty roll and Stilton.

'I do like being spoiled. What did you think of the Dutch cruiser?'

'Fabulous. We're going upmarket a bit, aren't we?'

'We certainly are,' replied Greg. 'How would you like to accompany me when I show Mrs Lucas around this afternoon?'

Nobody heard the huge black Bentley silently turn into the yard. It was only when its massive wheels crunched loudly on the gravel that Mary, whose ears seemed better tuned than most, detected the arrival of Mrs Lucas.

She was petite, with a huge blond coiffure, dripping with jewellery and expensively dressed (and not for boating). Greg had her as an actress, and dissuaded her as she left her car from swapping her low-heeled driving pumps for four-inch stilettos.

"Fraid it was Massingham's day off today and Alan won't let me drive the Ferrari,' she said when Greg had greeted her and introduced her to Mary.

Greg put Mrs Lucas at about forty-five years of age. She had a natural charm. He had guessed Mr Lucas was seventy, so another guess was that this was not the first Mrs Lucas.

Mary effectively took over from Greg as they boarded *L'Enterprise*. She showed talent as a salesperson that Greg never knew she had. How had a bunch of daffodils in a vase turned up on the saloon table?

'Very nice,' said Mrs Lucas, and turning to Mary she said, 'What do you think I should change to please His Lordship?'

'Why change anything until he's had time to think of the complaint?' Mary said with a smile and a wink.

'Actually,' replied Mrs Lucas, 'between you, me and the gatepost, he will probably sell it after a few trips. He gets bored very easily. It's very nice as it is. Looks very expensive to me, and please don't tell me the price. He never discusses business with me – so ignorance is bliss.'

Greg's pleasure at this nearly completed sale was doubled at the thought that they would probably have the boat back to sell for the second time after Mr Lucas had played with it a bit. "One for the price of two" came to mind.

Mrs Lucas departed. After she had gone Greg hugged Mary tight.

'I'm not sure that I'm needed here at all. Where on earth did the flowers come from?'

'Oh, gosh. I borrowed them from Flossie. Glad you reminded me.'

Mary clambered back aboard *L'Enterprise*, recovered the daffodils, and returned them from whence they had come. Greg heard Mary and

Flossie laughing about something as he left the office to see Harry.

Harry had bad news.

'I haven't heard a word from Selby. He's made enemies in his time and I'm worried. It's been over two weeks since he went to London in the van saying he'd be back in a couple of days. If he intended to stay away longer, he would have contacted me.'

'Have you tried to contact any of his friends or customers?' said Greg.

'I've been through his paperwork to find a contact in London who might have seen him. Drew a blank with the exception of a small furniture removal company he did business with in Hammersmith. I've phoned them twice and they repeated that they saw him the day after he left our cottage when he delivered a couple of sofas. They haven't seen or heard from him since. Look, Greg, I need your help. I don't want to bother my brother.'

'What can I do for you, Harry?' said Greg.

'I need advice. I feel that I should report Selby missing. My worry is that as Selby and I have criminal records I will immediately become a suspect if I do and the police will be round digging up the garden and God knows what.'

'The way I see it, Harry,' said Greg, 'is that the longer you don't report him missing the more likely they are going to wonder about your own behaviour. You've convinced me that he's probably in trouble somewhere. Just think about this. What if something has happened to him? His body turns up in the Thames, or his van is found abandoned? What if this happens after six months or more?'

'The police are going to find it very difficult to understand why you haven't reported him missing. You're living with him; he's your pal. I know you are going straight. If he got mixed up with a bad lot that's his affair; but if he's in trouble, you'd never forgive yourself for doing nothing to help.'

Harry went quiet.

'You seem to be saying that I should tell the police.'

'You must,' said Greg. 'You really don't have any choice. The risk of putting yourself under suspicion gets greater as time passes. If you need a character reference at any time, you can count on me.'

'Thanks, Greg. I'll go straight to the police station on the way home this evening. You are right.'

Harry was back on Monday, early, before work. He banged on the caravan door.

'Come in, Harry, and have a cup of tea.'

Harry's first remarks were to thank Greg for the advice. 'Things went much better than I could have hoped at the police station. I was surprised to learn that they knew all about Harry and myself, our address and history. However, the desk sergeant was pleasant and sympathetic. He promised to contact me should they receive any information. Mind you, it didn't cheer me up when, as I was leaving the police station, he called out to tell me that a dozen or so people go missing in London every day.'

* * *

The Commander answered his phone.

'Commander Williamson? This is David.'

'Ah,' said the Commander, 'I trust you are well. What can I do, Captain Worthy?'

David explained that it was a matter best discussed in the Commander's office and that he, David, had to be in London the next day if that would be convenient.

Yes, it would.

So it was that at eleven the next morning David found himself outside the unmarked door off Waterloo Bridge Road, entered, and was ushered up to the Commander's office.

Greetings completed, David said, 'I have a matter upon which I would seek your advice. I have an operator whose name you know: Greg Norfield. He proposes to marry a girl by the name of Mary Rowlinson. I have mentioned her name to you before. I would not be telling you this if it were not for the fact that this Miss Rowlinson is employed by HM Customs & Excise in Southampton. She is a highly intelligent woman and it looks as if she will be living inside the very secure premises which I have chosen for future operations out of Dartmouth.'

'I'm sorry, David, but what do you expect me to do about it?'

'Quite simply,' said David, 'I would like your opinion as to whether it would be a good idea to bring her into the organisation? What I fear is that, being the sort of person she is, because of her training she may become a threat unless we do just that. Also it would be kinder to her future husband, Greg Norfield, if he didn't have to operate for us under the constant worry of his covert behaviour being found out by his own wife.'

'Captain Worthy,' said the Commander, 'being kind is not what we do very well, but you wanted my advice. It is this. My considerable experience of people in these circumstances tells me that in this particular case you have nothing to worry about. Leave matters as they are. I do not think a problem will arise.' And with that the Commander stood up and shook hands with David. 'Miss Kershaw will see you out.'

As soon as David had departed, the Commander had Miss Kershaw put in a call to a Mr Nicholas Wroughton, asking him to phone back on the private line.

'Nick,' said the Commander when the call came through, 'some time ago you traced for me the whereabouts of a Mr Gregory Norfield and gave him, albeit rather circuitously, my instructions. They were carried out entirely satisfactorily. I now require you to tell me everything you know about him. Please go ahead.'

'Mr Norfield first came to my attention a couple of years ago as a frequent sailing visitor to Salcombe. As far as I could glean he was a freelance journalist. I understand he has a base at a Dartmouth shipyard. I believe he is a divorcee. He told me he came here for peace and quiet, was always single-handed and used to hole up in a creek further up the river. He got to know a local family and they told me he was a regular straight and decent guy. When you asked me to find someone to assist in Operation Troag I figured he exactly fitted your requirements. Did I make a mistake?'

'Not at all, Nick. Thank you.'

The line went dead.

Being in love was taking its toll. Greg was showing signs of lack of concentration. He completely forgot a client who had an appointment to look at a boat one morning. It was Flossie who had to search the yard to remind him. When they got back to the office the man had left. He had to phone an apology, but the man did not come back.

On another occasion he lost two hundred pounds on a sale by the simple act of typing a bill of sale himself with the wrong figure in it. The client must have known the agreed price but wrote his cheque for the lower amount.

His mind was not on the job. What price the deception of the one he loved and could not bear to think of losing?

'I'm the luckiest so-and-so on earth,' he said one morning out loud to himself in the privacy of the caravan. 'I am not going to let anything stand in the way of our lives together. To hell with David and Troag.'

He was sitting at the table writing up the details

of a new client's craft when the phone rang. It was David.

'Just called to let you know that Mr Lucas has agreed to purchase. I will tell you when his payment has gone through and then you can arrange with him direct how and when he will collect the boat.'

'Great stuff,' said Greg. 'I signed up *my* first customer for QC this afternoon, so that's one each,' he said smugly. 'And whilst you are on, I can report that building work on the sales office is nearly complete. We are on schedule. Of course,' Greg continued, 'all this is subject to approval by my assistant office manager, who will be here to scrutinise the progress on Friday.'

'Ah, the delightful Miss Rowlinson! When will she become a permanent feature of the establishment?'

'Not sure yet, David. We have not fixed a date for the wedding and she will be working in Southampton for nearly two more months.'

After David had rung off Greg wondered what was behind his question.

Harry called in at the caravan on his way home. He'd not heard anything from the police since he'd reported Selby missing but now he was worried about the legality of his occupying the cottage. Greg told him not to worry as he believed he had every right to live there, but he told Harry he had a solicitor friend with whom he would check.

'I'm sorry,' said Harry. 'I know I've said

uncomplimentary things about your fiancée in the past but things are quite different now. I want you to know I wish you every happiness. My wife dumped me when I went to jail.'

Harry departed to his empty cottage.

It was Mary on the phone: 'I'm not waiting until tomorrow. I know a super shop in Ringwood that stays open late,' she said, 'I'm going to stop there and bring our supper for tonight with me. Make sure you've got the wine in the fridge.'

'You think of everything, my darling' was all he could get out before she rang off.

He checked the fridge: plenty of wine.

'How lucky can I be?' he mused out loud. 'I will have my beloved Mary with me tonight.'

Harry was on the phone again, and in some distress: 'The police in London have found Selby's van, apparently abandoned, in Richmond near the river. They told me that the van was empty and that an initial search had revealed nothing, but it has been towed away for Forensics to check.'

'Poor old Harry!' was Greg's first thought. 'Hope he's up to taking the inevitable bad news when it comes.' Greg had always thought that Selby would come to a sticky end. In fact at one point he had prayed for it.

With Mary's arrival late in the evening Greg's mind cleared of the week's problems. They were in each other's arms again.

'Plenty of time for that.' She grinned. 'I'm starving.'

'You're always starving.'

'That's because I seem to spend most of my time belting around after you.'

Their happiness pervaded the caravan as they tucked in to the cold supper that Mary had brought with her. She quizzed him about all that had been going on and he listened to her news. Conversation was all about their hopes for the future together, about the success of the new business adventure – and even about how many children they might have.

That mood changed when Harry banged on the caravan door early the next morning and Greg invited him in.

'You may talk freely with Mary here,' Greg said, 'I have told her about Selby going missing.'

What Greg didn't say, however, was that she did not know the reason why Greg knew the man in the first place.

Harry blurted out, 'Two policemen came round last night and asked if they could go through Selby's papers in the hopes of finding a clue as to his whereabouts. I gave them complete freedom to search where they liked. I showed them all over the place including the outbuildings and shed where Selby used to keep the van. They were there over an hour. As far as I could tell they turned up nothing that would help. I'm still worried how long I can go on living there.'

'Well, don't be,' said Greg. 'I have checked with my friend. Until Selby is found there is absolutely no way anyone can get you out.

Once again Harry thanked him and asked him not to tell his brother what was going on.

'I think you are making a mistake there,' said Greg. 'I've been happy to help you but he is your brother and I think you should tell him. Take my advice. He is your brother, as I just said.'

Harry nodded agreement and left with more profuse thanks.

That weekend Greg and Mary inspected the shell of the new office being built alongside No.1 Shed. With the floor and walls complete, and the shop windows in place, they could visualise where the display stands were going to be seen from outside the big windows, and where the signwriters were going to paint on those windows, in gold lettering, "QC Ltd. International Yacht Brokers" and other information. Standing outside the empty building they were lost in their thoughts and each other as, unabashed, they hugged and kissed.

'Aye aye,' called Chris Curnow as he hung over the balcony above them, and Mary blushed. 'I guess I'm going to have to get used to this going on all over the place from now on. Come on up, you two – I'd like to bring you up to date.'

They went round and climbed the stairs.

'Sorry Flossie's not in this morning to make the coffee,' said Chris.

'Good grief!' said Mary. 'Show me where the things are and I'll make it. You men are absolutely hopeless without a woman around you.'

Chris pointed to the cupboard, sink and shelf

in the corner of the office.

'She's right,' he said with a chuckle, hunching his shoulders. 'Greg knows how I have valued his work here. I promised him a directorship and now I am going to implement that promise. It won't give you any money until we can afford to pay directors' fees but it would give you some authority and, as agreed with QC, it will cement Curnow's interest in the brokerage.'

Chris continued: 'The fast patrol boat will bring in valuable income. I'm confident we can obtain an order for another. The income from the QC rental should give us a good return within a couple of years or so. Things are moving in the right direction.'

They left Chris's office for some quality time together before Mary had to return to Southampton.

'Please take great care, my love,' called Greg as she drove off.

* * *

On Monday morning Miss Kershaw took the phone call.

'I will see if the Commander is available, Mr Carruthers. Just hold the line, please.'

A moment later the Commander came on the line: 'Good Morning, Don. I thought you were retired. It's been a long time.'

'Does one ever retire?' came the answer. 'But let me not waste your time. I imagine you will recall a young woman I commended to you some years ago.'

'Please continue,' said the Commander.

'Well, I called you because I have information that may be of interest. The woman in question was a protégée of mine, and I recommended she took over part of my job when I retired. She has now handed in her notice because she intends to get married and move away from Southampton. She is an intelligent and clever person. She has told me who she is to marry. In fact she has intimated that she wanted to ask me to the wedding. The point I am making is that I met the man she is to marry last year. I feel you should know the circumstances of that meeting.'

Don went on to tell of the events in the Solent that led to his own meeting with Gregory Norfield.

'Most interesting,' said the Commander.

'Now, of course, I don't know what action you took about my recommendation of Mary Rowlinson and I'm convinced my decision at the time not to take proceedings against the person who is now her fiancé was right, but I thought you should know that this man is obviously a bit of an adventurer. His name is Gregory Norfield. Please don't misunderstand me, Commander; it's just that I care for her well-being and I still maintain my high opinion of her ability. She must be very much in love with this man. I had evidence of this recently when I met them together, but to give up the job for which she had worked very hard strikes me as being out of character.'

The Commander answered, 'I am grateful for your call. It was the right thing to advise me. Thank you for the information. I wish you well with your retirement.'

The call was terminated with mutual goodbyes.

The Commander chuckled as he replaced the receiver. What he always wanted from his operatives was what he called "acute observation". What amused him even more was the prospect of five of his people all together at a wedding and only any two of them knew about one or two of the others' secret lives. None of them knew most of the others. He saw it as a test of his own judgement as to whether they could all maintain the "two's a crowd, three's too many" golden rule that he insisted they all observe.

He'd have to wait and see. By the nature of this rule there was nothing he could do about it. Or was there?

On Tuesday evening Greg was preparing his supper in the caravan and listening to the radio. The phone rang. It was David.

'Are you on your own?' were his first words.

Greg affirmed that was so.

'Is this line secure? I know it goes through the Curnow office.'

'Yes,' replied Greg. 'The procedure is that the last person to leave the main office puts the line through to me before locking up and setting the alarms.'

'Listen carefully if you would, please, Greg. You have entered the world of covert operations.

I have been part of that world since I left the Royal Navy. I have consulted those higher up about your forthcoming marital status.'

'I believe you are properly motivated to be of further service but I will emphasise, as I did on *Amity*, so take this in. You will be on your own if you are uncovered. Should you be prosecuted for illegal behaviour you will be disowned. You will not be provided with any defence or immunity whatsoever. Some people like to gamble on the gee-gees. You and I make a little money from what we both know is a good and just cause – our country. *It is still a gamble. Nobody is forcing you.* There are risks involved. In my opinion those risks will increase once you have a sharp and intelligent woman living with you on the premises.'

'I hear what you say. Just one thing before you go any further,' said Greg: 'What's with Troag?'

'Transport of Arabic Gentleman. We probably won't use it again,' said David. 'By great fortune we now have at the Curnow Yard the perfect set-up. You and I are in a legitimate enterprise that operates worldwide. Dartmouth is a comparatively quiet backwater. We can bring craft to those pontoons at any time of the day or night from anywhere in Europe. The site is secure. You live on site and you have already dipped your hands into murky waters. The time has come for you to decide how secure that site will be in the future.'

Greg replied, 'I have made certain promises to my friend Chris Curnow. It is through him that I got this job—'

David interrupted. He spoke with some vehemence: 'Stop. I know about your promises – and please don't ask how – but only you and I know our purpose for this particular location. It is only you and me who risk losing anything. The law will accept that nobody (but nobody) else – and that means anyone at QC or the Curnow Yard – knows, or can say they knew, what we were up to unless we tell them; and we are not going to. That means that we both have to deceive everyone else we know. Politics is a dirty business. I am in no way interested in party politics but I do believe that what I am doing is wholly in the interest of my country. I feel no different about this than I did when I served my time in the navy. Are you in or out?'

'I'm in, with certain exceptions. I will have nothing to do with banned substances, kidnap, torture or murder. I am also having misgivings about deceiving my future wife. Right now, I am in.'

'I promise', said David, 'that I will not ask you to do anything other than serve your country. I gave you assurances during our last trip. The Cold War may not be recognisable as what most perceive as war. It is, of course, a political war. Should the sabre-rattling turn into action we would face global annihilation. The Soviets are still a threat, as are terrorist factions emerging from the Middle East. Is this a fair assessment?'

'Absolutely.'

'A very good night to you, Greg, and may your future be a happy one.'

CHAPTER NINE

Partnerships

By the first of June the new office structure, with wiring and decorating, was complete. Greg was officially on the QC payroll. In No.1 Shed the hull and deck sections of the fibreglass patrol boat had been mated up after installation of the engines, propulsion gear and fuel tanks. Half of the Curnow workforce of boatbuilders, shipwrights and fitters were employed full-time fitting out this one craft.

That weekend Mary brought with her the news for which Greg had been waiting: 'Two weeks before the official opening of the office here I will have finished in Southampton, my love. The letting agents have found me a tenant. My personal stuff will be locked up in the second bedroom, and I will bring down my final bits and pieces over the next couple of weekends. How does that grab you?'

'It grabs me more than you will ever know, my darling. Come and have a look.' He guided her to the new office building. 'It's echoing a bit at the moment but the carpet will be fitted by the manufacture next week followed by delivery of the furniture and equipment from QC. You'll have to tell me how to operate it all.'

'What do you mean *operate it all*?'

'Well, my beautiful fiancée, you've proved to me that you aren't just a pretty face. I have lost touch with technology when it comes to office stuff. They keep talking to me about computers, word processors, printers, and mail-merging, and all sorts of stuff about which I haven't a clue.'

'Look, my treasure, I think you need a secretary more than you need a wife. Which is it to be?' she teased him.

'Both, please.'

That weekend they visited the garden centre and ordered rectangular wooden containers of miniature box-hedge plants to go outside the office and the caravan as Mary had suggested. She also studied the list of office equipment that was to be supplied and to Greg's relief told him that it was similar to that which she had in her office in Southampton.

'When you come down next time,' Greg said to Mary, 'I will have checked with the registry office in Totnes. We both have to attend in person to give notice. How about we go next Friday?'

'You know why all this is going so well, don't you?' Mary said, and, without waiting for his answer, 'It's Daddy, I know it is.'

'I think you are right, my love,' he said, 'but while you are on the subject of your father do you think that he would approve of us marrying in a registry office?'

She grimaced, 'Of course he would, you silly old fool. He married people on board ships, all over the place, and anyway, don't forget, we're going to have our marriage blessed in the chapel of the College on the hill that he knew so well – he'd approve of that too. Oh, Greg, my darling, I just know we're going to be so happy. I can't wait until Friday. I'll be down late on Thursday.'

'Don't forget your birth certificate,' were his final words after kissing her goodbye on Sunday afternoon before she drove away.

On the Tuesday Greg made a phone call to David.

'How does this grab you?' he said to David, who grunted, 'If all goes to plan I'll have the office up and running in a couple of weeks. You wanted to open on July first. Well, the first Saturday in July is on the sixth. I didn't earn the nickname of The Masterplanner for nothing – now tell me what you think about this.'

'Go ahead – I'm all ears.'

'Subject to Curnow plans not being altered, Chris has told me that Sheikh Samad of Qatar is coming over that weekend for the start of the patrol-boat sea trials. I, as publicity manager for both companies, have a cunning plan. I suggest we have a grand opening party for QC on Saturday, the sixth of July. I know who to ask so as to wring maximum publicity locally for our new office. My plan is to ask the Sheikh to be a guest. According to Chris he cuts quite a figure. He is very sociable and media-savvy. We will have his patrol boat on the pontoon for all to see. Much more interesting for the local rag than just another office opening. I reckon it would raise the profile of both companies. What do you say?'

'Pretty good, I say' was David's reply.

Greg had a twinge of conscience after ringing off. He hadn't told David that part of his cunning plan was to get married to Mary the day before, on the Friday, and hold his wedding party in the new office. This way he would get the grand-opening caterers to throw in a wedding party at minimal cost to himself.

After the carpet had been fitted the next day Greg found time to go to the registry office in Totnes and book the appointment for him and Mary to sign up on Friday morning. He rang Mary from the caravan that evening.

'How about the fifth of July for our wedding?' he started.

There was a squeal of delight from the other end. 'Can I tell people?'

'Better be a bit cautious. We've got the appointment with the registry office on Friday morning first. Only then will we know if the date is certain.'

Mary arrived by seven o'clock on Thursday evening with a number of suitcases piled up in the passenger seat and the back of her little car.

'A fortnight tomorrow I will say goodbye to Southampton' were her first words. 'Don has said

I can finish on that day and he let me off early this afternoon.'

Greg gave her all the news of the week.

The forecast for Friday was warm and sunny. Small cumulus clouds were forming. Flossie was going to look after the brokerage. They set off in Mary's MG after breakfast. She had insisted that Greg should experience "real motoring" as she put the top down. They travelled through the wooded countryside to the registry office in Totnes at Follaton House.

This grand old country house was converted to council offices some years ago and provides an old-fashioned background to a modern ceremony. The registrar was a charming woman and despite the plain and stark furnishings of her office, she made the procedure of notification much less daunting than they had expected. Having provided all the details "in person" as required by the law, they took the opportunity for some retail therapy.

'Come on, Greg – let's look at the shops while we are here. Work can wait, just for one day.' With free car parking at the council offices they took the twenty-minute downhill walk into the town with its narrow streets and variety of shops.

Over coffee in a small deli in Fore Street, Mary placed her hand on Greg's.

'I don't need a ceremony to make promises to you or you to me. But the law is the law. Greg, I am so happy.'

'You once said to me,' Greg whispered back in

her ear, 'all this happiness is not one-sided,' and, oblivious to others seated around them, he placed his lips on hers for a lingering kiss. Hand in hand they walked back to their car, each knowing that their new lives were beginning.

Driving back together they discussed whom they were going to invite to the wedding party. Greg told her that he had already mentioned it to the Trehairnes and would like to ask Nick Wroughton.

'That name rings a bell,' said Mary.

Up in the office, on their return from Totnes, Chris greeted them with the news that the patrol boat would be ready for launching next week, when they would run engine trials. This meant that they were on schedule for the arrival of his customer Sheikh Samad, for full sea trials on the first weekend of July.

'I think I told you,' continued Chris, 'the Sheikh is bringing his crew, who will put her through her paces over several days and then, all being well, they will take her round to Southampton, from where she will travel as deck cargo to the Gulf. Before the boat leaves Dartmouth we will receive final payment. This will ease our cash flow somewhat. Together with the down payment and first rent from QC, we'll be back in the black again.'

Mary looked at Greg as they linked arms and left Chris's office. 'I just can't wait to be down here, darling Greg. I want to be part of all that's going on, as well as with you.'

'I reckon', Mary said the next morning, 'that if the signwriter is coming next week to do his stuff on the windows, he'll expect them to be clean; so out with the Windowlene and the Marigolds, my lover, as they say in the West Country. Let's get cracking.'

After they had finished that task Greg had another idea: he decided to introduce Mary to the Trehairnes.

That afternoon they motored over to Salcombe. Julia was outside the farmhouse as they drove up to the front door. He introduced Mary to Julia, who took a long searching look at her.

'Mmm, so you're the one who's going to take him away from me?' All that Greg had ever dared to say to Mary about Julia had been that he thought she had a crush on him, and that she was a bit "forward" for her age.

Mary replied to Julia with a smile, 'How's university going? If you learn nothing else whilst you are there, you will certainly learn about men.'

Hearing conversation, Joan and Frank came out of the house before Julia could comment further. After hugs and handshakes all round Mary and Greg were invited in.

Frank took Mary off to show her what they did there. Greg stayed behind with Joan to give her their latest news and issue invitations for them all to come to the wedding.

'Yes, that would be lovely,' said Joan, 'duties on the smallholding permitting. Are you going to ask Nick Wroughton?'

'Absolutely – just haven't got around to it yet. It was only this morning we could firm up on the date,' said Greg.

On their way back to the yard Mary told him how much she'd enjoyed meeting his friends. 'Are you sure, Mr Norfield,' she said, 'that you never got up to some hanky-panky with that girl?'

'A man wouldn't be a man if he didn't find her attractive,' Greg replied, 'and I won't say I didn't, but I'm practically old enough to be her grandfather for goodness' sake.'

'You're old enough to be my father,' replied Mary.

'True,' he said, 'but ask yourself, who is it I am going to marry?'

They laughed together and Greg knew it had been a successful afternoon with another ghost laid to rest.

True to their promise the QC van arrived with the furniture and office equipment on Wednesday. The men unloaded, leaving a pile of boxes on top of the desks and chairs in the middle of the new office.

When Greg phoned Mary that evening she said, 'Get the stuff out of the boxes. Dump all the packaging and wait until I get down on Friday to give you a hand. We'll sort it out together. I'm sure you've got plenty else to do in the meanwhile.'

'Bless you,' was all he could think to say.

The launching of the patrol boat was not a champagne occasion. That was to come for another day, and for another reason. Greg took photos when she was alongside. This boat looked very workmanlike, in her two-tone grey livery with a dark blue cove line and white boot top. Greg was going to make full use of her build as publicity for The Curnow Yard. He already had shots of the boat in various stages of construction. When Mary came down the following Friday, she saw the evidence of much activity that had taken place in her absence. She parked her car next to the telephone engineers' van outside the new office. The door was open. She could hear voices from inside. One was Greg's.

'You will have to wait until the boss arrives,' he was saying, followed by 'Here she is now.'

Greg met her in the doorway with a huge hug and an uninhibited kiss.

'I heard that bit about "the boss",' she said, smiling. 'I didn't know that's what you call me behind my back.'

She looked at the other two men present.

'Glad you turned up, miss. He hasn't stopped talking about you and won't let us get on with our work. We need to know where you want the sockets put for the telephone-line connections – one for the fax and one for the telephone – and it says here we need to check the extensions to a caravan and the office upstairs.'

These men had come to fix the phone lines but within two minutes she had them helping

Greg and herself move everything around until satisfied. She looked at Greg for approval. They left the two telephone engineers to get on with what they came for. As Greg and Mary went outside to continue their postponed loving greetings, they heard one of them say, 'Cor, just like my missus, poor sod, and they aren't even married yet!'

'Come and have a look at this,' said Greg to Mary as he pointed to the pontoon, which was almost all taken up with the two craft tied there: *L'Enterprise* and the Qatar patrol boat. 'How's that for raising the profile of the place, eh? Furthermore I have arranged that when the press come here for our grand opening those boats will be there and also present will be Sheikh Samad and his entourage, to say nothing of Alan Lucas turning up in the Ferrari to take his boat away.'

'Remove that smug grin, my treasure – it's your job.' She tried to say this with a straight face but didn't succeed.

Neither of them had noticed Chris hanging over the balcony above.

'Come on, Mary,' he said, 'he's been buzzing around like the proverbial fly these last few days. He deserves a little praise. I tell you what, you two lovebirds: Flossie and I will deal with any enquiries and the telephone guys. Why don't you take advantage of the weather and push off in *Amity* for a few hours? You won't get the chance again, I suspect, for a long time?'

They looked at each other as the suggestion sunk in.

'Done,' they chimed almost in unison.

And so they had a lazy sail on the flood tide. Halfway up the river to Totnes they turned round, picked up a mooring at Dittisham, and rowed ashore to have lunch in The Ferry Boat on the quay. The last couple of miles downriver back to the yard took them an hour against the last of the flood.

'Greg, my darling, go and play with your boats whilst I have a look at this word processor,' said Mary upon their return to the new office. 'When I come down next weekend it'll be for good. I'll have plenty of time before we open to help you sort out the equipment. And by the way, you are taking an awful chance not telling David about us having our wedding party in the office, aren't you?'

'Not a bit. I just didn't want to complicate the issue. He'll work it out himself when I fax him his invitation. He's got to come down anyway. My guess is they'll consider it "enterprise". Excuse the pun. They wouldn't expect less.'

Just five days later Mary was back from Southampton. Her car was loaded with the last of her personal goods. The little silver ship was found a place of honour on a shelf in the caravan. She had Greg fix the crucifix on the wall above their bed.

'I've read all the instruction manuals,' she said

as they went into the new office. 'Now then, before the morning is out you will be as proficient on this computer as you are at navigating your way round the oceans.'

While Mary was away Greg had loaded the display boards with the material supplied by QC. The two double-sided stands were positioned so that one side could be read through the windows and the other from within the office. Each stand contained fixings for thirty-two printed details of craft on either side. Over one hundred and twenty craft could be displayed.

The gold lettering high up on the big picture windows proclaimed the name of the owners of the brokerage and other essential details. As Mary and Greg came out of the office they met Chris and John Dalton outside.

'A classy act that,' said Chris, admiring the frontage. 'It will not do this yard any harm at all. Do you mean to say, Greg, that if you sell any of the craft displayed you will be credited with the brokerage fee?'

'Absolutely. But don't forget most of them are based somewhere else. If a buyer is serious, I may have to get that boat back here to conduct a trial sail or inspection. There is a little more work involved than might first appear.'

'Tell me' continued Chris: 'what happens if you are away collecting a boat from, say, Brighton? There's one on the board there that says it is "Afloat Brighton".'

Before Greg could answer Mary stepped

forward. 'Now, you are an intelligent man, Chris – why do you think I am here?'

On the day prior to the wedding Chris would be driving to Exeter Airport to collect the Sheikh and his crew from their private jet.

The wedding at the registry office was to be at twelve fifteen in Totnes on the Friday. The wedding party was to be at two o'clock that afternoon in the new sales office. The next day would be the QC Ltd grand opening.

With barely two weeks to the busiest two days the yard would ever see, *L'Enterprise* and the patrol boat on the visitors' pontoon were being made "Shipshape and Bristol fashion", as the saying goes. Greg had invited all the press he could persuade to come.

He rang David to update him. He added, 'I hear that you are booked into the Livermead Hotel. Don't you think it might be a good idea if you were in the same hotel as a Qatar sheikh whom you might – by chance, of course – bump into during your forty-eight hours there?'

'Good thinking, Greg. Where's he staying?'

'The Imperial, David.'

'When I called you the Masterplanner, said Mary, overhearing the conversation, 'you didn't like it.'

'Just business, my love, just business.'

A few days before the wedding Mary realised she had not brought with her – actually she did not even own – anything suitable in which to get married. Greg had the one suit, which he said he had saved for funerals.

'Charming' had been her response to that information.

Chris Curnow's wife, Rosemary, who was to be one of their witnesses at the registry office, said to Mary, 'Let's go into Torquay. I'd love to be with you to choose your wedding clothes.'

Mary had jumped at the idea.

The two of them spent a morning together in the shops.

'What do you think about this one?' said Mary after they had seen several outfits.

'No,' replied Rosemary, 'blue is your colour. I once saw something in the shop over the road. Come on – let's see what they have.'

The assistant in that shop eyed Mary from head to foot.

It took the three of them to carry the boxes out to the car an hour later.

'Rosemary, I could never have done that on my own. You're a pal,' said Mary, as they drove back to the caravan.

'Remember,' said Rosemary, 'tell Greg we want him out of the caravan on the big day *before* we get back from the hairdresser's. I'll keep all this lovely stuff for you until we get back. We'll need an hour to have you looking a million dollars.'

Mary smiled as she looked at Rosemary. 'Greg and I are so lucky to have such good friends.'

Just before Rosemary drove off home, she said,

'If I don't see you before, I'll see you on the day. Phone me if there's absolutely anything you'd like me to do.'

* * *

Came their big day.

'I'm off,' Mary said to Greg after an early breakfast. 'I love you dearly, but I don't want you in the caravan when I get back.' She drove off with Rosemary at the wheel of the Curnows' own car.

She was in the hairdresser's in Torquay at eight thirty. The girls there had vied for the privilege of doing the bride's hair.

'Don't attempt to suggest a different style,' said Mary to the proprietor of the salon that Rosemary had recommended. 'Just apply your art in the best way you know.'

The owner had opted to do the job herself, she would stake her reputation on it.

At the yard, Chris, who was to drive the four of them to Totnes in Greg's white Rover, was putting the final shine on the car and attaching white ribbons when Rosemary drove up to the caravan with Mary. She spotted Greg nearby and, after telling Mary to stay put, she got out of the car and ushered him back to the offices, with dire threats should he dare come back to the caravan before she phoned over to say he could.

'I'm nervous enough as it is without having him fussing around' was Mary's reply as Rosemary set about helping her to dress. The caravan curtains were partly drawn but they could see Greg outside the offices with a red rose in the buttonhole of his only suit.

'He looks pretty cool for a man on his wedding day,' said Mary.

'Well, what do you want –' was Rosemary's reply, 'a dithering wreck?'

Their laughter broke the nervous tension as they made for the door after Rosemary had phoned her husband to bring the car and the bridegroom. Mary was wearing a navy-blue two-piece with an embroidered white blouse and mid-calf matching skirt with white piping, white court shoes, and a gardenia in her hair at the top of her long blond ponytail. Her hair had been styled around a tiny scallop-shaped dark blue velvet hat. She took care as she stepped out of the caravan.

'I knew you were lovely,' he said as he met her at the bottom of the steps, 'today you look like a queen.'

They hugged and her eyes became moist.

'Now look what you've done to my mascara.'

They got into the Rover. Rosemary and Mary sat in the back, and Greg, in the front with Chris, was told not to listen to the girl-talk going on behind them.

When they arrived at the council offices the sight of Follaton House with its classical-style portico softened the characterless features of the very functional registry office.

Fifteen minutes later they were on their way home. This time Greg was allowed to sit with his bride in the back.

Chris had done his own bit of organising. As they drove through the shipyard gates the whole of the yard workforce formed a guard of honour, waving and clapping all the way to the caravan, where David was waiting with a bucketful of confetti and the local press photographer.

A bit of a freshen-up was in order and they went to greet their guests in the new QC office.

With a few bunches of blue and white balloons, some ribbons and vases of flowers, the office was transformed into a cheerful venue for a wedding party.

Laid out on the white-clothed tables was a comprehensive buffet. There was discreet background music. David had with him his cine camera to record the happy event for posterity, as he said.

The Trehairnes and Nick Wroughton came together in one car.

'Something small,' said Joan Trehairne as she handed over their present. 'We know space is at a premium in your caravan. We hope it gives you a smile.' Joan told them that Julia had volunteered to stay behind to look after the stock, and sent her best wishes.

Greg warmly shook Don Carruthers' hand. 'I want to thank you for being so kind and understanding to my Mary. You could be forgiven for thinking she had let you down.'

'It is more than compensated for by seeing her so happy, said Don. 'Our daughter would have been about her age had she lived. Sadly she was taken from us only months after she was born. Perhaps that has something to do with it.'

Mary was moving toward Nick Wroughton at the other end of the room. 'Now I remember where I met you,' she said.

Nick looked fazed.

'You were a deck officer on a tanker we boarded at the Fawley refinery many years ago.'

'Sorry, my dear,' said Nick, 'but who is "we"?'

Mary explained that at that time she had recently joined Customs & Excise. It was her first routine boarding of a ship. She was one of a party of four.

'Well, I'm damned,' he said. 'That must be nearly ten years ago. Of course – the fair-haired, blue-eyed young girl with a ponytail.'

'That was me,' said Mary.

'Are you still in the service?'

'No, I quit, to marry Greg. I'm going to be his assistant in the office here – when he can afford to pay me,' she said with a laugh. 'Meanwhile I'll still be here in the office!'

Greg came over to the two of them and put his arm round Mary.

'Either you are chatting up my girl,' he said good-heartedly, 'or you are giving away all my secrets.'

'Well, yes, if you call having a pint in the pub

on a Saturday night a secret,' said Nick. 'Actually she reminded me that we met about ten years ago when I was first officer on board a tanker in the Solent.'

'Really?' said Greg with a grin. 'When I was on board a boat in the Solent she nearly had me arrested and then saved me from going to prison. I've had to marry her out of gratitude!'

'Tell me,' said Nick: 'who is that older gentleman over there with the carnation in his buttonhole? His face is familiar.'

'That', said Mary, 'is Don Carruthers, my old boss. I'll introduce you.'

'No need – I'll introduce myself.'

Nick moved away toward Don. David swept the room with his cine camera.

'Lovely party,' said Joan as she and Frank Trehairne came over, 'but needs must when the Devil drives and all that. We have goats to milk etcetera. Uncle Robert is enjoying your champagne to the extent that we are afraid he might break into song any moment and that would spoil your do! If you two ever get to sail to Salcombe, make sure you drop your hook in Robbie's Creek and give us a bell. There's a welcome for you any time'

They collected Nick Wroughton, as well as Robert, on the way out. Other friends decided it was time to go, offering their thanks and best wishes to the bride and groom.

Chris, John, and Flossie from the offices upstairs had each taken the time in turn to look in and add their wishes. David was the last to go.

'May the future for you both be happy and fruitful,' he said, 'putting his arm round Mary and kissing her on the cheek. As for my own immediate future, I think I will explore the potential of the Imperial Hotel!'

Back in the caravan they opened their presents. The one that intrigued Mary most was the brass ornamental three monkeys: "Hear no evil, see no evil, speak no evil", from the Trehairnes.

The caterers had insisted at the close of the party that the couple took with them two cold bottles of champagne and a big box of the best of the buffet. And so they spent the rest of their wedding day mulling over events as they mellowed under the influence of so many goodies.

With the practical necessity to be up early for yet another party, which occasion would be work, it wasn't long before they were supremely happy in each other's arms.

In the morning Greg said to Mary, 'Today is the official start of our new lives in so many ways, Mrs Norfield. I just thank God we are in this together.'

'Amen to that,' she said.

CHAPTER TEN

Foul play

The grand opening was at ten o'clock. Greg, Mary, Chris and David were on duty well before that. They had attached boat details to over a hundred of the spaces on the display boards. First to arrive, well before ten, were Brian Hope and Tom Sinclair from QC in a large Daimler, which Brian was driving. He went round to the boot and produced an enormous bouquet of lilies tied with a blue ribbon. He walked toward Mary, waiting with Greg outside the office door.

'Mrs Norfield, I presume? Please accept these with my very best wishes for the future.'

Mary took his hand and managed to balance this huge spray in the crook of her other arm.

'I hear from David and Greg', he continued, 'that you had a great deal to do with getting this office together.' And, looking at the shrubs in boxes along the front, he said, 'That's a very nice touch.'

David pointed his finger very obviously at Mary.

'Let's have the grand tour, then,' said Brian.

They all went in and it was clear from his looks and head-nodding that all he saw pleased him.

'And within budget?'

'Of course,' said Mary before anyone else could utter a word.

Next to arrive was the mayor and his wife, who, logged by the local press photographer and reporter, cut the traditional ribbon across the entrance and wished the enterprise good fortune.

'Good for your company, and good for the towns of Kingswear and Dartmouth,' he said.

The arrival of a dark brown Rolls Royce, driven by a young Arab in mid-blue matching jacket and trousers, and a dark blue pleated turban, drew much attention. He stopped the car outside the office door, went round to the passenger side, and opened the door for Sheikh Samad. He added a sense of quality to the occasion, wearing the traditional white thobe and chequered gutra headdress. Chris introduced him to the mayor with his ornate gold chain and badge of office.

'I am most privileged to meet an English mayor,' acclaimed the Sheikh, to which the mayor replied, 'As am I to meet you, Your Highness. We are pleased that you have chosen this shipyard to build your patrol boat.'

'Come,' said the Sheikh – 'please call me Sam, and I will show you.' He waved his hand toward the nearby pontoon where the boat lay. He took the mayor by the elbow.

Chris led the way. As they walked down the gangway they could be heard chatting like old friends. The photographer had a field day, and

Greg managed to manoeuvre them into a position where *L'Enterprise*, the next boat along, would be included in shots he took of the Qatar craft.

Alan Lucas, the new owner of *L'Enterprise*, had thanked Greg for inviting him to the QC opening. He arrived in the Bentley to collect his new purchase. He was accompanied by three young men dressed in white roll-necks, navy slacks and deck shoes. Although short, he looked the part in his dark blue blazer and white well-pressed trousers below which showed his top-of-the-range doeskin deck shoes. He was clearly pleased to be introduced to the Sheikh but declined the hospitality on offer.

'This is my son,' he said to Greg as he introduced the shortest of the three young men. 'The other two who have gone aboard are my crew. I would like to get under way, please.'

David was on board, briefing the crew about the controls. Greg and David helped them to cast off. Sheikh Samad took much interest in what was going on.

During that afternoon they had a steady trickle of visitors. The caterers kept the buffet freshly stocked and made sure the champagne didn't run out. Sheikh Samad, glass of orange juice in hand, seemed to be genuinely enjoying himself, chatting to everyone.

'Look, this is your event and we seem to be hijacking it,' Chris said quietly to David and his boss, Brian Hope.

'Not a bit of it,' replied Brian, looking toward the Sheikh. 'I think we should be paying you for the star attraction.'

Chris explained to David that the next day, Sunday, would be the first day of the sea trials and that the Sheikh would drive over from Torquay every day with his crew. He intended to go to sea with the boat each time. Chris hoped that three or four days would see the completion of the trials.

'I'm rather afraid', said David to Greg, 'that Alan Lucas may not be enjoying his trip round to Fowey. The forecast wasn't bad but, with wind against tide, I think his idea of a gentle cruise may not be quite that.'

The caterers cleared up at five o' clock and Greg left a notice on the door: "Open for business from ten a.m. Sunday." It had been a hard but highly successful day.

Brian Hope's departing remark was heard: 'Let us see that it carries on the way it has started.'

That is the way he was: short on words, high on expectation.

David motored back to Lymington on Sunday morning. Before he left, he called back into the office and advised Greg and Mary that they were entitled to a weekday off together in view of the need for the sales office to be open at weekends. QCs experience with their other smaller offices was that they had no complaints if the office was closed on a Wednesday. A message on the answer machine and a notice in the window to this effect would be in order.

A few people came into the QC office on Sunday – including Bob Berry, who was the owner of the Fisher 34 they had signed up to sell. He tied the boat up on the visitors' pontoon and after he left Greg was quick to go down to the pontoon and tie his first QC "For Sale" signs on her.

This yacht with her tan sails and dark varnished brightwork looked in good condition and he hastened to get the photos he'd taken earlier together with details off to Lymington for them to produce the print for the display board.

Early on Monday morning, as Greg and Mary were about to open the QC office, Chris leaned over the balcony.

'Can you spare a minute, Greg?'

Mary said she would open up and look after things as Greg climbed the stairs to Chris's office. Chris's face showed that something was wrong.

'I had a phone call at home last night from my restaurant friend Antonio Favresi to tell me that the police called on him to ask about Selby Somerfield-Smythe. It would seem they were investigating his disappearance. I didn't know at that point anything about Selby's disappearance so of course I phoned Harry. He explained why he hadn't wanted to bother me.'

'He was concerned that you and the yard should not be implicated in any way,' said Greg.

'Well, we could be,' continued Chris. 'Antonio, you and I are implicated. I think it a good idea if we sort out our next move. Antonio has said all the right things to the police. Somehow they had found the name and address of his restaurant and faced with the direct question "Do you know this man?" he told the truth. He told them that he'd known Selby because a customer, he couldn't remember which one, in a conversation with him about where he obtained his fresh fish, had replied that he got it from a merchant in Torbay. He told the police that this customer had sent Selby to see him about bringing the stuff up from Brixham. The truth, however, according to Antonio, was that Selby had tried to blackmail him into giving him business on the threat of revealing to the police the source of the two or three deliveries of your "bits of trade" that he'd made from the Curnow Yard.'

All this came as no surprise to Greg. Selby was a blackmailer. Hoping to cheer Harry up, and with no Flossie in the room, he used the internal phone to contact the warehouse. No reply. Greg wanted to tell him that whatever happened to Selby he would have the right to live in the cottage for at least thirty years before he could be challenged.

There was a clattering of footsteps on the stairs. Harry burst into the office.

'They've found Selby!' he exclaimed.

He sank into the nearest chair, his hand

clasped across his mouth, seemingly unable to say any more. His distress was obvious. For a moment none of them spoke. Chris placed his hand on his brother's shoulder.

'And?'

'They found him stuffed down a bloody sewer in Putney,' Harry shouted. 'They wouldn't tell me any more, other than that the forensic report after checking his van revealed signs that he had struggled in the driver's seat. That and marks round his neck led them to believe he had been strangled some time before his body was discovered. Because I was the last known person to see him alive they're sending someone down right now to interview me.'

'What can we do for you, right now, Harry?' said Chris.

'I need to get home. They'll be knocking on my door. Then they'll be round here. I know how these things are. I've been through it all before. I am so sorry, Chris. I've let you down.'

'Come on, Harry – I'll drive you home. I want to be with you when the police arrive. Greg here will let the others know where I am.'

John Dalton, and then Flossie, turned up shortly after Chris and Harry had left the yard.

'They've left on a family matter. It's to do with Selby's disappearance,' Greg told them. 'I'll be up again in a minute to explain. I must pop down and put Mary in the picture.'

This he did, but omitted the gruesome details. Revelling in the luxury of having his wife look after the QC business, he went back up to the Curnow offices to explain further to John and Flossie.

Would Mary ever forgive him for being relieved that the question of *what to do about Selby?* was now resolved?

Chris and Harry returned after lunch. Harry wanted to work to keep his mind occupied with matters other than his pal. Chris found an excuse to ask Greg down to the pontoon, where they could not be overheard.

'The meeting at the cottage with the police went well, Greg. I didn't detect any bias against Harry because he had a criminal record. I was able to reassure them that myself, as well as a number of people here, could vouch for Harry's movements and whereabouts since Selby went missing. I told them all of us here would be happy to cooperate.'

'What about his deliveries to Antonio in Soho?' said Greg.

'There is no evidence. Selby had no paperwork from here. It was all for cash. Harry was the only other person to know and he's not telling, is he? Let's put it behind us, Greg. I don't believe we can blame ourselves in any way for his death. It seems to me that he must have fallen foul of some very unpleasant people for one reason only – he was trying or threatening to blackmail them about something he had discovered.'

'Do you really believe that, Chris?'

'I'd put money on it. The impression I got from the police this morning was that they knew the perpetrators were a terrorist gang in London. They hinted that the manner of Selby's death and disposal carried the gang's hallmark.

Greg chose to hide his anxiety about the Selby affair from Mary and was not comfortable at the deception about his own dubious past activities. He was pensive that afternoon – so much so that Mary asked him if anything was wrong.

He knew what his feelings of guilt told him to do. He might withhold from the police what he knew about Selby but then Selby wasn't deserving of the truth and wasn't alive to care either. Mary was.

In bed that night Greg held Mary tight.

'I have a confession to make,' he said. 'You won't like what you hear but I believe there's a bigger chance of losing your love if I don't tell you.'

She wriggled round to face him. The little bed light was still on.

'I've been waiting for this all day,' she said. 'I knew there was something wrong this morning. In fact, I think I've known for some time. Nothing you tell me will ever stop me loving you, my darling Greg. We promised each other we would share everything in our lives together; please God he doesn't let either of us fall at the first hurdle.'

There was moisture in her eyes as she waited for him to continue.

'In revealing something to you my lovely, I am

breaking a promise to someone else, but it's you I care about most. Please let me get to the end of what I have to tell before you say anything. Some time ago I was asked to do something for my country. A covert operation to which I was sworn to secrecy.'

At this point Mary raised two fingers and placed them on his lips. He understood the gesture but not why she had done it. He thought maybe she needed to say something as he had asked her not to speak. He frowned.

'It's me that should be making a confession, my darling one,' she said. 'I didn't know it was possible to love you any more than I do. You are prepared to break a solemn promise because you love me.' Tears came to her eyes. 'It should be me that has to confess, you lovely old fool.'

Greg was totally confused and it showed on his face.

She continued: 'Do you trust me, Greg?'

'You know I do, absolutely.'

'Then do not say any more. I also am bound to secrecy over a matter I have not told you about. It has been bothering me ever since our wedding day. Bless you for what you have said. Now that we know that each of us is committed to a pledge we should not break I would like to sleep on it till the morning. That's what my father told me to do when I was a child.'

They cuddled up together, relieved of something each had thought would come between them.

'I've been thinking,' said Mary as they sipped their coffee in the morning.

'Hope it didn't hurt, my love.'

Mary smiled. 'You're being facetious again, darling. I am serious. About last night: 'the way I see it is that we are morally obliged to keep a pledge. All the time we trust each other we have no problem. Should either of us behave in a way likely to raise doubts in the other we simply say we are on duty.

'I like it' was Greg's response.

'However, if I catch you with another woman, don't you dare tell me you are on duty!'

Greg put down his coffee mug.

'One more thing, my love. I think you need to know the full story about Selby. I know you'll understand why I haven't told you before, but Harry only recently came out of prison. We are all doing our best to help him back to a normal life. Selby was his cell mate and they became friends, sharing Selby's cottage in Buckfastleigh when they came out of Dartmoor together. It seemed right at the time, when I found out, not to break a confidence by telling you.'

Mary got the breakfast on the go.

'Thanks for that. You know you can rely on my discretion. My! Look at the time. We've got work to do.'

The patrol-boat trials commenced. The Sheikh and his crew turned up each day for runs in the boat outside the harbour in the morning. They all then went back to their hotel for lunch and prayers. They returned in the afternoon if a further run was needed.

One morning the specialists from the German engine manufacturers accompanied them and explained about their service facilities in the Middle East. On the fifth day the trials were signed off and the crew of five took the boat to Southampton docks for onward transmission. The crew were going to travel with the boat in the freighter on which she was to be loaded as deck cargo.

Chris took the Sheikh to his aircraft at Exeter Airport. He was buoyed up by the prospect of another lucrative order for a similar craft. This second order depended on the performance of the first, which was still in Southampton. After that, who knows? However, the workshop had plenty of commissions for maintenance and repairs during the winter.

* * *

With an invitation from the Trehairnes to join them on Christmas Day, Mary and Greg decided to sail round to Salcombe. As soon as the yard closed for the holiday they cast off and headed west. Well clear of the harbour, snuggled up together in the cockpit, Mary looked at Greg.

'This is what sailing is all about: away from the hassle, master of your own destiny, and a welcoming landfall ahead.'

'Aided, to no small extent,' deemed Greg, 'by a north wind giving us a calm sea in the lee of the land, good speed through the water, and could we ever forget that sight ahead of us as the sun drops down toward the horizon and a ribbon of shimmering light on the water guides us to our destination?'

'Poetic,' said Mary, 'but true. I shall not forget this day.'

The spectacular cliffs at the entrance and the picturesque run up the river past the town to the quay were new for Mary. With no commerce taking place at the town quay on Christmas Eve they had a peaceful night.

Christmas Day dawned bright and cold but a relight of the cabin heater soon had them warm again. Never had bacon and eggs tasted so good, and the prospect of the day with friends cheered them even more.

Came a knock on the deck.

'Permission to come aboard?'

Greg slid back the hatch to see a familiar face. It was Nick.

'I'm your chauffeur,' he said. 'Happy Christmas.'

Greg started to make the introductions when he remembered, and Mary interrupted: 'We're old friends' she said, laughing.

'Yes,' said Greg, 'I remember now. You were reminiscing at our wedding party – something about on board a tanker.'

'Nothing for you to be jealous about,' said Mary.

'After ten years he couldn't even remember me.'

They climbed into Nick's Land Rover and made off up the hill. They were greeted warmly by the Trehairnes. Already seated by a roaring log fire in that huge old fireplace now surrounded by holly rich with red berries, were Uncle Robert, Julia, and Joan's sister Ruth Davidson, with whom Julia was living whilst at Exeter University.

Mary noticed Greg looking at Julia as they entered the room. As if to pre-empt her thoughts he spontaneously gave Mary a big hug and a smile that said it all.

Nick knew everyone present. It was only Ruth Davidson who had to be introduced to Greg and Mary. Joan elaborated by telling them that her older sister had been widowed some ten years now and lived on her own. She was enjoying having her niece to stay and the two of them got along like a house on fire.

'Penny for them,' said Mary to Greg. 'Thought I'd lost you there – you were miles away for a few moments.'

'I was thinking just how lucky I was to have married you,' said Greg truthfully, as Frank produced a jug of scrumpy.

Frank told them that this particular vintage, made from last year's home apple crop, was special and that as he knew they could all keep a secret he would tell them what that secret was after they had tried it. Greg read something more into the phrase "keep a secret" than was intended.

'Well,' said Frank, raising his mug, 'I know it's Dickensian but a Happy Christmas to us all,' followed by 'What do you think?'

All pronounced that it was the best yet.

Frank revealed that this year's secret ingredient was – rose petals.

It was a fantastic feast the Trehairnes laid out that Christmas Day. The nineteenth-century room, with low beams generously decorated with holly and mistletoe, and lit candles on the table, provided a warm feeling for the family and friends sat around it. Nobody doubted Mary when she said it was the finest Christmas meal she had ever had.

Joan wound up the proceedings by playing "Auld Lang Syne" as they all stood around the piano and sang, holding hands in the time-honoured way.

The family refused offers of help to clear up. While Nick and Ruth Davidson sat down by the fire to chat, Mary and Greg opted for a walk down to the creek.

As soon as they were out of earshot, Mary said, 'It doesn't need an ex Customs officer to know that the wine and Calvados weren't bought in this country. I guess that was the outcome of what they call moonshining in the West Country.'

'Now come on, my lovely, lovely lady. Presents are exchanged at Christmas; this is a fishing port. I've seen French boats in here.'

Mary stepped in front of Greg, reached up and put her arms round his neck and her lips to his.

When they had finished their lingering kiss she said, 'I was only joking.'

'Oh,' Greg replied, 'I thought for a minute over lunch you were going to produce a pair of handcuffs and march them off to the brig.'

They chuckled.

Arm in arm they walked down to the creek. Standing on the landing, Mary was able to share a little of the peace and beauty of the place – the green rolling fields, the lapping of the water, and the throaty gurgles of Brent geese. Greg promised he would introduce her to Old Sam the seal when they sailed here together one day.

Driving them back to the boat, Nick told them a little about himself: 'I love this job. I have plenty of responsibility. I meet a lot of people and I look after my old and infirm mother. She insisted that I had Christmas lunch with my friends, but I am going back to spend the rest of the day with her. Hope I didn't drag you away before you wanted to leave,' he said.

'Not a bit,' replied Greg. 'Better to get back before dark.'

'I'll be round early in the morning to collect your harbour dues,' said Nick with a grin and a wink as they got out of the Land Rover and waved him off.

They cast off before first light to catch the east-going tide and to get back whilst the weather held. It was marvellous, Greg thought, to have someone below making the butties and coffee whilst he, enjoying being under power from his quiet and smooth new engine, motored *Amity* down the harbour and out into the open sea. There was practically no wind, so they continued to motor whilst they sat close together bundled up in their warmest gear on a benign sea.

'I reckon you fancied Nick,' said Greg as they recalled the events of the day before.

'No harm in you being a bit jealous.'

Before they reached Start Point a gentle breeze sprung up and they were able to turn off the engine and sail the rest of the way on port tack. Today was Boxing Day. They had three more days of holiday.

As they sailed northwards across Start Bay Greg asked Mary if her father had ever told her the story of Slapton Sands, visible only a mile or so to the west. He had after all seen much tragedy at sea.

She shook her head from side to side.

'Toward the end of the last war in these very waters, here in Start Bay and to the east in Lyme Bay, over nine hundred, mainly American, troops and sailors died during exercises for the D-Day landings in Normandy. They were ambushed by German fast E-boats. Only last year a Sherman tank was raised from the bottom here where it had lain ever since. It is to be placed on shore as a memorial to that dreadful event.'

They were silent for a long time as Mary remembered words from the service of Burial at

Sea uttered by her father many times: *"They that go down to the sea in ships: and occupy their business in great waters"*. She mouthed a silent prayer for those who would still be remembering their lost loved ones forty years later: Americans; who gave their lives for us.

It was a thoughtful couple who, the day after the celebration of the birth of Christ, sailed gently up the calm waters of the Dart remembering those who risk their lives at sea to defend our freedom.

'Let's go a little way upriver,' Mary said to Greg as they glided past the steep wooded cliffs. 'It is so peaceful. Just the two of us. We have everything we need for another day. Let's find a quiet spot, drop the anchor, and count our blessings.'

'I'm all for that,' he replied, and well beyond Dittisham, upriver, they found their sheltered spot in an isolated creek where Greg knew it to be safe to drop anchor and later to take the ground. There they would be undisturbed except by seabirds and the creatures of the shallows.

They knew that due to work and the weather it was likely there would be no more sailing until the spring.

It had been a fantastic two days, and snug in the forecabin, keeping each other warm, they thanked God for his mercies and their love for each other.

Back at work on New Year's Day Greg's hunch proved right. They had several visitors, with enquiries from prospective buyers and sellers. The New Year had started with promise. Two days later the yard opened after the long break.

Harry came into the office to tell them that he was required to attend the inquest into Selby's death in the West London Coroner's Court during the second week in January, after which the body could be released for burial. Harry would have to make arrangements in London for the cremation in Torquay.

'Do you think', said Harry 'that one of you at least, if you both can't get away at the same time, could come to the service? It seems terrible, but as far as I know Selby had no friends or relations that I can contact and that means only myself and Chris will be attending the service.'

Mary promptly said she'd be pleased to go, leaving Greg in the office. She knew how Greg had felt about Selby. After all, they had promised to support Harry in any way they could. Chris came down to join them and let Harry know that Rosemary and Bill Fossett and his wife would go along as well.

Early the following week Harry had to go to London to identify the body. Chris went with him. The day after their return Chris told Greg that the police would release the body to Harry for burial after the inquest. A verdict of "killing by person or persons unknown" was almost certain. This would mean that the case remained open with the Metropolitan Police.

CHAPTER ELEVEN

Deception

David answered his telephone at home one evening.

'Good evening, Captain,' said the voice. 'This is the transport department.'

David recognised the Commander.

'It's OK to talk,' replied David. 'This is my wife's bridge night. She's out.'

'Now we've got that formality over,' said the Commander, 'do you have what I wanted?'

David replied that he had the only copy of the cine film that he had been asked by the Commander to take of Mary and Greg's wedding party. David wanted to know if his boss would like him to mail it or take it to his office.

'Oh no, no' came the reply, 'I don't wish to have anything here. I wonder if you could arrange for me to have a viewing in the near future somewhere?'

'Are you willing to come down here, where I have the projector and screen etcetera?' David asked the Commander. 'In a couple of weeks my wife will have departed for Australia to see our daughter and grandchildren. She will be staying out there for a month or so. We will be undisturbed.'

'That will be splendid. Call Miss Kershaw from a secure phone in a couple of days to fix up the meeting. I wish to bring a colleague to see the film and to whom I will introduce you.'

'Commander, what about the golden rule you were at pains to remind me about last time we spoke?'

'Oh, my dear friend, you've been around long enough to know the rules of management. We make the rules; you obey them. Only we are allowed to break them. I look forward to seeing you again soon.'

The line went dead.

* * *

At the inquest, Harry was glad of his brother's company. He gave evidence of identification of his friend and he was asked to say how he had met him in the first place – a matter which made Harry and his brother to later wish they had sought legal advice, as they were in open court with press reporters in attendance.

The courtroom reminded Harry of a school classroom. The coroner sat at a table with three clerks taking notes or handing them to him. To his left was a witness box like a raised pulpit with a Bible on the shelf. Harry was required to hold the Bible in one hand while he swore to tell the truth (reading from a card in the other hand). After he had finished his evidence of identification he stepped down to listen to the next witness, a police sergeant.

'The victim was reported to us as a missing person by the last witness. We subsequently found the victim's van by the river Thames. An extensive search over many days failed to find any trace of the victim. It was not until a resident in the Borough of Putney reported a drain blockage that the victim's body was found in a sewer. The marks found on the victim's neck and legs by the forensic pathologist, together with blood samples we found in the victim's van, led us to the conclusion that the victim had been strangled as he sat in the driver's seat. There was evidence that he had put up a considerable struggle before his life was extinguished.'

Harry broke down and sobbed. 'The bastards,' he cried as Chris put his arm round his shoulders and helped him out of the room.

As predicted, the verdict was unlawful killing, and the body was ordered to be released for burial. Chris and Harry found the police sergeant who had given evidence to be very kind and helpful. After the conclusion of the inquest he said he was sorry that his evidence was upsetting to Harry but that unfortunately it had been necessary. He gave them the name of a local funeral director, who they visited to make the arrangements for cremation in Torquay. Chris and Harry did not get back to Buckfastleigh until late that night.

The funeral service in Torquay took place a week later. So it was that Bill Fossett and his wife, Chris and Rosemary Curnow, and Mary set off for the crematorium. Mary elected to drive Harry in Greg's Rover. She thought that she, on her own, was the most likely of them to alleviate his distress at this time. The other four went in Chris's car. Greg stayed behind to man the office.

On the coffin lay a sole sprig of heather which Harry had picked on Dartmoor the day before. It had seemed to him to be appropriate – life for Selby had been much better in Dartmoor Prison than was meted out to him after his release.

As they drove out through the gates of the crematorium they were surprised by a man wearing a belted beige raincoat and a flat cap. He was carrying a large press camera with flash and closed in on them as they moved slowly out into the main road. The flashes from the camera made it impossible to recognise or remember details of the photographer. In indignation Chris pulled up in the road outside but by the time he'd got out and run back to the gates the photographer had jumped into a car and been driven off.

The following Sunday the *News of the World* carried a picture taken from the nearside of the Rover clearly showing Harry in the passenger seat and Mary driving, under the headline "Putney Murder Victim Buried by Cellmate".

Chris drove over to the cottage at Buckfastleigh immediately after Harry's phoned request.

'What can we do about this?' Harry said to his brother.

Chris thought for a moment before replying: 'Probably nothing. Batten down the hatches comes to mind. It's a huge violation of your privacy but the gutter press do it all the time. Sooner or later your conviction had to be known. It wouldn't surprise me if some at the shipyard outside of myself, Greg, and John Dalton knew already. Sorry, Harry, but that is how it works.'

After hearing the news, Mary and Greg both knew people who might not be pleased one little bit by that photograph in the newspaper.

The Commander was one, because he recognised Mary Norfield and wondered about her involvement with a crook. Another was Captain David Worthy, RN retired. A third person was Nick Wroughton, who had not known about Harry's past history but had met him at the wedding party. He only knew Mary as Greg's wife. He also did not know that the Commander knew Mary. As for the Commander, he knew that Mary didn't know that Nicholas Wroughton was in "the service" and that Nick didn't know that she was. On top of that, none of the others knew that Don Carruthers was one of them and it was Don who had recruited Mary to the organisation and who raised his eyebrows a long way when the picture was drawn to his attention at work the next day.

So many people, bound by an oath of secrecy,

had been drawn into a web of lies spun by the Commander. He knew all of them, and yet most of them did not know each other.

The Commander may have been pleased with his network but he wasn't pleased about the fact that he had not been told by Mary of her association with a certain Selby Somerfield-Smythe, deceased, and ex-Dartmoor Prison.

* * *

A week after the *News of the World* affair David phoned Greg to report his good news.

'I didn't tell you the outcome of my 'accidental' encounter with the Sheikh in the Imperial Hotel because I thought it might be tempting fate. However, I am flying down to our Monte Carlo office next week to finalise the details for one of the largest yachts we have ever sold. I am arranging for it to be crewed through the Suez Canal to the obliging Sheikh Samad in the Gulf. If it hadn't been for your tip-off about the Imperial Hotel, this sale would not have happened. I've allocated five thousand pounds from our fee to your office.'

'More good news,' said Greg: 'we will be selling *L'Enterprise* for Mr Lucas. He says that he just doesn't have the time to make use of her. I did not, of course, mention when he phoned me that Mrs Lucas had already predicted that course of events.'

'You are well aware, Greg, that discretion is part of every job.'

CHAPTER TWELVE

The Commander

Two weeks later David's wife departed for Australia and the evening for showing the film of the wedding to the Commander at David's house near Brockenhurst had arrived. Miss Kershaw had said that the Commander and his colleague would be there by 6.30 p.m. They were.

'Step inside, please,' invited David.

The Commander introduced Captain Leonard Montague, RN retired. Captain Montague was on the short side but lean like his companion, though with little hair and a distinct limp. David had him at about his own age or a little younger.

'Captain Montague is happy to be known as Monty,' continued the Commander.

They moved into the dining room, where David had set up his cine equipment.

'We only expect to be here just long enough to see the film. As you know, I have arranged a private dinner party for the three of us in my private suite at the hotel, not more than a couple of miles or so down the road from here.'

David's projector was at one end of his dining

room and the screen at the other. The two visitors sat either side of the table in the middle of the room, where they pulled pads and pencils from their briefcases preparing to make notes.

The opening shots showed the arrival of the bride and bridegroom. David's two guests leaned forward with keen interest.

'Please give us a running commentary, David,' said the Commander, 'particularly the names of those filmed.'

There was no soundtrack. From time to time the Commander spoke to Monty. As David announced the names of the people in the film the other two present were writing them down. Several times the Commander asked for the film to be stopped, or for a rerun or freeze-frame to study. The total running time was only about five minutes, but with stops and brief questions it took about three quarters of an hour to get to the last frame.

The Commander spoke again: 'You can now destroy that film, please. You will find a suitable excuse to tell the happy couple, if they ask, why you failed in some way to get it developed. Neither you, myself, Monty, nor anyone else, will keep that record. It was entirely for Monty's benefit. He is taking over from me. Miss Kershaw told you, I think, that I have a sitting room in my suite at the hotel where we will have a farewell dinner together and can talk in private. Come with us in my car and I will arrange for you to have a taxi back.'

The Commander had a well-stocked minibar in

his private sitting room and invited them to help themselves whilst he visited the bathroom.

With a Scotch in his hand, Monty was quick to fill David in on his own service background: 'I'd been in submarines for nearly twenty years when the Commander invited me into the firm. He probably thought that stealth and silence came as second nature to me.'

They laughed at that together.

'My spell underwater came to an end when I ignominiously fell down the conning tower.'

David managed to disguise his suppressed mirth at the thought of the skipper falling down his own companionway.

'The limp?' he said, mustering a look of concern.

'Quite.'

Monty continued by explaining that he had finished his service in the Royal Navy Procurement Office, which taught him bureaucracy of monumental proportions.

'Glad you two are getting acquainted,' said the Commander on returning. 'There will not be another opportunity for the three of us to socialise; and no, I am not going to hark on about the golden rule. We all know why it's there.' And turning to Monty he added, 'David has rendered valuable service over many years, as I have told you, so this occasion fulfils two functions: a chance for you to meet one of our most successful operatives, and an opportunity for me to say thank you to David, and farewell. Tell us all you know about the Harry character, please, David.'

'My guess', said David 'is that you saw a recent front page of the *News of the World*.'

The other two nodded in agreement.

'He is the brother of Chris Curnow, the shipyard and marina owner with whom we at QC have a brokerage agreement. Greg Norfield is our sales manager. Mary, as you saw in the film, is Greg's wife. The article that went with the picture was correct about Harry's past, but I am satisfied that he is now totally reformed. His brother has given him a responsible job at the shipyard and keeps a close eye on him.'

'I realise', said the Commander, 'that there was nothing anyone could have done to prevent either the photographer doing his job or the consequences. The golden rule was invented to protect all of us. What can you tell us about the late Selby.'

'Absolutely nothing, other than what you have read in the paper. I was as surprised as anyone when I saw the picture. I am now making discreet enquiries.'

The Commander reached for a pile of menus. 'Let us turn to more prosaic matters,' he said as he invited them to study what was on offer from an extensive menu.

A waiter was summoned to take the order and at the Commander's suggestion they went along with the "Chef's Choice" on the menu and recharged their glasses.

'Commander,' said David, 'you have instructed me to destroy my film. I have never knowingly disobeyed any order from you and tonight you have spoken well of me. I am now asking you for a little discretion. I fully understand the reason for your order. I know Greg Norfield and his wife very well, as you can imagine. I wonder if you would allow me to let them have a gift – just the first minute or so of my film, which features only the bride and groom. I will explain to them that I stupidly made an alteration to a setting on the camera resulting in the rest being unprintable. They are very much in love and would still have a memento, however short, of their big day. I will destroy the unwanted remainder of the film. Nobody else but they will be featured.'

The Commander looked to Monty with raised eyebrows. Monty nodded his assent.

'There – you have your answer.'

At this point the waiters entered the room. It may have been that David and Monty had wanted to please their host but for whatever reason the "Chef's Choice" turned out to be excellent.

After the meal and exchanges of their naval service experiences the three of them settled into more comfortable chairs.

'I have a reputation for being brief,' said the Commander as he lit a cigar, 'and I know at times my manner has been taken for rudeness; the latter never was my intention. I believe the very nature of the job calls for brevity. However, I would like to take this opportunity to just say a little on what I think about the future and how it may affect our operations. The Chernobyl incident last year concentrated minds in the Soviet Union,' continued the Commander to his guests. 'I can see an end to the Cold War. I think Britain will become more interested in the Middle and Far East, where threats to our country are on the increase. Finally, a free press is both a friend to democracy and an enemy to security. You sit, as you have seen, uncomfortably between the two.'

He rang down to reception to arrange a car to take David home. When the call came that the taxi was ready he took David's hand warmly.

'Monty will run things his way no doubt. I hope I haven't put you in too much danger during our long association. Goodbye and good luck.'

'It is a paradox', said the Commander to Monty after David had left, 'that we tell as little as possible to those we trust most. That way our enemies, and the public who pay us to protect them, and our operatives, are least likely to foul up the whole dirty business.'

'Tell me,' said Monty: 'would you agree that you have succeeded in hiding from our friend just departed the fact that at the party he so ably filmed were two of our operatives of whom even he was not aware?'

'Absolutely,' replied the Commander. 'Quite amazing really that five of our people should be in that same room together and none of them aware of more than two others present. Quite an achievement really. Perhaps I'll get a seat in the Lords one day!'

CHAPTER THIRTEEN

The French Connection

At the end of April with the change in the weather came a welcome change, as far as Mary and Greg were concerned, in the modus operandi of the Intelligence Services. Neither of them had been contacted that year so far. Then one day, after a visit by David to check over the QC order book with them, David asked if they could go to their caravan at the end of the day for a private chat.

'I have had a long session with Monty,' began David, after they had settled comfortably with the coffee Mary had produced.

'Who is Monty?' exclaimed Greg.

'Glasnost has spread a little into our own Intelligence Service,' continued David. 'I have to tell you that should you two have talked to each other about the transport department it is of no concern to the powers that be, nor to me.' Without waiting for comment he went on: 'Monty is the new boss. He has taken over from the Commander. He is a very astute man in my opinion and has concluded, as had I, that for a couple like you two, so obviously in love, it would be a miracle if you had not shared your secrets or it would have been most distressing for each of you if you had thought you could not. I do not want your comments about that now, please. There is a job in the offing, which, as always, requires the utmost secrecy.'

Mary and Greg both knew when to keep quiet, but their exchanged glances told David what he wanted to know.

'Go ahead,' said Greg.

'There are no other operatives who could attend to this job with a better chance of success. Please, Mary, wait until I have departed, and let Greg explain as much as he cares to. Monty has a more open mind about the golden rule. In this case he broke it himself by telling me something about Mary I did not know. The task in question involves a defection to the West. You are asked to help *transport* a Russian woman and her baby from East Berlin to England. The woman in question has refused to go anywhere without taking her child with her.'

Greg interrupted: 'Via Dartmouth is hardly the shortest route.'

'Greg, we don't do the planning; we just carry out orders. She is the wife of a Russian diplomat. The husband is presently working at the Soviet Embassy in London. She is a highly respected nuclear physicist in her own country but she fears for her future, having had a brush with the KGB involving a visit to the Lubyanka where she was "advised" not to leave Russia. Her transportation to the USA with her family is being organised in conjunction with the CIA. Her child, who was born prematurely, is scheduled to have some form of medical procedure in East Germany. Their escape from the hospital in Berlin involves an overland journey to Cherbourg, from where I wish you two to transport them back here.'

'Transport them in what?' was Greg's question.

'*Amity*,' came the answer. 'You two fit the bill perfectly. The Soviets will never think they would travel overland to Cherbourg and then by yacht to England. It will be just one link in their journey to asylum in America. We will *collect* her husband from London to join his family on the last leg to freedom.'

Mary, who had been listening carefully, decided to speak: 'This sounds decidedly risky to me. Furthermore, it is also probably illegal, assuming the woman in question will not have the proper travel documents.'

'Mary,' David pleaded, 'do not make assumptions, please. This woman's life is in danger. If you don't like your country's methods, at least consider that this is a humanitarian exercise. We have had to make risky plans to ensure that her husband does not come under suspicion the moment she disappears from Berlin. Life is risky.' David held out his hands, palms up, in a gesture of frustration at Mary's questioning.

'How are we going to explain the time', asked Greg, 'that we will require to sail to Cherbourg and back? This is a much bigger task than anything I have done so far.'

'Agreed. I have arranged a plausible cover for you. I am granting you a week's delayed honeymoon during which you will sail *Amity,* via the Solent or the Channel Islands, to Cherbourg. I will come down to look after the office in your absence. The Cherbourg part of your trip will only be known to me. You will return to Dartmouth with the "*goods*". Having Mary on board to help the passenger and her sick baby would be a huge asset. There are three lives at stake here. You will not get much notice. Mull it over this evening. I must have your answer by 10 p.m. Phone me at my hotel in Torquay. I have to back in Lymington early tomorrow morning.'

Mary was unaware of all that Greg had done previously and showed it. David got up, shook hands and left.

Before Greg could open his mouth, Mary spoke: 'We've agreed, my love, not to discuss details. Please don't tell me about all your previous exploits. Maybe one day but not now. Let's consider this one. As far as I am concerned I don't like the sound of it. On the other hand David is our boss in more than one sense of the word. He made it sound more like a rescue mission.'

'Sounds more like a free honeymoon to me,' grinned Greg.

'I don't find that very funny, my love,' Mary said.

Greg grabbed her.

'What's happened to your sense of adventure –

to say nothing of duty?'

'OK, you win. Over this issue you are the boss. Let's get some grub. There's not much time to think?'

What came clear in their discussion before and after dinner was that Mary didn't like the idea at all but Greg did, only he wasn't telling Mary about the fat "fee" that he expected at the end of it. Before they retired for the night Greg phoned David their agreement.

There was no escape from what Mary had not wanted to hear.

The next Friday, David phoned to tell them that their honeymoon started on Sunday. He'd booked himself into a hotel in Torbay for Saturday night and would be with them on Saturday afternoon to catch up with brokerage affairs and "have a chat".

Greg was in the middle of doing some promotion work for the yard, which meant he would have to come up with a good story for Chris as to why at the last minute he would be dropping it for a week. He hated lying to Chris and hated even more to be seen as putting himself first by suddenly taking time away, as if on a whim.

Chris took it rather well as Greg pursued his elaborate deception by telling him that, some time ago, David had offered to stand in for them for a week so that they could have a delayed honeymoon.

'I expected more notice, Chris, but I won't get

another offer like this. I'll get on to your media promotion campaign the moment I return.'

'You know how bad I felt lying to you in the past,' he said to Mary later; 'now I have had to lie to my best friend.'

'I don't feel good about this venture at all' was Mary's response.

David arrived as promised on Saturday afternoon. Mary held the fort in the office whilst David and Greg retired to the caravan, where David explained what would happen when they arrived in Cherbourg. He also produced a large battery pack.

'This', he said, 'will power the cellphone which we installed in the boot of your car last year. I take it that installation has proved to be a lot better than the old rubbish you had before?'

Greg agreed it had been very good. David told him that all he had to do was unplug the unit in the car, slide it out of its mounting and plug it into the fully charged battery pack, which came complete with aerial. It was rechargeable from the boat's electrics.

They would not be required in Cherbourg before Wednesday afternoon, but the deadline for the flight out of this country for the Russians was midnight Thursday. They were to phone him from a call box, once they had tied up in the French port. He would then give them final details of the arrival of their guest and baby. He had arranged for a "very friendly" official to board the boat and complete the customs and immigration formalities upon their arrival in Cherbourg.

He continued: 'Down on the pontoon you will have a noisy visit from six "old French friends", one of whom will be Natasha. They will bring with them gifts and be carrying a couple of canvas sailing bags. In one bag will be the baby. Get Natasha and the baby down below and cover up any crying from the child with a radio and your noisy, if necessary, group of Frenchmen. Any questions?'

'I've been thinking,' responded Greg: 'how about we sail from here to Lymington and berth on a QC pontoon before setting sail across the Channel, thereby establishing our presence in the Solent? We may even put about some misinformation about sailing east instead of south.'

'Good planning!' said David. 'I approve. Leave it me to reserve you a berth. At no time, except in extreme emergency, should you contact either the coastguard or the coast radio stations at Niton Radio on the Isle of Wight or Crossmar Jobourg on the Cap de la Hague. Both of these stations can get a fix on transmissions from VHF/RT marine frequencies. Use your cellphone to contact me. I am satisfied that the public network both here and in France is secure.'

They cast off very early the next morning, raising sail as they left Dartmouth Harbour entrance.

This hurried release, leaving the worries of the business to their boss, came as a relief to the two of them as they cuddled up in the cockpit. Temporarily forgetting the purpose of the mission, they let the Autohelm do the steering. Tide and wind were in their favour. The prevailing south-westerly meant easy sailing on a broad reach and a good speed over the ground. They tied up in Weymouth for the night.

After supper on board Greg finished preparations on deck to sail at first light next morning.

As soon as he went below Mary spoke what was on her mind: 'We have everything we could possibly want, my darling Greg. Why are we doing this dangerous thing?'

He grabbed her to him as she looked into his eyes, her question still hanging in the air.

'Everyone is entitled to a honeymoon, aren't they?' was his reply.

A frown came over her face. 'You know what I mean.' She lowered her voice and moved her head closer to his. 'This could get us into a mountain of trouble if anything goes wrong. It could ruin everything.'

'Oh, ye of little faith,' he said. 'You are with me, remember. Nothing will go wrong, I promise you.'

'Greg, my love, you know that misquoting the Bible makes me cross and you are promising something you know you cannot guarantee.'

Greg apologised and after much hugging and

kissing they tucked up for the night.

Out at sea again in the morning, Mary seemed to put her misgivings out of mind. They sailed close along the Dorset coast between Weymouth and St Alban's Head. Only close inshore is it possible to see the entrance to Lulworth Cove and appreciate the splendour of the cliffs and their layers of different colours, the great arch of Durdle Door and the tiny cliff-bound anchorage at Chapman's Pool. That day the thunder of the guns on the Lulworth ranges, inland beyond the cliffs, was supplemented by the whining of a shell ricochet overhead. Greg laughed when Mary looked alarmed.

'The odds of being hit are about the same as finding the proverbial needle in a haystack,' he said as they headed for the passage inside the race off St Alban's Head.

'I have described you in the past as an adventurer, Greg my love, but this is more like gung-ho.'

With the last of the flood tide they ran straight from Anvil Point to Hurst in just over a couple of hours. The passage north of the Shingles bank at high water means one sails so close to the steep-to shore that it is possible to have a conversation with people on the strip of beach round Hurst Point.

Once past the imposing gun emplacements of Hurst Castle it is a short run up the Solent to Lymington and QC's pontoon berths. Brian Hope had spotted their arrival and came down to the pontoon to welcome them and wish them a good stopover.

They walked hand in hand into the town that evening for an early drink at the Ship Inn on the quay. They opted for a Chinese dinner in the restaurant opposite the pub before wandering back to the boat. Fully clothed, they lay on the bunk for a short sleep before the alarm woke them at eleven thirty. This was the time to cast off and catch the first of the ebb taking them west out into the Solent and English Channel beyond – not east as declared.

Once past The Needles and moving out into the full force of the west-going tide they had to lay off their course to Cherbourg by about thirty degrees to the east. Satisfied that they were on track, the westerly breeze put them on a beam reach with full sail up and a log speed of about six knots. At this rate they reckoned they could be in Cherbourg by lunchtime next day.

'We should be grateful for a clear night,' Greg whispered in Mary's ear. 'This passage across busy shipping lanes is frightening in bad visibility. On a night like this, with the stars above, a friendly sea below, and the girl you love so much in your arms, I ask for nothing else.'

They abandoned their resolve to do turnabout on the helm whilst the other slept below. Huddled up together in the cockpit they sailed on through the night.

At first light it was Greg who went below to make the tea and bacon butties. Thus fortified, and in daylight with safer visibility, they took turns below to snatch some sleep.

They arrived off the French coast around midday. The sight of the long outer wall of Cherbourg Harbour was a relief – more so as the very strong cross tide frequently encountered as one nears the harbour entrance was taking them to exactly where they wanted to be, at the eastern end of that wall.

Many a yacht has been caught near the entrance with an engine not powerful enough to make up for the speed of the tide sweeping the boat away.

They tied up in the inner harbour as directed. Greg knew of a public phone in its own booth in a restaurant on the quay. He also knew the restaurant owners. He left Mary to deal with the French Customs formalities. Joking that if she couldn't keep them happy nobody could, he set off to make his call to David.

When he returned to the boat, with a bag of sandwiches, he had news for Mary: 'Change of plan. Our French friends will be here late this afternoon, rather than tomorrow as planned. We'll grab some rest before they arrive. We may have to adopt plan B. I won't know till I make another call to David.'

'What is plan B?' said Mary.

'I'll tell you later. Sufficient for you to know for

the moment that our sailing instructions may be altered yet again, and I won't know what they are until we have the goods safely on board. They should be with us about five o'clock this evening French time. She is disguised as a young man. The whole party of six are to be known as Jean, Jacques, Louis, Alphonse, Paul and Pierre.'

They arrived just after five thirty local time, laughing and chatting and making as much noise as would hopefully drown a baby's cries but not so much as would draw too much attention. They approached along the pontoon and the charade of being old friends, which they had all rehearsed, was enacted as they climbed on board at Greg and Mary's invitation.

Jacques, the oldest of them, was carrying a length of chain in a bag, which he gave to Greg. He was clearly in charge as he indicated all of them to go below. He remained in the cockpit with Greg. The pretence of old friends greeting each other was continued down below until Jacques was satisfied that nobody on nearby boats was in the slightest bit interested in them, nor were they going to be overheard. Jacques called down for Mary to come up from below. He sat between them in the cockpit, an arm round each of their shoulders.

With head bowed he drew them close and spoke quietly: 'I have bad news, I am afraid. The baby, he die. We bury him in France. We have just crossed border from Belgium. We find him not breathing. We do our best. The lady, she is very sad and crying. We have discussion what to do. She agrees we must not delay or her husband in England will be in great danger. We left her in the what you call motorhome, to make her goodbyes. Meanwhile we dig grave to bury baby.'

Mary immediately went below to comfort their guest. Natasha was in the forward saloon behind the closed curtains. She could be heard quietly sobbing. Mary went forward to her past the four men in the main saloon. They embraced, and with their arms around each other they wept together.

Jacques went on to explain to Greg that they were travelling as French tourists in a large motorhome. They had crossed from the Federal Republic into Belgium and were nearing the French border when they made their sad discovery. This whole operation was with the cooperation of French Security. It was essential they cross the border into France as quickly as possible. Once in France they pulled into an empty lay-by and buried the baby by the roadside behind a stone wall. They were near a church outside a remote small village. Natasha (as she is now to be called), the mother, despite her extreme distress had suggested this herself. They had been able to dig a deep grave as they carried a pick and shovel as part of the vehicle's touring kit.

They emptied their metal toolbox and used it as a coffin. They were satisfied that this way the grave would not be disturbed by human or animal action. It was still dark and the large parked vehicle had ensured that they had not been observed digging behind the wall. There was plenty of leaf litter around to disguise the fact that the ground had been disturbed. Natasha would come back as an American citizen to arrange a proper burial.

French officials had assisted their safe border crossing, thus Jacques believed that once the circumstances were known to the authorities there would not be a problem about the later reburial. He went on to say how incredibly brave Natasha had been during the whole journey. Members of the group took turns to rest or drive, as planned, but he was sure that Natasha had not slept at all. He thought it would not be long before she broke down.

Natasha wore typical yachting clothing. Her dark hair had been cut short like a man's and she was wearing a soft knitted hat pulled well down when she came aboard. She could easily pass as a young man. Mary guessed her age to be in her late twenties. She had beside her the canvas bag which she had carried aboard. From the bag she pulled a small photograph of a newborn baby in her arms. With tears streaming down her face she showed it to Mary.

'Baby boy,' she sobbed. 'Alexander. He just nine week. He die in night. We bury.' Mary held her tight. 'We go now to England, yes?'

She wiped her eyes with a small damp

handkerchief clasped in her fist.

'Stay here. I will go up to see my husband,' said Mary.

She joined the others in the cockpit, who were saying their goodbyes, maintaining the bonhomie in a manner according to orders, despite the tragedy of the moment.

'Au 'voir, mes amis. Bon voyage!'

'See you next year,' cried Greg as they made their way along the pontoon.

Nobody around would be counting that there were now only five. Mary went below to their guest and Greg went ashore to phone David again.

When Greg returned to the boat he found Mary with Natasha still in the forecabin but she seemed in a calmer state of mind. She had eaten very little in the past twenty-four hours and was enjoying the sandwich and coffee that Mary had made. Natasha looked pleased, and Mary looked surprised when Greg whispered that the plans were changed and that they were going to cast off right now. Natasha understood that until they were clear of the outer harbour she was to stay in the forecabin, where she could not be seen, with the porthole curtains still closed. With very few words they started the engine and cast off.

They made a good team – Greg on the helm and Mary on deck releasing harbour ties from the sails and sheets and checking lashings. They did not unwind the sails until well clear of the outer harbour wall. Greg reckoned their departure would be less obtrusive and quicker that way. It would be dark soon. They lowered the French courtesy flag from the hoist and set their course for Chichester Harbour. Mary went below to check on Natasha. She found her looking at a number of personal possessions that she had taken from her canvas bag.

'Would you rather be alone?' enquired Mary.

'No, no. I take last look at old life. Soon, my husband and me, we start new life America. We start life of peace. No more fear. You tell, please, when deep water. You have chain to put in bag?'

Mary was puzzled and frowned.

'You put all this', said Natasha, pointing at her possessions and the bag, 'into deep water. Jacques explain, no?'

Mary raised a finger as she said, 'Wait a moment. I will go up top and speak to my husband.'

'Yes, that is right. I have instructions to put that bag overboard in deep water,' said Greg. 'All evidence of her identity must go. The anchor chain that Jacques brought with him is intended to weigh down Natasha's canvas bag.'

He had experience of this procedure when he had brought *L'Enterprise* back to Dartmouth with David as they dumped their passengers' overalls.

Mary went below to confirm with Natasha that it would be done. Natasha nodded her head very slowly to acknowledge what Mary had said.

'All my old life in bag – everything that is me. My clothes. My identity. My photographs. My hair, they cut. I told I take nothing to England –

nothing. If caught, I have no identity.' Tears began to well up again.

'I will help you pack your bag,' said Mary.

'No, no. Please, it private. Bring chain. I pack bag with chain, OK?'

Mary reported all this to Greg when she returned to the cockpit. With a steady force three to four westerly they were making good and comfortable way toward their destination under full sail. The boat rolled gently as they followed their northerly course. Both Greg and Mary knew it would be several hours yet before they could dump the bag where the water was deepest in the middle of the traffic separation zone and where divers did not normally operate.

Greg gave the chain to Mary, who went below. The chain weighed about forty to fifty pounds. It would have to be placed in the middle of the contents in the bag. They would then have to ensure the canvas was correctly laced up so that nothing could escape. Mary took the chain into the forecabin and with great patience explained to Natasha what had to be done. She also told her that it would be a good idea if she lay down on the leeward bunk and tried to get some sleep. She made Mary promise to wake her when the time came to sink the bag.

Mary went up to join Greg on the helm. She asked him about plan B.

'Something has gone wrong with the Dartmouth plan. I was not informed what. However, they are also having problems at the American Air Force base from whence they are due to fly the two Russians to the USA. Our new destination is Chichester Harbour. Have you not noticed the new heading?' There was just enough light to see the smirk on his face as he said this.

'You don't question orders you receive. I don't question the skipper's actions.' She was smiling when she gave this reply. She reverted to a serious tone of voice: 'This is madness, Greg, my love. We have an illegal immigrant on board. We are about to dispose of a bag, and do not really know what's in it. We have already broken French law, and if I know anything about it we are soon going to break the law in our own country.'

'It sounds to me, Mary, that you have lost your motivation. I can understand. The sight of that distraught woman is enough to distract anyone; however, we are past the point of no return. Please, I beg you, help me to complete this mission. We knew the risks before we started.'

Several minutes passed before Mary put an arm round her husband's shoulders.

'I'll stick with you, my darling. Yes, of course we are in it together. What happens next?'

'Next we dump the bag. I sailed this evening because, although we do not have to put Natasha ashore in Emsworth until tomorrow night, I prefer we do our hanging about in familiar, and hopefully more friendly, waters. Also, surely it is better for Natasha to be in England as soon as possible?'

'Why Emsworth?' asked Mary.

'Because when I heard of the potential difficulties at the American airbase in the east of the country I suggested that, to save time and risk, they might consider the drop-off in Emsworth and the use of Lasham airfield, barely an hour's drive north of Emsworth. Lasham is a gliding centre but within the airfield, is a servicing facility for large passenger aircraft, which come and go at short notice, drawing attention from nobody. There are no security gates or barriers at either Emsworth Yacht Harbour or Lasham, and, as far as I know, no immigration control either.'

Shortly after midnight Mary went into the forecabin to wake Natasha as they were in the middle of the Channel, where the bag was to be dropped. She was not asleep. The bag was by her side securely laced up, as far as Mary could see by the dimmed night-light. It was, with the chain inside, very heavy. Mary returned to the cockpit to take the helm so that Greg could go down and bring the bag up. Natasha watched his every movement and followed him up the companionway steps as he heaved the bag into the cockpit.

'Please,' she said, 'me put in sea.'

'I will help you,' said Greg. 'It is too heavy for you to lift over the rail.'

Greg took his sailing knife from the holster on his belt and opened the marlinspike. He set about stabbing holes in the bag.

Natasha screamed. *'Nyet, nyet!'*

He had to constrain her as he explained it was to ensure that the air came out to allow the bag to sink quickly. She was grief-stricken, her cries of anguish hard to bear. It had to be done. The boat was headed into wind to slow it down. Greg and the Russian girl had the bag balanced on the stern rail. Mary clung to Natasha round the waist as the bag was tipped overboard, fearful that she might choose to go with it. She did not try, but her body was wracked with sobs.

'Dasvidanya!' she cried, and remained peering over the rail at the spot where the bag hit the water and quickly disappeared below the dark waves. Her sobbing was now accompanied by convulsions. She was clearly overcome.

Mary comforted her as best she could as she helped her down below.

'Now you start a new life, Natasha. Tomorrow you will be with your husband in England and the next day in America, where they will welcome you both. In a few hours we will be in English waters. I am going to make us a warm drink. We will be on this tack for the rest of the way. Lay down on the starboard bunk where you cannot fall out and try to sleep. It is done.'

Mary gave her a handkerchief and brought her a mug of hot chocolate and a soft blanket. She showed her where the switch was to turn off the dim blue night-sailing light in the cabin. When Mary noiselessly checked on her half an hour later, the hot drink, the gentle motion of the boat and complete exhaustion had done its work – she was fast asleep under the blanket. Mary turned off the light and pulled the curtains closed behind her as she returned to Greg in the cockpit.

Mary and Greg stayed close to each other as they had done on the trip the day before, only this time in silence – together for warmth; in silence because there was a sense of something they could not, or would not, discuss. They just wanted to be quietly together.

The flashing of the lighthouse on St Catherine's Point was a welcome sight on the port bow as the dawn became visible in the east. Time to phone David about their progress. To Greg's relief the mobile phone worked perfectly six miles offshore. The light on the Nab Tower to starboard confirmed their position an hour later. A further check on their guest showed her still sound asleep.

'What's the plan now, skipper?' said Mary.

'We'll drop anchor in the little bay below Culver Cliff on the north edge of Sandown Bay. Get some breakfast and some shut-eye for a couple hours, until there's enough water over the bar to safely enter Chichester Harbour.'

They tried not to wake Natasha, but with the tramping on the deck over her head and the anchor chain running out, she woke. Still with the blanket round her shoulders she looked out from the main hatch. She looked up at the cliffs towering above them and then to Greg and Mary in the cockpit.

'England?' she questioned. 'This is England?'

'Yes, Isle of Wight,' answered Greg.

She came up the steps into the cockpit and threw her arms around them both.

'Oh, tank you, tank you, tank you,' she cried.

Greg hastily ushered her down and out of sight into the saloon again. It seemed cruel to worry her that they were not completely safe yet. Her whole demeanour had changed and he did not want to spoil her mood. Mary set to in the galley. Greg explained that they would rest up for a couple of hours after some breakfast before getting under way again.

'Trust us,' he said gently to Natasha. 'Stay below for the rest of the journey. Enjoy England through the portholes and windows as we sail to the mainland. Soon we will take you on the last part of the journey and you will be with your husband tonight.'

CHAPTER FOURTEEN

England

They enjoyed that breakfast. Mary demonstrated her skill at French toast and used their last six eggs. It was a joy to see Natasha tuck in. The sleep had clearly done her good. They told her they were going to catch up on their own sleep before heading for the mainland when the tide was right.

Mary felt that Natasha had spent enough time on her own. She suggested that she would join her on the other bunk up forward so that they could chat.

Natasha's face lit up as she nodded approval and said, 'Yes, please.'

Greg lay down on the seat opposite the galley and went out like a light to the sound of the two of them quietly talking behind the curtain.

Greg awoke as Mary came aft and held her forefinger to her lips.

'She's fallen asleep again,' she whispered.

They climbed up into the cockpit, started the engine, hauled anchor as quietly as they could, and motored out from the little bay. The sun was high enough for its warmth to be felt as they cleared Bembridge Ledge and set sail for Chichester Harbour on the flood tide.

The sound of powerful engines and the slapping of a hull hitting the waves caught them by surprise. One moment they were sat sleepily in the cockpit close together, happy at the sight of Chichester Harbour entrance only a few miles ahead; the next, they were frozen with fear at what they heard coming from astern.

Memories from two years previously in the Solent came back to Greg – memories of the sound of a powerful launch and detention by HM Customs.

'Keep looking ahead, and take the helm,' he shouted at Mary.

His brain told him to appear casual as he slowly turned his head to see what was coming up from astern. His heartbeat quickened. The bow of the fast-approaching craft threw foaming white crests to either side. It was only about fifty yards away when recognition dawned on Greg as it altered course to overtake them.

A dark blue hull and orange topsides: the Bembridge lifeboat. A cheery wave from a crew member on deck. The throaty roar of the engines faded as it powered past and away from them.

The strain of the last twenty-four hours showed on their faces as they put their heads together and Greg muttered, 'Thank God.'

He expected Mary to admonish him. She didn't.

Her relief also showed.

An hour and a half later they were through the harbour entrance and headed for a little used narrow creek, known to Greg but few others, where they anchored.

Away from prying eyes, they caught up on some more sleep and had time to learn much from Natasha about life in the Soviet Union and why she and her husband had decided it was not the country in which they could bring up their child. Her eyes became moist at the mention of the baby they had now lost. Her husband had met many American government officials during the course of his work at the Soviet embassy in London and from that had come the invitation for him and his wife to join the Metropolitan Research Corporation (MRC) of Iowa, USA.

This company was mainly engaged in the design of nuclear power stations. As a nuclear physicist of the same discipline Natasha could be a valuable member of their team.

Natasha's husband was a highly qualified statistician as well as a diplomat. MRC was convinced that the political scene in Russia would soon move away from the old communism and that there would be cooperation between the USA and Russia over the peaceful use of nuclear power. The two of them had been promised asylum from the US government, well-paid jobs, and a house from MRC of Iowa. Maybe one day they would be able to return to their country as free people. That was their hope.

Greg made his final call to David.

'The honeymoon is going well. We are pleased to be back to old haunts in the Solent. Arrange the taxi as you promised. Your girl has promised to be on time.'

They cleared away after a supper which had been almost without conversation as the importance of the next few hours was on their minds.

At ten they hauled in the two anchors, one forward, one aft, that held them in the middle of the narrow creek and motored out into the main channel. From there they headed northwards towards the marina. Greg was familiar with the navigation marks in the Emsworth channel that led through the moorings. He had kept a boat there himself for many years.

As one approaches Emsworth, some five miles inland from the harbour entrance, the many shore lights help to show the way into the marina. Once inside, the pontoon lights are the only guide to the fuel quay, where they were to disembark their guest. They called Natasha to come into the cockpit as they approached the quay. She had no baggage.

All was in darkness as Greg came alongside the narrow floating pontoon attached to the refuelling quay. Mary was on the side deck guiding her skipper with the powerful torch. It was a rerun for Greg of the time he dropped Troag in Dartmouth. Several shadowy figures held *Amity* firm against the pontoon as Greg gave the boat a touch astern from the engine to stop the forward movement.

Natasha just had time to whisper, 'Tank you, I will always remember,' and after hurried kisses from her crew she was helped over the side and up the vertical iron ladder by those ashore.

Greg felt the boat being pushed away from the quay and a few seconds later heard the car, which had been waiting on the quay, depart.

'Let's get out of here,' said Greg as he turned the boat round and retraced their way back out into the main channel.

Once clear of the moorings they headed down the channel and dropped anchor about a mile from the harbour entrance. Mary hung the anchor light on the jib sheets over the foredeck.

'Mission accomplished,' said Greg.

'I'll tell you what I think, my darling Greg, in the morning.'

The tone of Mary's reply was not only wistful but cynical, thought Greg.

'We both need some sleep, my dearest Greg. When I say "in the morning" I mean "in the morning".'

Greg knew not to push her further. They put the infill in place between the two bunks in the forecabin and thus, snuggled up together without undressing, they were soon asleep. It was daylight when they woke.

'Do you realise', Greg said to his wife, 'we have not been out of our clothes for three whole days?'

'As far as I am concerned we can stay here in

this bunk for another three days. I'm shattered.'

'Well, I am hungry,' said Greg as he made his way aft into the galley and put the kettle on.

Mary joined him a minute later.

As they sipped their tea in silence, Greg finally spoke: 'Mary, my lovely Mary, something is on your mind – please tell me what it is.'

'It's Thursday, isn't it?' she said.

Greg nodded.

'We don't have to be back in Dartmouth until late Sunday, do we?'

Another nod from Greg.

'May I make a suggestion?' questioned Mary. 'I'm tired, dirty, and could do with a shower and a good meal. Yes, I do have a lot to say. I need a little more time to think. Would you mind if we sorted ourselves out first today, and then found somewhere quiet to hole up on our way home tonight? Then I will tell you what's on my mind.'

At this point they heard the sound of an engine followed by a bump. Looking out of the window they saw that a launch strung with fenders was alongside and a young man was leaning over to tie up to their cleat amidships.

'Harbourmaster!' came the call from the young man.

Mary looked distinctly frightened as Greg made for the cockpit and nonchalantly bade him good morning with a smile.

'Did you stay overnight?' said the young man as Greg caught site of his own anchor light still hanging in the foresheets.

No arguing there. Greg indicated in the affirmative.

'Just the one night, sir?' went the questioning. 'What is your overall length?'

Greg knew what was coming and despite his belief that to be charged for laying to one's own anchor was a racket this didn't seem to be the occasion to protest, so he paid up. At least he received a piece of paper that said he'd paid his harbour dues in Chichester Harbour for *Amity*, and, better still, the lad had forgotten to date it. He had evidence of having gone east as announced.

And so it was that they hauled up the anchor after a rather meagre breakfast of what little food they had left. Once clear of the bar beacon they had the tide in their favour and four hours later they tied up in the marina just inside the entrance to Cowes. Mary had said little about anything other than the sailing.

They felt a whole lot better after hot showers in the marina and lunch in the restaurant opposite. Then they renewed, rather extravagantly, their depleted ship's stores from the local shops. All through this Mary remained unusually quiet.

Greg suggested, 'Let's motor up the river to the fuelling barge. We need to refuel, then head further down the Solent to Newtown River. It's only an hour or so out of Cowes.'

Mary pursed her lips and nodded her approval. Newtown is on the Isle of Wight, and here there is a series of creeks, the tops of which mostly dry out at low water. It is owned by the National Trust, isolated and quiet at that time of the year. Greg felt it would be the right atmosphere for Mary to tell him what was on her mind.

'Yes, that will be lovely. I used to go there with my father. We'll cuddle up together, feed the ducks and I'll tell you what's bothering me – and don't frown like that!'

The entrance to Newtown River is narrow and not easy to spot against the low cliffs along the coastline and high hills in the background.

Once inside they followed the channel hard to port and dropped anchor at the farthest point permissible in Clamerkin Lake opposite the old saltings. With the rolling Isle of Wight hills as a backdrop, amongst the nesting seabirds on the muddy banks, and farmland right down to the water's edge the anchorage was a haven of peace: no roads, no people. As they settled in the cockpit that peace was broken only by the ducks arguing amongst themselves, the gulls more vocal about their disagreements, and the inimitable twittering of a skylark as it rose from a nearby field and then dived back down into cover again.

'Which would you prefer first,' said Mary gravely, 'the good news or the bad?'

'Bad' came Greg's reply as they drew closer together.

'I have decided that I will not take part in any more covert operations. That is not to say that I will fight against you should you wish to continue on your own. You are entirely responsible for your own conscience and I will love you until my dying day whatever you do.'

There was a long pause as Mary waited for Greg's reaction. Greg digested this statement. There didn't seem to be anything for him to say. He knew she had thought long and hard before telling him. He knew that there was nothing to be gained by arguing.

All he said was 'Like to tell me why?'

'Yes, the baby's body was in the bag that we dropped overboard in the Channel.'

'Whoa!' interrupted Greg. 'Just a minute. I don't believe it.'

'You won't be able to convince me otherwise,' she said.

Greg found he just could not accept what had been said.

'How do you know? What proof do you have?'

'I don't need any proof; I just know.'

Greg tightened his arm around her shoulders and kissed her cheek gently. He had to remind himself there was everything to lose by arguing.

'I can't agree with you, my love, but I promise I take what you have said seriously. What are you going to do about it? Or what do you want me to do about it?'

Mary shook her head from side to side.

'Nothing. What is done is done. I have said my prayers and sought forgiveness. I shall never forget, but all the arguments in the world about what is in the national interest will not persuade me to take part in any such operations again.'

'What about the Cold War, then? Are you not frightened by what may happen if we do not deter the Soviets from the use of their nuclear weapons?'

They sat there for some time in silence before Mary spoke again.

'Greg, it's politics, and you know it. In a shooting war, what we have done may be justified or sanctioned, but, in my book, not so because of a *threat* of war.'

'How about prevention being better than cure?'

'We're not going to see eye to eye, Greg. Let's agree to differ.'

'Mary, my love, we must not let this come between us.'

'It won't' was the reply as she looked up at him sadly.

'What about the good news, then?' he whispered into her ear.

Her grave look changed to a smile. 'I'm pregnant,' she said.

Greg gave her a questioning look.

'Yes, yes, really.'

'Oh, you lovely, lovely wife,' he cried as he squeezed her tighter.

She looked up at Greg seriously. 'If it's a boy, we'll call him Alexander.'

'And if a girl?'

'If a girl we'll name her Alexandra Natasha.'

Greg thought for a moment. He could see where

all this came from but wasn't sure where it might lead.

'I know what you are thinking, my love,' Mary said. 'Of course you have as much right to name our child as I have. I'm not insisting, just suggesting.'

'Mary, oh lovely Mary, it's a great idea and the names are fabulous. What I'd like you to think of is that recent events have influenced your thinking. Could we just give it a little more time before we make up our minds?'

'How about six months?' Mary laughed as she said this, and the tension was broken.

They laughed and hugged and Greg said he was ravenous. So they went below to celebrate their good news and plan the future, now as a family.

Greg's cellphone rang. It was David. He told Greg that Natasha and her husband had arrived in America. He wanted to know if they would be back to open the brokerage on Monday morning as he should return to Lymington immediately after closing the office at five o'clock on Sunday afternoon. Greg assured him that they were on schedule and asked him to hold the line for a few seconds.

He held his hand over the mouthpiece and turned to Mary: 'May I tell him the good news, my love? I'm busting to tell everyone I know.'

Mary looked delighted and nodded her approval. And so it was that within twenty-four hours everyone at the Curnow Yard also knew.

As they set about preparing their supper their mood became more normal. The conversation was all about the future with junior. Apart from telling her that the Russians had arrived in America Greg had decided that he would not say more about the Natasha affair unless Mary raised it. She did.

Replete from the steaks they'd bought in Cowes, accompanied by Greg's sauté potatoes with onion, and fresh Isle of Wight asparagus, they took the last of the red wine into the cockpit to watch the flat lines of cloud turn to flames of orange then red as the sun dropped below the hills. The gulls dived for the scraps they threw over the stern and a pair of large, brightly coloured shelduck paddled up to compete with the coots for the snacks.

'I guess Robbie's Creek is a bit like this?' questioned Mary.

'Yes, you wanted somewhere away from the crowds where we could be with our thoughts.'

Mary was quiet for a moment, then: 'I had quite a long talk with Natasha. I promised her that we would always be friends. The more we spoke the easier it became to communicate with her. She was very brave over the loss of her baby but was determined to find a new life with her husband. She confirmed that she was younger than me, and I said she was young enough to have another child. I told her to get a move on about it when she got to the States so that our two children would be the same age when they met!'

'You told her before you told me?' exclaimed Greg, teasing her.

'Yes. Somehow sharing this with her at that particular moment gave her tremendous pleasure and strength. I am glad I told her. It was a gamble that could have gone the other way. I was guided by my father. He was always comforting people, and down in the cabin with Natasha I felt his presence. Will you promise me, Greg, that one day we will make every effort to see her again?'

'I promise, my lovely Mary, that I will move heaven and earth to do just that.'

They were both dog-tired. With barely another word they tidied ship, frapped the halyards, hoisted the anchor light, and went below.

In the bunk, limbs entangled, Greg whispered into Mary's ear, 'Goodnight, you two.'

The next day, by silent mutual assent, the subject of the cross-Channel trip was not mentioned. Once out of the narrow river entrance with the wind north of west they took a south-westerly course down the Needles Channel. Close-hauled, this took them outside the race at St Alban's Head. A change of tack brought them close to the sheltered anchorage in Lulworth Cove by late in the afternoon.

'Let's not go on to Weymouth as planned,' Mary said. 'I've never been into Lulworth; and anyway, you suggested that a caravan was not the place for a baby. Well, I want to talk to you about that, and the sooner the better.'

'OK,' agreed Greg. 'The entrance is difficult enough to see at the best of times. Now we've found it, let me concentrate on getting us safely inside.'

Lulworth Cove is like a small oval lake surrounded by tall cliffs covered with scattered vegetation. Greg likened it to sailing into a crab's mouth with large rocky claws either side as you enter. The pool inside is the shape of the crab's shell. The only sign of life is the beach to the west and Lulworth village. It is like being in the middle of a volcano except for the narrow entrance. With a bit of north in the wind that day, the water inside was calm.

Mary had a mischievous grin on her face practically the whole of the time they took to anchor, tidy ship, and get the kettle on.

'I've got it all planned,' she said as they settled in the cockpit with their tea and biscuits.

'Got what planned?'

'You may think that I told everyone but you first, but it was not my intention. You see, I suspected more than a month ago. So I chose my moment to have a word with Chris. I did not mention anything at all about babies. I told him how much I loved being where we were, how I loved the terrific view across the river, the closeness to our work. I told him as far as I was concerned the whole set-up with the caravan was idyllic. "Get to the point Mary," Chris said to me with a huge grin. "When are you going to come to the *but*?" So I asked him what the chances might be to have a bigger, more comfortable caravan on the same site. I showed him some brochures I had of really beautiful static caravans, as they are called. They have proper bedrooms and showers and toilets that can be flushed if ducted to a sewer.'

Greg interrupted: 'But a caravan really isn't the place to bring up a baby, my love.'

'Of course it is,' Mary nearly shouted. 'Travellers and gypsies have been doing it for centuries!'

'Ha,' said Greg, 'I bet Chris guessed what was up.'

'Sorry,' said Mary, 'I think he did. He didn't actually say anything about my being pregnant, but when he held his grin a bit too long and said he knew what I was getting at I think I blushed. I could feel the warmth in my cheeks. I'll tell you something, Greg: after me, he's your best friend.'

'I know that, so what did he have to say?'

'He was very sympathetic after he realised I'd been doing my homework. I told him about an elderly prospective customer who came to the office one day to enquire about selling his boat. This old boy talked to me about his childhood days just after the First World War. His father knew the man who owned a small boat-repair business which is now the Curnow Yard. When he was a young lad living nearby the old owner gave him the freedom of the place. He spent hours playing amongst the boats and sheds and along the riverbank.'

'Mary, love, now *I* am going to say it: get to the point.'

Greg took her hand gently and kissed it.

'Apparently, where our caravan is now, the old owner lived in a railway carriage. Behind that, where all the junk is dumped, was a cesspit. So I had a little scout around and found the remains of same. We could have a static caravan with proper drainage, and running hot and cold water. I gave Chris some brochures showing what I had in mind. He promised to look into it.

'And how do you think we are going to pay for all this?' said Greg.

'Oh, ye of little faith. It was you who said that to me recently, my sweetheart, my lover, and father of our child. Surely you do not think I would be talking to you this way if I hadn't known it was affordable?'

Greg was suitably admonished.

She continued: 'I have some investments from my inheritance as well as the income from the flat in Southampton. The most important investment I can make now is in our future and that of our child. I can afford the cost of preparing the ground for our new home as well as the deposit on the new caravan. The bank hopefully can provide the rest and my income from the rent of the flat will help pay off the loan. If this plan works as Chris thinks it might, and if I've done the sums correctly, it will cost less than a quarter of what it would cost to buy a house. The price of houses around Torbay is ridiculous anyway.'

'Don't you think this is pushing Chris a bit too far?'

There was no damping possible of Mary's enthusiasm.

'We would have a residence with a view that people would die for. No travelling to work – and talking of work, I can be back in harness within a week or two of the birth. As well as the phone extension from the office we can have a babysitting intercom on the desk. One of us can move from the desk to the baby in the caravan in less time than it takes to run up the stairs in a house!

Greg remembered the money he had in his bank box and the fee that was to come from this latest exploit. His own contribution could be considerable. The brokerage was becoming profitable. They would soon be able to pay themselves more under the terms of the agreement with QC. It was time to come clean with Mary about his "pension fund", as he called it. As he started to explain, Mary's eyes narrowed.

'Oh no, no, no!' she exclaimed. 'I will have nothing to do with your blood money.'

Greg was shocked – shocked at what she had said and shocked at the vehemence with which she had said it. She saw his look. She flung her arms around him.

'I'm so sorry, my love. You said this must not come between us and I can see that it has.' Tears welled up in her eyes. 'This should be a time to be happy. It really is possible to do it my way.'

Greg was lost for words. Again he knew this was not the time to argue. He wiped away her tears.

'This is no way to start a family, my love. Nothing will come between us. It just never occurred to me to even think about what you have proposed. It has all come as a complete surprise to me.'

'Well, of course it has,' she said. 'You didn't know. I have had weeks to think about it. Oh, Greg, it'll be tremendous fun. We'll have a new home, more room, modern amenities, no more having to go out in the cold and dark to the loos or showers. Just keep your fingers crossed that Chris can get permission. I know he wants it to happen for us. Please, please, leave it to me.'

'I will, I will,' said Greg.

'When we get back,' Mary continued, 'I will show you a brochure of a static caravan named Bungalow by the manufacturers. It has a cold-water tank in the roof. It would be easy for a clever chap like you to run our cold water to this tank instead of having to use the tap outside. We have mains electricity already. The Bungalow has built-in electric heaters for hot water to the galley sink and to a shower. It has built in electric panel radiators, two bedrooms, plus lounge/diner and about five times the storage space we have now. The galley is a dream and there are insulated walls, floor and roof. Shall I go on?'

'No,' said Greg. 'It sounds fantastic. As usual I am a complete idiot. Shall I speak to Chris about it when we return?'

'Leave Chris to me' was the reply. 'You keep to the brokerage.'

Greg decided to chance his arm: 'And who is

going to tell the powers that be about your other decision?'

'Me, of course,' she said with a frown. 'I told the Commander some time ago that I would never do anything against my principles. It is entirely my personal business. I do not have to give them the true reason I told you yesterday. That is between you and me. They are secretive; we shall be also. What happened about the baby is done and cannot be undone. There could be serious consequences for us both. For me it is a huge moral issue and I will feel guilty for the rest of my life, but, my dear Greg, I will not let it spoil our happiness or that of our child. In fact it is the total innocence of the child we are bringing into this world that has persuaded me to take this view. I have made my peace with God. Just think on this: what would we be inflicting on our baby if we were convicted of failure to report a death as well as disposing of the body and were sent to prison?'

Greg shook his head from side to side. 'You are truly amazing, my love. I promise you I have the greatest respect for everything you have said. I won't mention it again, nor am I trying to get the last word, but you should know that while I can see the reasons for your suspicions about the baby being in the bag I really do believe that he was buried in France.'

With that they hugged and kissed and went below to prepare their evening meal. The conversation was all about the new home they planned and hoped for. They bunked down early that evening and made a start for Dartmouth at dawn the next morning.

Greg hauled anchor and was on the helm as they motored out of the narrow entrance to Lulworth, while Mary busied herself in the galley. Greg put in a call to David to tell him they would be back a day early, which pleased him.

The wind was a touch north of west again, which gave them a long starboard tack toward Dartmouth and routed outside of Portland Race. They enjoyed that day. They knew it would likely be their last together on board for a long time. Just before dark, half a mile off the entrance to the Dart, they rolled up all sail and motored into the river. Enough room had been left for them to tie up on the visitors' pontoon.

Tired but now happy to be back where they could begin an exciting new episode in their lives, they worked together to tidy ship and unload their gear and the food that was left over from the trip. They checked the office, which David had locked. He had left a pile of notes on the desk.

The top one read, "All this shows I've been busy in your absence. Don't suppose you'll want to tell me about your honeymoon! Regards, David."

CHAPTER FIFTEEN

The Cabin

They opened the brokerage on Sunday morning and set about catching up on the items in David's notes. On Monday their first visitor was Chris, who came down from his office with a wide grin on his face. He looked at Mary as he asked diffidently if they had any news.

'More to the point,' she said, after they had exchanged greetings, 'have *you* any news? I've told Greg I knew you'd guessed ours when I spoke to you about the chances of a new caravan.'

Chris was still smiling. 'Guessed what, Mary? Surely there's not something you haven't told me?'

'Come on,' said Greg, 'you must be the only one round here who doesn't know, but I can see you are keeping something back – spill the beans.'

'You're in luck, I think,' Chris continued. 'I've been advised that both the new caravan and the cesspit revival would almost certainly be approved. A surveyor from the planning department will be coming out today to look over the ground. A detail that I had overlooked, however, was to do with who occupies the caravan. I was told that we were in the business of boatbuilding – not property development. Permission for a dwelling would most likely be conditional on the resident being an employee and not paying rent. You qualify as a director, so there will be no problem all the time you continue to do what you are doing.'

'Does that mean that if you fire me we have to move?' said Greg.

They looked at each other in turn and broad smiles came over their faces.

'Mmm,' mouthed Chris, 'we'll meet that one when we come to it.' And he burst out laughing.

Mary leaped up and gave Chris a huge hug. Greg grasped his hand firmly.

'Pack it up, you two!' exclaimed Chris. 'You are embarrassing me. Oh, by the way, you still haven't told me what I was supposed to have guessed?'

'Late October' was Mary's reply.

'Wonderful,' said Chris. 'We can have another double celebration. Last week the Sheikh signed for patrol boat number two. Delivery mid-October!'

Greg assured Chris that he would get straight on to finishing the work for Curnow that he'd started before he went away unexpectedly. This he did whilst Mary attended to more action required as a result of David's notes.

Mary also faxed the manufacturers of the Bungalow to get a firm quotation for her specific requirements and installation costs, and, most importantly, the date for delivery if they placed a firm order.

At the end of that week Greg was summoned by David to be at Head Office in Lymington the following Monday. David said on the phone that he needed an hour or so with Greg privately before he went to Lymington but would not say why; he hinted that the "reward" had something to do with it. David told Greg to first meet him in the morning at his house near Brockenhurst, which would only take him a few minutes out of his way, and not to disclose this to QC.

Mary was very quiet when she heard Greg on the phone.

'There seems to be something going on,' she said.

'Yes, I agree. I'll find out on Monday, won't I?'

It was Friday afternoon when the fax arrived from QC. It was a memo and accounts from Tom Sinclair, the company secretary. He had drawn up draft accounts of the Dartmouth branch for the first nine months of operations. He asked Greg to give him a ring to clarify a couple of points. Greg phoned him.

'It's remarkable,' said Tom 'for the last six months from October to March, to see that the sales performance is so close to your original forecast.' Greg's own bookkeeping had told him this already but it was Tom's next remarks that made Greg wonder: 'With the downturn in activity within the leisure-boat industry it would be helpful if you would give some thought as to whether you should maybe downgrade your sales forecast for the next six-month period. See you Monday as arranged.'

Mary was very quiet for the rest of the afternoon. Greg knew she had something on her mind. That evening in the caravan Greg asked her if anything was amiss. His first concern was for her health.

'Are you OK – the pregnancy, I mean?'

'No, my sweetheart' she said, 'nothing to do with that at all. It was your conversation with David that bothers me. I'm thinking that maybe he wants you, or me, or both of us for another operation. Obviously I haven't spoken to anyone else about my objections on moral grounds but you know I am adamant. I think it's time they were told how I feel. What should I do?'

'I agree that they should be told as soon as possible, my love. Since you made it clear to me in Newtown River last week how you felt I also have done a great deal of thinking. You know I really do believe that the baby was buried in France. Only time will prove me right. However, I love you far too much to go against you. I have decided that I also am going to quit.'

With that Mary burst into tears. 'You would do that for me?'

Greg went over and put his arms around her and drew her close.

'Not just for you, my lovely Mary, but for the three of us.' She dried her eyes.

'Will you tell David or should we get on to Captain Montague first?'

'David is our man,' said Greg. 'Leave it to me. We have to face up to the fact that he is also our boss at QC. I do think we owe him the courtesy, and of course I'm seeing him on Monday in private at his home, which makes it much easier.'

'Oh, Greg, I am so sorry I have put you in this position.'

'You have nothing to be sorry about, my love. Let me tell you something else: speaking to Chris yesterday I gleaned that he'd been talking to Brian Hope, the QC managing director, you remember. Chris got the impression from Bryan that something wasn't quite right. Mary, my love, I've been thinking for some time that I'd rather be working for myself again. I just wonder if now is the time to see if I could somehow buy the brokerage from them. What do you say?'

'You must do what you are sure is what you want. Is it affordable along with our plans for the new 'van?'

Mary went on to say that they had the weekend ahead of them to think before Greg saw David. On Saturday the quotation for the new caravan arrived in the mail complete with floor plan to Mary's specification and an extensively illustrated brochure.

* * *

Greg easily found the house near Brockenhurst

on Monday morning.

David opened the door and greeted him warmly. 'Got the kettle on. Tea or coffee?'

Greg settled for tea and was invited to follow David into the kitchen. He explained his wife had gone up to London for the day and wasted no time in telling Greg why he was there. He produced a black leather briefcase and laid it on the kitchen table.

'There's fifteen thousand pounds in there. The sum reflects the risk taken by both of you and the use of your boat. The powers that be are well pleased with your part in the operation. When you leave here to see Brian you will have this case in your car and I will not have the slightest idea of its existence.'

Greg took a deep breath. 'David, before you say any more I have to talk to you about the future. You may not want me to have that briefcase after I have said what I have to say.'

'Go ahead,' said David, frowning.

Greg came to the point. He made it clear to David that neither Mary nor he would undertake any further covert operations. He knew David was a man of few words and to keep faith with Mary's request he did not give any reason for their decision. There was a long silence.

David looked Greg straight in the eye and said just one word: 'Final?'

'Absolutely,' continued Greg. 'I have great respect for yourself. You know that we will never discuss past missions with anyone. Can you tell me what the meeting at QC is all about?'

'Ah,' said David. 'The summons to see Brian today happened to be a convenience for me to talk to you about your fee in private. No, I will not tell you; I will let Brian speak for himself. You go to Lymington now. You have not been here. You have never been here. I will turn up half an hour after you have arrived at QC. Yes, I do know what it's all about, but you have to remember Brian is my boss as well as yours and it is to him that I owe my loyalty. However, Greg, because I also have respect for yourself and Mary I will give you one piece of off-the-cuff advice: listen carefully to what he has to say, especially in the light of what you will have locked up in the boot of your Rover. Furthermore, there is no question of you not keeping it. You have earned it. The future is another matter.'

Greg arrived for his appointment with Brian Hope well before noon. He was promptly ushered into Brian's office. The greeting was friendly. Brian arranged for coffee to be brought and waved Greg into the seat opposite the desk.

'I won't beat about the bush,' he said. 'We have been reviewing our policy in the light of our group results for the year ending thirty-first of March. We have concluded that the economic outlook is uncertain. I am expected by our shareholders to maximise profits and pay dividends. It seems to me that our operation in Dartmouth cannot show a fair return until next year at the earliest. And that's going by your original forecast. Am I right?'

Greg did some hard thinking before he replied. *They want out and I have a three-year contract with over two years to go.*

'Yes, you are right. I could not in all honesty offer you increased sales beyond my original forecast. Our fixed overheads will not go down and I think the salary that Mary and I share is absolutely minimal.'

'Thank you for an honest answer,' said Brian. 'Dartmouth was a good idea when I first thought about it a couple of years ago. I have changed my mind, because in the short term it doesn't fit our company group profile. I thought it best to talk to you first before speaking to Chris Curnow, with whom of course we not only have a rental agreement for the office and pontoon space but it was me who persuaded him to invest in building our office.'

'This is beginning', interrupted Greg, 'to sound as if you don't want to carry on with Dartmouth. Where does that leave me?'

Brian continued: 'Would you find it attractive to be relieved of your contract with us in such a way that the Dartmouth business became solely yours?'

Greg purposely hesitated before answering. He even managed a look of surprise. He could see things were going his way better than he could have possibly dreamed.

'I understand where you are coming from, Brian,' he said. 'This has come as a surprise. I personally still have faith in the operation becoming profitable in the long term, so the answer is that if we can come to some agreement, then yes, I would like to run the office on my own account. A problem is that I don't have a lot of spare cash. Chris will need the rent from the office. I need to think.'

'Good. I think you and your wife could make a fist of it. I will draw up what we think is a fair offer to effect the transfer. I will talk to Chris Curnow before you get back.'

Greg nodded his agreement just as David entered the room with an apology about being delayed.

'David knows what I had to say,' continued Brian. 'I have a lunch date, I'm afraid, but if you like to discuss this further with him he and I can talk later when I return. Subject to Chris Curnow's approval, I will get our proposition in writing to you quickly.' With that, Brian got up from behind his desk, shook Greg's hand and departed saying 'Buy our man a decent lunch, David.'

'Come on,' said David, 'I'll feed you before you drive back. I know a little place in Ringwood, which is well on your way, where we can talk in private.'

Over lunch Greg pointed out that Chris Curnow might not be happy about it. After all, he was getting his rent at the moment from a company of good standing.

'Greg, I don't believe there is any way that Chris

will turn down the proposition. He has complete faith in your ability.'

Greg decided to take David into his confidence: 'Mary believes that the baby's body was in the bag we buried at sea. I believed Jacques when he told us it was buried in France. Mary calls any fee from that operation *blood money*.'

'There is a term 'white lie', said David. 'I certainly have no doubt that the baby was buried in France. I think that within a few months Natasha – and that is not her real name, as you might have guessed – will have successfully applied for American citizenship. She will then come back to Europe to arrange a legitimate burial of her son. When that happens I will let you know. Then your reward will no longer be seen by Mary as blood money.'

That was good enough for Greg. He thanked David. 'We'll have to cut this lunch short. I must get to my bank in Dartmouth before it closes.'

In the car park as they were saying their goodbyes and out of earshot of others David spoke quietly: 'Don't worry about the use of Curnow's for future landings. I've been advised that Emsworth is perfect and in many ways more convenient than Dartmouth. We have you to thank for that one. I will inform Monty immediately of your dilemma and Mary's decision. Like myself, I know he will think the problem is temporary. I look forward to our continued friendship.' He gripped Greg's hand. '*Bon chance.*'

Greg drove back to Dartmouth at a rather faster pace than his usual. He pulled into an isolated lay-by to check the briefcase. Not to check it was all there. He had no doubt about that. What he needed to do was to assess whether he had the necessary amount of space available in his bank deed box. He got to the bank with quarter of an hour to spare.

As he left the bank they closed the doors behind him and he found himself in the street holding the empty briefcase. He remembered that down a small side street was a pawnbroker. He got five pounds for the case, mumbling to the man that he'd be back.

He bought an enormous bunch of red roses, which he held out in front of him as he entered the caravan. Mary's eyes lit up.

'You've had a good day,' she declared as she manoeuvred herself round the flowers to kiss him.

'You bet,' was his reply. 'David took it well when I told him we were quitting intelligence operations,' Greg went on to explain everything, except the briefcase. He said that the meeting at David's house was in the way of a favour to tell him to listen carefully when he met Brian Hope. They spent that evening discussing details of the tactical advantage gained by QC approaching them, rather than the other way around.

The next day Greg's first duty was to see Chris.

'Look, Greg, I can tell you now, we did not expect to get back costs involved in building the sales office for at least three years. If you and

Mary believe that you can keep up the rent payments, I am happy to have you as tenants. We do not want ownership of the brokerage ourselves if we can avoid it.'

'Good,' said Greg, 'because they really want out. I believe I will get a good deal from QC. I know that I will have the bank behind me.' (When he said this he smiled to himself as he thought of his deed box.)

Chris looked pleased.

'Big moment for you, Greg. I think it's all going to work out fine. Now, here's some more good news: my informant tells me that planning permission will be granted for your new caravan, but, before you put down any money, sweat it out till I get confirmation from the council in writing.'

Greg went straight to the office to tell Mary. 'What did I tell you, Greg, my love? It's going our way. Nothing is going to spoil our future family plans.'

Two days later they heard from Lymington. The offer was to sell the brokerage to Greg: "Goodwill, sales records and data, plus all the hardware in the office including fixtures and fittings, for the sum of ten thousand pounds." A clause in this offer was that Greg's company would become an agent for QC and that one of the four sides of the display boards in the office would be dedicated to QC sales and successful referrals from either company to the other would result in a 3.5%

commission subject to an annual review. The date for commencement of the contract to be the 1st of July.

They had a meeting in Chris's office.

'Sign it, Greg. It looks in order to me. I'm happy with the terms.'

'We are nearly home and dry, are we not, my love?' said Mary, all smiles. 'The furnishings and equipment alone in the office are worth what they are asking. Add the value of the goodwill and continuing association with the company – it's a great deal.'

'No doubt about it,' said Greg.

The three of them shook hands all round.

'Just one thing, Chris,' continued Greg: 'Let me have a word with the bank before you and I sign anything.'

In the caravan that evening Greg and Mary talked over the new plans. Greg told her that he could pay QC and that he would make all the arrangements with the bank manager as soon as possible.

'Promise?' she said with a smile.

'Promise what?' was his reply.

'Promise that even if you pay them from your previous ill-gotten gains, not a penny will have come from our Cherbourg trip. AND promise that you will let me arrange the financing of all the initial costs of our new home from my own resources?'

Greg was choked with emotion. He had wiped his past clean as far as she was concerned. He was certain that, if it took years to prove it, he would be able to wipe the 'blood money' idea from her mind. He laughed as he reached for her and held her tight.

'I promise. And I promise that I will love you for ever and ever.'

Only when Greg woke in the morning did he realise that he had to think of a way of converting his used banknotes into currency that QC could accept. He made an appointment to see the bank manager that afternoon.

'Got any idea what we should call the new company, my love?'

'How about Devon Yachts? Got a nice ring about it,' she said.

Armed with this suggestion Greg set off for the bank after lunch.

He was ushered into Mr Haythornthwaite's oak-panelled office. The walls were covered in black-and-white photos of men, presumably previous managers. The branch had been there for over a hundred years. He had only met the manager once before but remembered him well, mainly because anyone meeting Mr Haythornthwaite would instantly guess he was a bank manager. Apart from the pinstripe trousers, dark grey jacket, white shirt with stiff collar and maroon bow tie, he was rather rotund with hair swept over to cover a balding pate.

He had a jolly and welcoming ruddy face, and he peered at them over glasses on the end of his nose. He signalled Greg to sit down, placed his elbows on the desk with his hands as if at prayer and asked what he could do to help.

Greg explained what was going on between him and QC, fully aware that it probably called for more than usual attention from the manager because this was the same bank where Curnow had their account. He also knew that Greg was now a director of Curnow's. Greg told him that he would like a personal loan for his wife and himself for the purchase of the static caravan plus two new accounts for "Devon Yachts Ltd", the company they were going to form to own the brokerage. Greg didn't need to explain it was best practice to separate the "client account" from the current business account.

'As regards the loan, Mr Norfield, I will grant it provided that you and your wife pay 20% toward the cost of the new caravan first. I take it that it will be in your joint names?'

'Ah. You see, Mr Haythornthwaite, I have to confide something very personal to you about my past.'

The manager raised an eyebrow.

'I have only been married to my lovely Mary for less than a year. She is now pregnant; the baby is expected in October. She is a person of high Christian morals and I love her dearly. You will realise that she is much younger than me. What I have to confess to you is that in my past I was a bit of a gambler – horses, you know. I've put all that behind me now of course, but she would not take kindly to knowing what I am telling you. Even more so as to how much I had won. She does not believe in gambling – do you?'

When the bank manager replied that he had a flutter himself from time to time Greg knew he was nearly there.

'Please, Mr Norfield, would you tell me how this is relevant to your reason for our meeting?' said the manager.

'Yes, indeed,' was Greg's answer. 'My money is in my box in your vault. My wife would, in her present delicate state, not like to know about that. It is all in cash. I'm telling you because I need to draw twelve thousand pounds from the box and place it into our account. Once I have formed the company I will transfer that sum into the new company account and write QC Ltd a cheque. May I do that initial cash transfer now?'

The manager raised both eyebrows.

'Mr Norfield, it is not my business to know how you got your money in the past, provided it was honestly obtained. I assure you that what is discussed in this office is entirely between us two. I would also add that it is also not my business to know what is in your deed box. I will confirm the loan for your dwelling when I have proof from you that you have put down the 20% deposit. I will write to you in a couple of days to confirm the new company accounts and as soon as you have the company registered at Companies House let me have a copy of the certificate so that I can order the necessary printing.'

'Thank you, Mr Haythornthwaite. I understand.'

'Meanwhile, I will phone through to my head cashier to tell him that you will be making your cash transfer right away. I will tell him to use our interview room for this purpose. May I wish you and your wife the very best for the future, both in the new business and personally.'

Once outside the bank the face that Greg had managed to constrain in the manager's office broke out into a grin. He had slain his worst fears about being able to use his cash and cleared the air with Mary. He went into the off-licence, bought a bottle of Moët, and went home to tell Mary the good news.

She was obviously pleased with what he told her. Very interesting was the fact that Tom Sinclair had phoned whilst he was at the bank to ask about their initial reaction to the offer. She had cautiously said 'favourable' and told him that her husband was discussing the matter at the bank 'right at this moment'.

'You are a genius,' said Greg. 'Let's go through it all again. We can fax the signed agreement tomorrow.'

* * *

A busy few days followed. By the end of the following week Mary had completed the paperwork with Companies House and the name 'Devon

Yachts Ltd' had been registered. The bank had opened the new brokerage accounts and transfered Greg's twelve thousand. They then faxed Brian Hope their acceptance of the proposals to take place officially from the 1st of July and told him they expected to send him a 'Devon Yachts' cheque in a few days.

The *Dartmouth Chronicle* reporter turned up one day and reminded them that he'd been at the QC opening the previous September. He said that he'd since dug into the paper's archives and would like to do an article about the Curnow shipyard site going back over one hundred years. Greg had used this paper to advertise boats for sale locally but this was going to be a timely piece of free publicity.

Two weeks later, in mid-June, they received approval to go ahead with their residential plans. Mary paid the deposit on the new caravan. They now owned the brokerage. The caravan builders sent a man to check the site and access for the delivery. The contractor moved onto the ground at the back of the caravan and started work on the waste water and sewage sumps.

Harry turned up at the office the morning that Greg and Mary were busy changing various name signs from "QC" to "Devon Yachts".

'It has occurred to me', he said, 'that you two might have a problem of somewhere to live during the changeover. I would be happy to put you up in the cottage, and there's plenty of room for you to temporarily store all your personal stuff.'

Mary gave him a hug.

'That's very thoughtful of you, Harry. We'll take you up on that, but it might be for two or three weeks if that's OK. The cesspit and soakaway should be finished in a few days. Greg has found a buyer for the old caravan and is busy checking over its roadworthiness. Our new home can be delivered before the end of July. We ought to allow a week for connecting up the services and teething troubles and then you and your brother shall be our guests of honour at the house-warming.'

'You're on,' said Harry.

The next two weeks flew by for Mary and Greg. The high point of the brokerage was the return of *L'Enterprise.* Alan Lucas expected to get what he paid for it. He also expected them to come and fetch the boat from Fowey.

Greg asked Nick Wroughton to crew for him when he brought it back from Fowey. He guessed Nick would enjoy the trip. He wasn't wrong about that, and soon the fine Dutch steel cruiser was tied up again on their pontoon "For Sale".

Greg knew that this boat was in a price bracket that would have more appeal to QC customers. Three and a half per cent on a craft that would return more than treble his average sale didn't require a genius to work out that his new deal with QC was a winner. He phoned David to get it on their books.

With fifteen weeks to go Mary had a good report at her next visit to the prenatal clinic and she was booked in for the birth at Torbay Hospital. What thrilled her more was the news of the delivery date of their new home at the end of the month. Mary and Greg, with Harry's help and the loan of the Curnows' van, moved out of the "old caravan" and into Harry's cottage one Wednesday when the office was closed. The "old caravan" was collected by the new owner, and Greg cleaned up the concrete apron ready to take their new home.

The main double gates into the yard had to be opened to accommodate the width when it arrived on a low-loader. They were amazed that this huge (to them) construction, ten feet by thirty feet overall, was winched on its own wheels into place by just the crew of two that came with it. Within a couple of hours they had it jacked up level and showed Greg how and where to place brick supports for a more permanent installation.

Bill Fossett, as he had promised, sent a couple of his guys round with a set of three stout wooden steps complete with handrail that had been made in the workshop for the door access. Mary would not let the delivery crew leave until she had checked every nook and cranny inside. Greg sat down with her in the "living room".

Inside was more like a luxury yacht than a caravan. To add to their pleasure it received the highest praise from Bill Fossett after he had inspected the quality of the joinery. The woodwork was in ash and gave a light and airy feeling. The many drawers and fitted cupboards in all rooms had a quality "feel" about them. Yacht-like, every seat, bunk, and bed had stowage space underneath.

However, there was much to do before they could move in: connecting up the mains services as well as installing all their possessions. Over the coming few days Greg was allowed to man the office whilst Mary prepared their new home.

Three days after the delivery Bill came into the office and gave Mary a varnished mahogany name plaque that said quite simply "The Cabin". Greg attached this beside the door and put it around that from henceforth they would be living in The Cabin and not in "the caravan".

In reality it took another week before they could actually move in. They chose a Wednesday, when the office was closed, to move. Pride of place in the saloon was the little silver ship. Mary saw to it that her father's crucifix was above the baby's room bedhead. Moving day was the second Wednesday in August. Every time they had come to work from Harry's cottage in Buckfastleigh they had brought some of their belongings with them.

They sat with their coffees, holding hands, surveying the new surroundings. The view was better. The windows were larger and lower. The floor was about a foot higher than the old caravan. That small increase in elevation made a huge difference. They could better see the craft moored in the river and beyond to the wooded hills on the other side, atop which sat the impressive Royal Naval College.

'I just want to sit here with you and do nothing,' Mary said.

'And that is exactly what we will do, then.'

'You are forgetting that we've invited half the yard over later.'

Harry, Chris, John Dalton, Tom Fossett and the crane crew all came over at about five o'clock. Flossie followed. Then came Joan and Frank, and Robert Trehairne. A little later Mr Haythornthwaite, the bank manager, arrived. A complete surprise was the arrival of David with several bottles of champagne in a cool box. He opened one and made a short speech. He finished with 'And may God bless all who sail in her.' He then dribbled the first rush of champagne out of the bottle over the name plaque.

Tom had loaned them his elaborate Calor gas-fired barbecue and volunteered to be chef. Clad in a large blue and white striped cook's apron he dispensed succulent fare from just outside The Cabin front door, where all the tables and chairs they could beg or borrow had been placed.

The party went on for a couple of hours. Nobody was in a hurry to go. David was staying nearby overnight and in the morning he took more photos of *L'Enterprise* for a prospective customer.

'Give her a good clean-up, Greg. We'll leave her here until I have time to take her back to Lymington for my customer to inspect. My guess is', he said, 'you'll be banking over three grand on this one.'

'My guess is that *you* will be banking double that' was Greg's reply, and they both grinned knowingly.

* * *

What with the new home, a great deal of welcome activity at Devon Yachts, and the forthcoming baby, Mary and Greg knew there would be no time for sailing *Amity*; so when Chris wanted to lift her out, before the crane got busy at the end of the season, they readily agreed.

As promised, the boat was put down on wooden railway sleepers adjacent to The Cabin with the mast down on trestles above the deck. With a big tarpaulin over all she was snug for the winter and placed where Greg could do the hull work conveniently. No way was Greg going to allow Mary, now six months pregnant and showing it, to do antifouling as she suggested.

'Come on over to No.1 Shed when you can,' said Bill Fossett when he stuck his nose into their office about three weeks after they had moved into The Cabin.

No, it wasn't the patrol boat Bill had invited them to see. Bill had designed, and the guys had built, a porch with a four-foot overhang to keep out the rain. They were going to fit this in front of The Cabin. They had also built a low shed with sliding doors to go alongside, big enough to take a pram and a pushchair, all finished to master-shipwright standard.

'If it's alright by you,' said Bill, 'the lads would like to come in on Saturday morning and carry this lot over to The Cabin and fit it into position.'

Mary addressed Greg: 'Now perhaps you know what I meant when I said the other day that we should count our blessings.'

Greg's reaction, when he learned that the porch/shed was a present from Chris and that the workforce had made it in their own time, was to phone Frank Trehairne. He chose a moment when Mary was not in the office. He gave Frank the news about all that was going on, including the fact that the boat was out of the water.

'I need four dozen bottles of champagne to give as presents to all the staff here for Christmas. Do you think Robbie could fulfil my order?'

There was a bit of a pause and spluttering. 'Did I hear right? I thought you were going straight.'

Greg replied, 'So I am; it's not for me!'

There was a roar of laughter from the other end of the phone, followed by 'I bet you don't tell Mary.'

'Too bloody true. I'll work out a way of picking the stuff up from Salcombe if Rob's answer is in the affirmative. I'd rather you kept it for a bit. I don't want it here until nearer Christmas,' said Greg.

'That's OK,' answered Frank barely suppressing

more laughter. 'I'll get him to leave it at the local police station for safe keeping!'

Mary's big day grew nearer. The clinic gave her a date and each visit to their GP reported all was progressing well. They had fun with the expected date of November the 5th but Greg's attempt at a joke about if it was a boy calling him Guy was met with withering contempt from Mary. She reminded him that they had agreed on Alexander.

Mary drove over to the Naval College. She had no problem getting to see the chaplain after telling them her father's history.

On returning to The Cabin that evening she told Greg she had arranged the christening in the chapel and, perhaps more importantly to her, beforehand a short private blessing of their marriage – something she had wanted when they discussed their wedding the previous year.

The conversation turned to choosing godparents. They asked Chris and Rosemary Curnow, who were delighted, particularly as they had no children of their own.

CHAPTER SIXTEEN

Sergei

Nick Wroughton called on Frank Trehairne for an "urgent and private" talk. They went into the cider house, where they would not be disturbed.

'A little birdie tells me that our friend in Dartmouth has retired,' said Nick.

'Depends what you mean by retired.'

'The powers that be up in The Smoke have another very important project,' continued Nick. 'They say that our friend is the only one who can do the job. They say that he retired to please his wife. You know the two of them better than I. Do you think it would be possible for you to persuade him to do a little job?'

'You are testing my loyalties now, Nick.'

'That's easy: put your country first.'

'The answer to your question is "possibly",' said Frank.

'I need an explanation for that, it's contrary to what those above are saying.'

Frank paused for a few seconds.

'When Christmas comes and you and your old mum are enjoying at your table the fruits of

Robbie's labours out to sea, so also will our mutual friend – via my "wholesalers", of course!'

Nick's subsequent conversation on the phone with David echoed Frank's opinion.

'The answer as to whether I could persuade Greg to help with Operation Sergei is that it is possible. I am prepared to try.'

David outlined the operation, which involved the use of *L'Enterprise* en route from Dartmouth to Lymington, under an agreement made with Greg for QC to sell her. However, on the way they (meaning Nick and Greg) would be "picking up Sergei" mid-Channel and offloading him in Lymington.

'Sorry, Nick, old chap, but *try* isn't good enough. Sergei won't go with anyone other than Greg or myself. Sergei will be holed up in a safe house near Cherbourg any day now. The route we have chosen through Europe to Cherbourg has been proved to be secure. Our agents in the East have already laid false trails down through Austria and Switzerland. The only possible crew on *L'Enterprise* is Greg and yourself. I have to be here to organise the "taxi" to whisk Sergei away on a plane to the States. Sergei has been one of us for many years. He speaks several languages including a number of Arabic dialects, Russian, and English. He is nearly round the bend believing that the KGB is on to him. He is on his way to Cherbourg now. We must not keep him in a safe house there for long.

'Give me another very good reason, David.'

'Tell him that Sergei has been negotiating on behalf of the Soviets to supply arms to an organisation in the Middle East. We have excellent intelligence to suggest that this weaponry is for use against the West, and America in particular. Sergei is our man in serious danger. Tell Greg the man is Troag – the very same. Mary need never know anything other than that *L'Enterprise* is required urgently back here in Lymington. Tell him from me that one white lie deserves another.'

'There is another way, if push comes to shove,' said Nick. 'I just don't tell Greg what's up until we're well under way. What do you think?'

'I thought of that, Nick, and don't like it one little bit. Firstly, he's quite capable of bringing the boat here single-handed and will wonder at your involvement. Secondly, only recently did he tell me personally that he wouldn't do another trip. Better that you approach him on the basis that you are both involved, and I know he enjoys your company.'

Nick phoned Greg. Mary answered.

'I need Greg over here urgently. I have a prospective customer for you, who doesn't want it put about he is selling his boat. I've told this guy I know just the man.'

Greg drove over to Salcombe that afternoon. They met in a quiet corner of the lounge bar in The Marine Hotel, overlooking the river.

'No matter what I have to say, Greg – will you hear me out?'

'Of course, but what's the mystery?'

'Your work for The Firm has been appreciated. You have been told that. What you have probably guessed is that I too am part of that organisation.'

'No surprise at all,' interrupted Greg.

'I'll continue please, Greg,' said Nick. 'We now have a more enlightened chief than previously. He believes that we may discuss operations amongst ourselves but still on a need-to-know basis. What you need to know is as follows – and please don't interrupt to tell me about your promises to your lovely wife, Mary.'

Greg remained silent.

Nick went on to explain about a fundamental Islamic organisation evolved from Maktab al-Khidamat in Afghanistan, believed now to be based in the Middle East, that called for global Jihad. There was clear evidence that they were now being supplied with arms and explosives by the Soviets and that they were turning their attention against the West, and the USA in particular.

'Paradoxically, the Soviet Union were fighting in Afghanistan the very brothers of those they were arming. The Soviets will soon be withdrawing from Afghanistan. They will sell their massive surplus of weaponry to the Jihadists for the purpose of attacking the West without firing a shot themselves.' Greg made as if to interrupt, but Nick held up his hand and continued: 'You have rightly guessed that there is one more job before you retire. Mary need know nothing about it. In order to keep faith with your promise to Mary there will be no reward, no fee, for either you or me. I forgo mine because I respect you both. Now I will tell you what it is we have to do for our country – in fact it would not be too strong to say for world peace.'

Greg poured them both some more coffee and said nothing.

Nick described the plan for the two of them to take *L'Enterprise* to Lymington within the next forty-eight hours. He told Greg how David would organise matters upon their arrival and how they could collect Sergei on the way without increasing the total time for the passage to Lymington; thus there would be no suspicions aroused. The extra distance they would have to travel to the rendezvous in mid-Channel could be achieved in the same time by increasing their normal cruising speed. They would arrive at their destination, no one the wiser as to where they had been on the way. A 10 a.m. departure from Dartmouth would allow a 7.30 p.m. arrival in Lymington as requested by David. He wanted them to arrive after his staff had gone home. Finally Nick told Greg that Sergei was the same man that he landed in Dartmouth on the Troag exercise last year.

'The Russian is adamant that he will not travel to Britain with anyone other than yourself or David. That fact is a non-negotiable part of his defection. Right now he doesn't trust anybody else, which is why David has to meet him off the boat. David told me to tell you that Sergei is a close friend of Natasha and her husband, and that his life is at risk.'

Nick waited for what seemed a long time.

'Look,' said Greg, 'perhaps you'd like to tell me what I am eventually to say to Mary. If I say yes to your request I'm certainly not going to tell her before the baby is born.'

'David said to tell you *one good white lie deserves another.*'

'Very funny.'

Greg said nothing more for what seemed a very long time. To save a life? Mary's father would say yes if he were alive.

'When do we go?'

'Come to my office now. I will make a quick call. David will phone your office to say that he wants *L'Enterprise* in Lymington either tomorrow or the next day. If Mary doesn't tell him where you are at the moment, he will ask her. If she hasn't phoned my office within quarter of an hour you will phone her to say that you have had a call from David and that I would like to crew *L'Enterprise* with you for the Lymington trip. Even I know that no man would want his pregnant wife, with only a couple of months to go, to be crewing on an eight- or nine-hour wave-bashing.'

'You knew I'd say yes, didn't you?' said Greg.

Nick smiled.

They went to the HM's office. Nick made his call and within five minutes Mary was on the phone.

'And you needn't think I'm going to spend hours, beautiful boat or not, being thrown around. I rang you straight away in case you wanted to ask Nick to crew for you.'

Greg was back in the Devon Yachts office before closing time. He looked at Mary, busy behind the desk.

'Nick's up for it,' he said. 'He's been itching to get on board again ever since the trip round from Fowey.'

'I'm glad you'll have a pal with you. Oh, and David apologized for the short notice.'

As they spoke David rang to say it was on for the very next day. He told them he'd checked on rail connections back from Lymington and suggested they took their sleeping kit and stayed overnight on board since it would be easier to get the train back the following morning.

Greg phoned Nick who said he'd get a lift to Curnow's by 10 a.m. as his Land Rover was in for service. He did.

They cast off before ten thirty. The forecast was force four, south-west. This would give them wind with tide for the first few hours. Once clear of the harbour they set off on an easterly course to pass south of Portland Race. Nick laid out his charted plans for Greg to check. They were to make for a point fifty miles on track for the Isle of Wight. This would take them to seven miles south-east of Portland Bill and clear of the race, from where they would call David using their cellphone.

If the phone was out of range they could still use the coast radio station on marine-band VHF ship-to-shore. It wouldn't matter if their position was located as they would still be on track for Lymington. This action would tell David that they were two hours from the rendezvous just north of East Channel One whistle buoy.

David would advise the French crew, which included Sergei. They would have ample time to launch the fast RIB from Cherbourg and meet as arranged. David's "crew" all worked at the RIB factory fringing Cherbourg Harbour, from where they spent much time on sea trials for their thirty-five-knot-plus craft.

They increased the speed on *L'Enterprise* after the successful call to David and altered course eighty degrees south of their original track. Their target whistle buoy had a radar reflector. Nick manned the Decca wheelhouse radar whilst Greg worked on the position by dead reckoning. As competent navigators they viewed this exercise as a bit of a competition. They were only half an hour from the buoy when Nick revealed his "secret weapon".

There was to be no radio communication that might be overheard between the two meeting craft. David had obtained from secret sources a visual strobe identifying binocular. It comprised a powerful binocular with a directional signal light and strobe connected to the boat's twelve-volt supply. The range was up to ten miles in good visibility. The RIB also had this equipment and thus they could send Morse signals to each other for identification, rather like the old Aldis lamp but hand-held and very compact. This would ensure they were approaching the correct party but could not be read by anyone else.

It worked. Just north of the buoy and outside its two mile no-go area they received the letters **B**ravo **S**ierra from a fast-approaching boat, low in the water, coming from the south. Nick aimed their reply signal at them. They were alongside within five minutes. As requested, it was Greg who positioned himself at the boarding gap in the safety rails, where he could be seen clearly from the approaching craft, whilst Nick remained at the wheel on the bridge deck.

There were six men in the RIB. Greg instantly recognised the one with the goatee, whom he had met briefly on the Troag trip with David. With one foot on the sponson of the RIB this man leaned across and peered closely at Greg.

'How is your wife?'

'Pregnant,' replied Greg, as arranged.

His proffered hand was taken as he helped the Russian onto the side deck.

There followed a large holdall heaved there by one of the French crew, who shouted, *'Bon voyage Sergei, bon chance,'* before they sped away to the south.

The sound of their two powerful outboard motors faded rapidly. Greg led his visitor down to one of the en-suite cabins.

He turned to Greg: 'So we meet again. Sergei is not my real name,' he said with the slight accent that Greg recognised, 'nor must I know yours or that of your friend on the bridge but I shall for ever be grateful for what you are doing.'

Nick had now pushed the speed up and set course northwards for the Isle of Wight. It was going to be a bumpy ride for a couple of hours or so. Greg showed Sergei how to avail himself of the facilities and change into the clothes he had brought with him.

Half an hour later, when Greg went down to the cabin as promised, Sergei had divested himself of the mechanic's overalls he'd been wearing as his cover for boarding the RIB in Cherbourg. Greg left him to enjoy the snack he'd taken him, along with instructions not to leave the cabin until advised.

Greg joined Nick up on the bridge deck. Moving around the boat was becoming hazardous. At the speed they were going with wind across tide *L'Enterprise* was rolling as well as pitching wildly.

Two and a half hours after picking up Sergei they entered the Needles Channel. The rolling stopped but the pitching increased as the ebb out of the Solent against the wind presented them with short, steep waves which were breaking on the Shingles bank to port.

It was too dangerous to get out of their secure seats and attempt to climb down from the bridge deck to see how their visitor was faring below. They were forced to slow down to make the motion bearable.

Once past Hurst Point in calmer water on the sheltered west side of the Solent Greg went below. Sergei had sensibly lain down on the bunk for most of the trip. He was cheered, he said, when he saw land out of the porthole.

Greg rejoined Nick. They passed Jack-in-the-Basket mark to port and followed the Yarmouth ferry up the river to their berth at QC. David was waiting to help them tie up and then, as Nick and Greg adjusted the springs, he went below to greet Sergei.

'Why you go to all this trouble and danger?' said Sergei.

'Because we must help those who help us seek peace and freedom' was David's reply. He called for the other two to join them in the cabin below.

'We have not used our real names, nor shall we do so,' he said, 'but Sergei wishes to thank you in his own words. I will go ashore now to arrange his taxi. Nobody here will take any notice of a guy coming ashore and getting into a car, just as nobody in Cherbourg was likely to notice that six mechanics went out in the RIB for speed trials and only five came back. When I return to the boat in a few minutes the three of you can come up on deck and say farewell to our friend as if you've known him for years.'

'I cannot thank you enough,' said Sergei. 'I was close – within hours, I think, of arrest. I know how everyone treat me since I leave Turkey three days ago that I move into better world. I thank Allah that I attend British university and learn about your ways of freedom.'

David called from the pontoon and they helped Sergei ashore with his holdall.

'May your God go with you,' he said quietly to the other two before David led him up the gangway.

From the deck they saw just the top of the car on the quay above before it drove off. David came straight back to the boat.

'Right, you guys, you will be pleased to know that I have brought forward some maintenance we have to carry out on a boat we sold last week. She's now berthed in Exmouth and it is better for us to send an engineer there to do the work than bring her back here. This means you don't have to suffer the tedious journey back by train in the morning. I have instructed Pete, our engineer, to first take you both to Kingswear by road in the morning and then do Exmouth on the way home. I have much to talk about with you tonight. I will push off down to the Chinese takeaway and bring back our supper while you tidy ship. On board here we can talk freely.'

'I like it,' said Greg, 'and whilst you are gone I will phone Mary to say we have arrived safely and tell her about the return arrangements.'

He phoned her. She offered to drive Nick back to Salcombe if it would help. They exchanged phone kisses. Greg once again felt guilty about his deceit.

Back on board, over the meal, David told them he'd decided to tidy up a few loose ends with them, mainly because he had talked Nick into persuading Greg to take part in the day's operation much against his (Greg's) earlier decision to quit.

'You'll be pleased to know, Greg, that I have had to rule out Dartmouth as a future point of landing or departure. I will explain. I personally made a mistake. I had used the College pontoon twice before the Troag exercise. Me, of all people, should have known that using a location more than once was risky. We had a helper related to one of the crew that met Greg and me on that pontoon. It was the third time this excellent and trusted operative had assisted. What he didn't know was that a remark he made to his wife about going to the College pontoon at night was overheard by his daughter and she almost certainly innocently quoted it out of context to someone at her place of work.'

'Her place of work being . . . ?' asked Greg.

'She works in the kitchens at Dartmoor Prison. We believe she must have been overheard by a prisoner who we will call Ahmoud. He was known to be a member of an Islamic terrorist cell in London and was serving fifteen years for possession of bomb-making materials. We believe that Selby Somerfield-Smythe, whilst in Dartmoor, was recruited by Ahmoud.'

At the mention of the name Selby, Greg nearly had a fit.

'Selby had no idea what he was letting himself in for,' continued David. 'He probably thought they were just a bit of low life like himself. But they knew that on release he would be running a courier business. After his discharge from prison he was given his first job by what he was led to believe were a London gang that shifted dubious goods around. He was also told to keep an eye on the College pontoon at night as they had reason to believe something illegal was going on there. He was bribed by promises of other work for his courier business.'

Greg had not told David of his encounter with Selby early one morning, but now that incident had been explained.

'He used his friendship with Harry Curnow to gain an advantage point from the shipyard on the opposite bank. He thought he was looking for smuggled goods. He had been told to look for any suspicious activity along the west bank north of the town quay. We are guessing that this was as a result of our innocent grass making a remark in the Dartmoor kitchen, overheard by Ahmoud. We believe that on a visit to London he contacted this gang and tried to blackmail them into getting a cut of whatever they were up to. Little did he know that in reality they were a vicious lot planning explosions and killings. They meted out to him the only penalty they knew for anyone who threatened to expose them. We have pieced all this together in cooperation with the Metropolitan Police and enquiries I have made recently from the authorities at HMP Dartmoor.'

Greg and Nick were enjoying their food as they listened to David. On a need-to-know basis, Greg decided it was not necessary at this moment to tell David about his encounter with Selby in the yard on the morning of the Troag incident.

'Selby's death is still an open case,' continued David. 'I won't be made privy to the extent of the exchange of information between the chief and the Met. However, you can see why we have decided Dartmouth is now a no-no. Now that we have arranged for it to be "leaked" to Ahmoud's lot that Dartmouth operations are closed down with the death of Selby we can breathe a sigh of relief. Also the gang in London are far too busy dodging the Met after Selby's murder to bother with, literally, a dead end. Closing down the Dartmouth facilities is sadly a fact, but the intelligence people find that feeding Ahmoud with misinformation is still of value. Any questions?'

'Yes,' said Greg. 'I am in enough trouble with Mary over one perceived illegal act, of which I know I am innocent. You assured me, David, that the transport department does not do "kidnap, torture, or murder" when I told you my involvement was conditional upon the exclusion of those activities. Selby's murder is unsolved. You have just given us your own explanation. Does your promise still hold good?'

'It does. The three of us here have relied on the trust of each other. I promise you that is still the case. I know of no other explanation for Selby's death.'

'Thank you for that,' said Greg. 'I feel a whole lot better. I'd like you two to know that I have no intention of talking to Mary about any of this until after the baby is born, if at all. I am particularly pleased to hear the theory about

Selby. I had a strong feeling he was a blackmailer long before I knew the reason for his imprisonment. He did not deserve the manner of his gruesome parting from this world but I have to admit I'm pleased he's not around any more.'

'A couple more points before I go,' said David. 'I am 99% sure that Alan Lucas will accept the offer I've had for *L'Enterprise*, Greg, which will put a few coppers into your new business. I like the agreement that we have and look forward to continuing to our mutual benefit. Tell Mary I apologise for a problem with the camera at the wedding party, which meant I failed to record most of the party, but I will let you have the opening few minutes of the happy couple on the big day. Finally, well done, you two. Have a good night, and of course be very careful what you say in front of Pete, our driver, in the morning. He'll make himself known at eight o'clock. Finally, one of you will have to make yourself comfortable in the back of the van!'

With that, David departed. Greg and Nick cleared the supper things away. It had been a very long day. An early night was in order, but before they settled down Nick looked at Greg with a grin.

'David doesn't know about your "bits of trade". I thought you were going to give the game away when he started to talk about Selby.'

'Look,' said Greg, also smirking, 'you don't know either, remember.' Greg went on to explain to Nick how Selby got involved through Harry with the "bits of trade" deliveries to London. He suggested that Selby had added two and two to make five and tied in the College pontoon episode with the "bits of trade".

'Hence I found him spying around the yard one Sunday. Now that my skulduggery is out of the link, Harry is no longer involved, and dead men don't talk, we are all in the clear. In the spirit of "need to know", ignorance is bliss!'

Nick, barely suppressing laughter, tapped the side of his nose with a forefinger. 'When you come over to collect your Christmas order from Frank's "wholesalers" perhaps we'll have a chance to discuss future plans – I mean seafaring, of course. Goodnight, Greg.'

In the morning, as promised, Pete greeted them on the pontoon. There was no danger of conversing together within the hearing of Pete, as Nick, who lost the toss, had to make himself comfortable on top of their sleeping gear amongst the tools and parts in the back of the van.

They arrived at Curnow's by lunchtime. Mary had made sandwiches for them and they recounted to her a slow, but uneventful, trip to Lymington, and passed on David's best wishes for her and the baby.

They were saved from telling more untruths by Chris coming down to say hello to Nick and to tell them that the launch of the new patrol boat would be at the end of October. Greg wanted the opportunity to talk to Nick further, so it was just as well that Mary said she'd rather Greg drove Nick back to Salcombe.

On the journey Nick told Greg that his four dozen bottles of "proprietary" champagne would cost him two hundred and fifty pounds – almost half the shop price. He said that Frank would keep it in the cider house for him to pick up the week before Christmas. The stuff would have come from his "wholesalers". Cash would be payable on collection.

Greg returned to Mary that afternoon with much on his conscience but little that disturbed him too much at that moment. He would square it all with her after the birth. She was so obviously happy with everything in their lives: the business, The Cabin, the baby, and their future. No way was he going to spoil it for her now.

Mary planned to be back at work within a couple of weeks after the birth, even if she was to work from The Cabin. They tested her babysitting apparatus, which worked perfectly. A microphone above the cot relayed the slightest sound over the phone extension to a speaker on the desk in the brokerage office. She had thrown out the old Atari computer and replaced it with the latest IBM desktop model. They were now able to email as well as fax, which greatly improved their communications ability.

Mary and Brian Hope's secretary at QC started talking to each other about domain names, the Internet, protocols and megabits – a language that Greg decided he would leave to Mary. As Mary got nearer her time and more tired, Greg would drive her on their Wednesday days off to the local surgery or the clinic in Torquay for regular check-ups.

At the end of October the second patrol boat was completed by Curnow's. There followed five days of sea trials and adjustments with the same crew from the Gulf, but this time Sheikh Samad did not attend himself. Either Chris or Bill Fossett was on board each time the boat went to sea. Once again, after signing off, she was to be shipped as deck cargo from Southampton.

'There goes one baby,' said Mary as they watched the patrol boat slip her moorings bound for Southampton, 'and here comes another.'

Greg gave Mary a quizzical look. She responded with a vigorous nod of her head.

They had prepared for this moment. Flossie was called for emergency telephone duty in the office so that Greg could take Mary to Torbay Hospital. She had packed her bag ready but insisted on phoning the hospital herself to discuss with them her symptoms and ask whether she should come in right away. The answer was in the affirmative.

She was in the maternity ward within the hour. Greg, fussing around like a headless chicken, was dismissed by Mary. She wanted to do this thing herself. She told him she'd get them to call him when she was ready. Greg gave her a hug and a kiss as she sat on the side of the bed.

'God bless you, my lovely Mary.'

'God bless all three of us,' replied Mary.

She looked anxiously at the nurse who was unpacking her things.

'We'll look after her, Mr Norfield. I have a feeling

this birth will go well,' she said with a smile.

Greg left the ward, blowing Mary kisses as he went. Secretly he was glad to leave the hospital. His ex-wife had insisted that he was present at the birth of their first child. He had felt utterly useless, and before the baby had appeared she had shouted at him to go away.

This time he was more comfortable going back to the office, where various people kept popping in to ask if there was any news. At the end of the day Greg put the phone through to The Cabin and got on with his meal. He waited until nine o'clock that evening, seven hours after taking her in, before he phoned the hospital. Their response was to tell him to go to bed and phone in the morning – all was proceeding normally.

Greg was woken by the phone at seven in the morning. He was surprised that he had slept so well.

'It's a boy, Mr Norfield,' said the voice. 'You may come whenever you wish. Your wife asked us not to disturb you until now.'

Greg looked down at Alexander Gregory Norfield in his arms. He had asked the nurse fearfully if he might take him from the cot beside Mary's bed. With tears in his eyes he looked at Mary. She was so obviously tired, but happy.

'You clever, clever girl, you.'

'Give me a little while and I'll do it again if you like.'

The nurse took the baby from Greg and assured

him that all was well. Mary would be moved to the general ward and, subject to conditions at their home, she could return with the child within a few days.

That is what happened.

After Mary's return from hospital Flossie turned out to be brilliant. She was like a daughter to them. Nothing was too much trouble. The work at Devon Yachts was not interrupted. When she wasn't taking over the phone calls whilst Greg was out and about, Flossie was at The Cabin offering any help that Mary wanted. She adored the baby. She was overjoyed when Mary asked her to be another godmother, along with Rosemary Curnow.

* * *

The christening took place in the College chapel at the end of November. Mary wore her father's cross around her neck on a plain silver chain that Greg had bought her as a "mum's present". In a simple ceremony, before the baptism, the chaplain conducted a short service to bless their marriage.

Alexander Norfield, wearing the white embroidered cotton christening robe worn by his mother thirty-five years earlier, was dutifully noisy at the font as the priest made the sign of the cross on his forehead. A quiet remark from Chris about another Norfield who could kick up a fuss when he wanted went unheard – except by Greg, for whom it was intended. The photographer from the local paper did his stuff outside the chapel.

They all managed to squeeze into The Cabin. The Curnows (including Harry), Flossie, Frank, Joan and Robbie Trehairne, and Nick Wroughton were all there. Mary fed Alexander, and after laying him contentedly down in his cot in "Alex's Room" (it said so on the door) she joined them in the saloon.

'I did not know', said Greg, 'just how happy a man could be until this day. A lovely wife, good friends, a wonderful home and job, and now a son. I truly count my blessings. Thank you all.' He embraced Mary with both arms as they kissed. 'You are gorgeous,' he said.

'Oh my, I nearly forgot,' said Frank. 'Hang on a minute, folks.'

He left The Cabin, went to his car outside and came back carrying a cool box which revealed three bottles of champagne packed in ice.

'Got to wet the baby's head with something stronger than holy water!'

Mary scrambled for all the glasses they were able to muster as Frank popped the cork.

"Alexander," they cried as glasses were raised and Mary was swamped with hugs and kisses.

As if on cue, a baby's cry was heard from a little speaker mounted in a corner of the ceiling. Most of the assembled company shook their heads in wonder as Greg went along to the baby's room and Mary told them all about her system.

She could hear practically every movement of the child from either there in the saloon, their bedroom, or the office across the way.

She went on to tell them that the telephone engineer, who installed it all in his spare time, was going to extend it so that they could have short-distance handsets operating on the amateur waveband. This meant either of them could keep watch wherever they were on site.

Greg returned to witness more heads shaking in wonder.

Nick said out aloud, 'If I were you, Greg, I should watch your step very carefully. You married someone with a propensity for surveillance!'

Many a true word is said in jest, thought Greg as Frank popped another cork.

The snacks they had prepared were produced. In good company it did not take long before they had drained the last of the champagne. It was Joan Trehairne who interrupted the merrymaking to remind them that perhaps it might be time to leave the happy couple and their offspring. Goodbyes and hugs were exchanged. Frank winked at Greg as he left and said loudly, making sure he was within Mary's hearing, 'I got the champagne from my wholesalers, Greg. It was very reasonably priced. If you would ever like some, just ask.'

'How did I ever find a pal like you, Frank?'

And so it came about that Greg drove to Salcombe a week before Christmas to collect his gift for the yard workers. Mary had produced, on her new computer, forty labels, which she attached to forty gift bottle-bags. The label said simply, "Thanks for your friendship. Merry Christmas from Mary, Greg, and Alexander."

Chris saw to it that everyone received their bottle. That was on the Monday. On Wednesday afternoon before locking the gates for the start of the holiday Bill Fossett went to the Devon Yachts office. He placed on the desk in front of Greg a little hand-carved wooden model of the yard's workboat. Along one side under the gunwale burnt into the wood was the message "Curnow Shipmates Wish You Well" and on the transom "HMS Bubbly".

Mary's progress had been remarkable. Within three weeks of the birth she was putting in a few hours each day in the office, and now regularly took over the incoming calls that were switched to The Cabin when Greg was out and about. They had a bell-push beside the office door and a notice that invited visitors to press if the door was closed. Flossie was on the receiving end of this facility and would call Greg or Mary or go down herself.

The few weeks before Christmas had been busy, both for the yard and for the brokerage. Chris and Greg decided that they would close both businesses on Christmas Eve and not reopen until the 5th of January because both Christmas Day and New Year's Day fell on a Thursday. Greg was looking forward to the long break and to making a start on *Amity*'s annual maintenance.

CHAPTER SEVENTEEN

The Reunion

Greg was working under the boat one day after Christmas when Mary came rushing out of The Cabin and shouted to him, 'Greg, come quickly. You're not going to believe this.'

Greg ran to join Mary, who had the phone in her hand.

With the other hand over the mouthpiece she told him that when she had answered the call a female voice had said, 'This is Natasha. I have come to see Mary.' Mary had asked where she was and she had replied that she was in a car outside the main gates of the yard with her husband.

Greg did a quick think and told her to say that they would look for the keys and be at the gate in a few minutes. This she did and turned to Greg.

'What do you think?' he said to Mary.

'I think this really is Natasha.'

'Tell her to wait where she is and close the call.'

Greg then grabbed the phone from Mary and dialled David's home number. David answered, but before he could finish his seasonal greetings Greg told him what had happened.

'Well, don't keep them waiting out in the cold, old man.' And as Greg started to explain that he suspected a trick he was interrupted: 'It was supposed to be a surprise. Everything is above board, I assure you. Don't spoil it for them.'

Greg pushed the phone into Mary's hand.

'Have a word with David,' he said as he grabbed the main-gate keys from the hook and shot out of the door. He ran past the yard offices and No. 1 Shed and headed for the gate. Outside was a silver Mercedes.

As he approached the ironwork gates a female figure emerged from the back of the vehicle. Yes, it was indeed Natasha, now smartly dressed, her dark hair down to her shoulders and curled under in pageboy style. She was almost unrecognisable compared with how he had seen her last, radiant and happy as she ran toward him. Greg fiddled with the lock and opened the gate. She stepped forward and grabbed him in a hug.

'Well, well!' was all Greg could think to say.

A tall elegant man with a mass of black hair flecked with grey and a Stalin-like bushy moustache then alighted from the back of the car. Natasha introduced her husband. He firmly clasped Greg's proffered hand.

'We have much for to thank you.' His English, near perfect, only just betrayed his Russian origins.

'I will open the gate fully to let the car through,' said Greg, 'and take you to our home just round the corner.'

'No, no,' said the Russian. 'Carl will wait here outside.'

He gave a signal to the driver, who proceeded to turn the car round in the road. The two Russians followed as he led them round the yard to The Cabin. Mary was waiting anxiously at the door. Natasha saw her. They ran to meet, arms outstretched to embrace and quietly call each other's names. The Russian girl's husband joined in and Mary was smothered by both of them muttering their thanks. All were smiling as Mary ushered them up the steps into the saloon. Divested of their topcoats, they settled into the seating.

'I never thought I'd see this day,' said Mary, her eyes moist.

'Not me too,' said Natasha in her faltering English with a broad smile.

Greg intervened: 'Mary, my love, I made you a promise. Remember?'

Mary looked thoughtful.

'We have new names now,' said Natasha's husband, 'and until our American citizenship is complete we can only travel outside America with personal bodyguard. We must be very careful to who we tell our names. You, of course, we may trust. We are booked into hotel as Mr and Mrs Theodore Roberts. We say we are on holiday, and on business, from United States. My wife is now Natalie and I am Theo. Carl Shultz, our driver, is also officially my personal assistant, and has his own room next to ours at hotel. He is bodyguard. We have American passports. We have much we wish to tell you. Will you be our guests for dinner tonight at hotel and then we tell our story – as much as we are allowed?'

Greg looked at Mary for approval.

'Why, yes, that would be lovely, wouldn't it, Greg?' she said.

He nodded agreement.

The Russian continued: 'We at Imperial Hotel, Torquay. Carl will call for you at seven o'clock, OK?'

Then Greg and Mary looked at each other in amusement as they realised they had both forgotten something. As Greg was about to speak Mary leaned forward and put the forefingers of both her hands on his lips.

'Natasha – sorry, *Natalie*' – she said, 'wait here a moment.'

She winked at Greg and made for the baby's room. She returned with their son bundled up in a soft blanket, still asleep.

She sat down next to Natasha and whispered, 'Meet Alexander.'

The Russian girl's eyes filled; a tear rolled down one cheek as she looked at the baby.

'May I hold him?' she murmured.

Then as she held the little bundle she gently swayed from side to side as more tears welled up.

In lowered tones Mary spoke close to Natalie's ear: 'I made you a promise on the boat that night.' A little louder, she explained that they would have to phone their babysitter about the possibility of going out that evening.

Natalie's husband intervened: 'Please. We have dinner in private apartment. You bring baby with you. Yes?'

'Oh, yes,' said Mary.

She was overjoyed at the thought of not leaving her baby behind, and it would have been very short notice for Flossie.

Before the Russians left they repeated how important it was to remember their new names, Theodore and Natalie Roberts, not Natasha. Carl Shultz would come back to collect them at seven o'clock. As they stepped outside, Natalie noticed the yacht on wooden railway sleepers next to The Cabin. She read the name on the stern. She grabbed her husband's arm.

'Look. There is boat that save my life.' she cried.

Theo looked amazed. 'So small. You sail from France to England?'

'Now you see how brave these Englanders.' Was her reply as she linked her arm through her husband's.

Greg led them back to the gate where the car was waiting.

'We have very much tell when you come for dinner,' Natalie said as they entered the waiting car.

Carl gave Greg a wave as they drove away.

Mary and Greg were as one as they shared the enormous surprise and pleasure of this reunion. They dug out their best clothes and the carrycot for Alexander, along with all his needs for the evening. They made themselves ready for collection by Carl. He was early and so were they when he called on his phone to say he was outside the gate.

Carl accompanied them in the lift up to the private suite high on the hill overlooking Torquay and the harbour. The tall Russian greeted them.

Natalie led Mary to the bedroom, where the baby would be comfortable in his carrycot. With the door ajar he would be heard if he woke or needed attention. The suite was sumptuous. From the bar in the living room they were invited to choose their drinks. It was clear to Greg that they had been treated generously by their new American hosts. Mary said how much she wanted to know all that had happened to them. They chose from the menu offered and Theodore phoned the order to the restaurant manager for serving an hour later.

Then he addressed Mary and Greg: 'It gives us more pleasure than anything that happen to us since we flee to West, to see you and tell full story how you save our lives.'

He raised his glass and looked to his wife; she did likewise.

'We salute two kind and brave people who give us new life. We also have to thank your friend, whose real name we now know is David.'

They sipped from their glasses and lowered them to the table.

'David, who arrange this meeting today, say we need keep no secrets from you. He say you took big risk for us. May we tell you all that happen?'

Greg nodded and Mary was quick to say, 'Of course, of course.'

'Please, I get you another drink. You tell them, Mllaya Moyna, my sweet, sweet wife. It was you they save.'

NATALIE'S ACCOUNT

While Natalie was staying with her baby after his operation in the Berlin (East Sector) hospital she was provided by the CIA with false papers for releasing the child into the care of specialist doctors. Natalie carried her little baby from the ward to the 'doctors' waiting outside in a motorhome with East German number plates. Supplied with false papers authorising specialist treatment in a German Democratic Republic (GDR) hospital near Leipsig, they cleared Checkpoint Charlie, and instead of heading south they made the shorter journey westwards crossing into the Federal Republic of Germany. Here at Helmstedt, now bearing French number plates, they became six tourists and a baby with French passports.

The CIA had laid a decoy trail from Berlin to Leipsig, and then south through Czechoslovakia and Austria to Italy in case the Stasi (the GDR state security force) suspected anything when they didn't turn up in Leipsig.

Shortly after crossing into Belgium near Aachen they discovered that her baby had died. It was imperative that they drove on westwards to meet

Mary and Greg in Cherbourg. During the drive through Belgium, and despite Natalie's distress, all six of them agreed that they would bury the child in a temporary grave in France. The five agents were French citizens working for the DGSE (Direction Général de la Sécurité Extérieure). They promised the mother that a legitimate burial would be arranged at a later date. They drove on through the night and crossed into France.

As luck would have it the lay-by they stopped at just over the border in north-east France near St-Amand-les-Eaux was adjacent to a small field next to the village church – a location that they could easily find later. They did not know at the time that they had actually buried the baby in consecrated ground. The field had been purchased by the church many years ago to be used one day as an extension to the graveyard.

The burial had been exactly as Jacques had told Mary and Greg in Cherbourg. They emptied the metal toolbox belonging to the motorhome to use as a coffin, on top of which they placed a heavy stone from the wall and covered the grave with further earth and leaf litter. The large parked vehicle had hidden them from view as they dug the small but deep hole on the other side of the wall with the pick and shovel that was part of their touring gear. It was just before dawn.

'You know what happen after,' continued Natalie. 'We go England.' She went on to explain, the pain from her memories evident and in her faltering English, how a few days ago she and her husband flew to France and met the five Frenchmen who had brought her safely on the journey from Berlin to Cherbourg. They had made all the arrangements for the exhumation, post-mortem, and inquest required by the French authorities. A burial permit was issued by the prosecutor. 'At that small church in Eastern France the priest laid to rest our little one,' added Natalie. 'The headstone reads "*Alexander – age nine weeks –1986*". We give to church money to maintain graveyard many years. It will always remind us price of freedom.'

At this point, Mary leaned across and took Greg's hand in hers.

'Oh, my dearest, I am so sorry. You were right,' she whispered very quietly.

'Come,' said Natalie to Mary, taking her hand. 'We see if Alexander OK.'

They went together to the bedroom to check on the baby. He was fast asleep. The Russian girl moved close to Mary.

With her arm around Mary's shoulder she whispered in her ear, 'I pregnant, I tink. You no tell husband when you tell me you pregnant. I no tell mine.'

They laughed softly together and rejoined the two men. Theo poured them more drinks as the staff knocked and came in to lay the table for dinner.

'After our dinner I tell you about me,' said the Russian. 'I tell you about good friend Sergei, who you also rescue. I tell you how all three of us knew that KGB had suspicions. We had to act in hurry.' He put his arm around Natalie. 'My sweet, she already scared when she was – how you say? – *interrogated* in Lubyanka, about me and our friends.'

Mary thought she had heard correctly the remark about Sergei being rescued. Greg *knew* that she had heard correctly.

The situation was saved for him by the staff returning with the food. Theo had spared nothing in his attempt to please them. The sight of caviar, served in ice-cooled glass dishes, brought memories to Greg of minor adventures compared with the part they had played in Natalie's dash for freedom.

The meal was superb. When all was cleared away the Russian lived up to the deep-red silk-faced smoking jacket he was wearing and produced Havana cigars and a beautiful silver cigarette box. The other three declined his offer. They did not smoke.

He asked if he might indulge, moved over to the large sash window and dropped down the top half, checking that the curtains were wide open. The lights from Torquay, right along Torbay, past Paignton, to Brixham in the distance, twinkled below. He chose a huge corona, which he pierced and then lit with much gusto and obvious pleasure. They settled to hear what he had to say.

THEODORE'S ACCOUNT

Theo was a senior diplomat at the Russian embassy in Kensington, London. He had been there for two years and only managed to see his wife in Moscow every six months or so. Several years ago he had been approached by the CIA. His first concern, however, was for his wife. She held an important post with the State Nuclear Energy Bureau. They had serious misgivings about the morality and ethics of their country's politics. Although offered inducements to defect, Theo would not consider it unless they could go together. The CIA contact was just an insurance policy.

On Theo's visit home for Christmas last year they had entertained their good friend Sergei at their Moscow flat. Whether it was because of the softening of the political atmosphere or maybe the excellent vodka before, during, and after their dinner doesn't matter, but no longer fearful of bugs in the apartment they had been more frank with each other than ever before.

Sergei, a bachelor, is a Soviet Union citizen of Arabic extraction and a member of Moscow's Middle East Section of the diplomatic corps. He travelled widely. In addition to English he spoke several dialects of Arabic. They did not know what drove him to reveal to them that he had been working for the West for some time.

'When he knew he had reached sympathetic ears,' said Theo,' he tell us that he had been recruited by the Americans as well as British long time ago. My wife, now four months pregnant, confessed she not approve of Soviet nuclear programme. She had concluded that there was more interest in arming the enemies of the West than the peaceful application of nuclear power, for which she had been trained. She talk of another nuclear scientist, Andrei Sakharov, Nobel Prize winner and famous dissident. He banished from Moscow, and still detained under house arrest after five years. We have doubts about our government ever telling the truth. The three of us know about leak of anthrax from biological-warfare laboratory, but denied by Kremlin. Over sixty people die.'

That evening on Christmas Day they formed a bond of like minds. Two weeks prior to the birth of her baby in April his wife had been "invited" by the KGB to "visit" the Lubyanka prison, where the questioning about her husband and friends was none too subtle. Then, after the birth, she had unwisely criticised the government to a friend about the withholding of information on the Chernobyl nuclear disaster. Shortly after that she received a visit from a so-called nuclear physicist, asking about her opinion on the incident. She could tell that this man was not versed in the study of physics. She knew that again this was the KGB. It was then that the three friends became aware that they were under observation and in great danger. They had to act.

Their French, American, and British contacts promised to arrange for their defection. The order in which they were each spirited away was dictated by the degree of imminent danger from the KGB. Another invitation to the basement of the Lubyanka for any one of them would have had them all exposed.

'You know, Soviets use any method to obtain

information,' said Theo. 'I was obliged to return to my embassy in London. Through my English contacts I say we have made our decisions. We were offered freedom, good positions in America, new identities, and comfortable homes. A month after baby Alexander born he diagnosed with serious heart condition requiring specialist surgery. My wife was told by authorities this only available in East Berlin. She know otherwise. This reminded her yet again of Sakharov, who had been force-fed for going on hunger strike because his wife was refused permission to go abroad for medical treatment. Natalie had applied to go to paediatric hospital in Geneva that had highest success rate in the world for procedure required for our son. This request was denied. She told to go hospital in East Berlin.'

There then was no doubt, in either Theo's mind or his wife's, that she was being restricted from going abroad, and confined to East Germany where the Stasi could keep an eye on her. Meanwhile Sergei had an assignment in Saudi Arabia, where he felt safe for the time being, but he knew that if Theo or Natalie were exposed for their views he would be recalled to Moscow purely on the basis of association, and then become subject to the regime's maximum scrutiny.

Danger for Theo and his wife had now reached "critical" level. Their decision to flee immediately was prompted by a promise, from the CIA, that the world's most advanced treatment for their baby son would be given the moment they stepped onto American soil. An elaborate plan was drawn up for her escape from the East Berlin hospital

As soon as the CIA learned that Natalie had successfully cleared into West Germany they informed Theo's English contact, who arranged for him to "disappear" before he came under suspicion in London. He was almost dragged out of bed from his Chelsea flat and transported to a safe house in Surrey. There he was assured that, with the Schengen Agreement in force since June of last year, having safely crossed into West Germany his wife and son would be safe on their journey to Cherbourg. They did not tell him how she or he would get to America. Later, in the middle of the next night, the two of them were reunited at an airfield in the south of England and seven hours later they were in Boston, USA.

They had time during that journey across the Atlantic to ponder on the morality of betrayal of their country, on who was to blame for the death of their son, and on the price they were paying for the cause of world peace. Even the joy of being reunited with their friend Sergei a little later could not remove their feelings of guilt and loss.

Theo drew hard on his cigar as he finished his narrative. He was looking sad. He took his wife's hand as he realised he had just reminded them of the downside to their decision.

He concluded, 'The French coroner made open verdict, so we never know if our son live if we take him Geneva or if he survive journey to America, and of course we have no way to check GDR hospital records.'

There was a long pause.

Greg broke the silence: 'If it is of any help to you – and I am much older than both of you – I have also been faced with difficult moral decisions about which I have had many doubts. Apportioning blame is a pointless exercise. It can destroy a marriage; and hindsight is a wonderful thing, but also pointless. Mary and I are saddened by the death of your baby son, but you are young and have each other. Could not making a new life together mean just that very thing?'

Without knowing what had passed between the two wives, Greg had touched on the secret that Natalie had revealed to Mary in the bedroom earlier. Natalie moved closer to her husband.

Mary rose to her feet. 'Come, Natalie – let us have a look at Alexander. He will need feeding soon. He has been so good and we really should be going home.'

When they were in the bedroom, Mary explained to Natalie that she had not said a word to Greg about her pregnancy. They joined the men again. The women did not know if Theo had replied to Greg's question. He gave Mary and Greg an address in the USA where "the Roberts" could be reached. Fond farewells were exchanged and big hugs repeated.

As they made to leave, Natalie whispered in Mary's ear, 'I tell him tonight.'

The Norfields said little as they were driven home and then, nearly at the end of the journey, Carl spoke: 'You guys may talk freely if you wish.

Captain Worthy is a good friend of mine. This meeting would not have come about if it had not been for him. He also arranged everything in France for them. He has told me a lot about you. We are all in this together. I was the *taxi* in Lymington who drove Sergei to Lasham.'

Mary gave Greg a quizzical look. This time she knew there was something that needed explaining. Greg for his part was beginning to think that the old Commander's policy of only discussing matters amongst themselves on a need-to-know basis was preferable. He knew that once they were on their own Mary would pursue the references to Sergei and Lymington. He reckoned he had barely five minutes to prepare his explanation. Was this the time to come clean?

The moment the car pulled up at the yard gate the baby started to cry, which mercifully for Greg took their attention. As they entered The Cabin Greg was quick to offer to feed the child and lay him down for the night.

'We've had a long day,' he said to Mary as he warmed the milk. 'Don't know about you, but I'm also ready for bed?' His raised eyebrows indicated this was more in the form of a question, and Mary understood.

'Greg, my darling, I feel terribly guilty.'

'So do I,' he said. 'Let's snuggle up in bed and feel guilty together!'

It seemed that by silent and mutual consent they fell asleep the moment their heads hit the pillow.

Alexander did not wake them that night until it was getting light. It took them a few minutes to realise they did not have to open the office until the following Thursday. Over a cup of tea they looked at each other and laughed.

Greg believed the best method of defence was attack: 'Do we open the confessional now, or wait until Sunday?' he enquired with a grin.

She smiled, put her arms round his neck and kissed him.

'I really am truly, truly sorry. I was convinced that we had buried that baby at sea. I can tell you now that as we pushed the bag overboard I muttered what words I could remember of the Burial at Sea service that my father had spoken many times. Why then did Natasha, as she was then, cry out so loud when you attacked the bag with your marlinspike?'

'In that bag', said Greg, 'was all that was left of her old life. She had been ordered to destroy every piece of evidence of identity including the only photograph she had of her son. There I was, actually carrying out the destruction in front of her very eyes. She was grief-stricken and desperately tired.'

'You know, my love,' said Mary,' you have far greater perception than I have given you credit for. You are right of course. You were right to believe her and not me at the time. Now you know why I feel so guilty.'

'My lovely, lovely Mary, I remember soon after we were married we lay in bed one night in that old caravan and had a long discussion about our involvement with the Intelligence Services. We are both guilty, and yet neither of us is guilty. To some, being economical with the truth is a form of lying. We have lied to each other. You are going to ask me about Sergei. To delay imparting information to someone can be interpreted as lying. We have both done it. It took you a very long time to tell me that it was actually you that got me recruited in the first place! I said to Theo last night, if you remember, about hindsight being a wonderful thing and how pointless it was trying to apportion blame. You are not guilty of anything, my darling, except maybe of loving me.'

'Good. That very definitely makes me guilty!'

'Now I'll tell you about Sergei,' said Greg. He told her everything about the Lymington passage in *L'Enterprise.*

She listened in silence. Then she said, 'I'm still not sure that the end justifies the means, but I remember we promised that night to keep faith with the cause. That cause was our small contribution to world peace. I think Daddy would have approved.

Blessed are the peacemakers for they shall be called the children of God.'

(Christ – Sermon on the Mount).

FIN

ENDNOTE

On the 19th of December 1986, as Mr and Mrs Roberts, defectors to the West, were making their plans to covertly return to Europe to bury their son, Andrei Sakharov, the world's best-known human-rights activist at the time, was released from nearly seven years' detention in Gorky by Mikhail Gorbachev, the new General Secretary of the Communist Party of the Soviet Union.

Greg, Mary, Theo, Natalie and Sergei, the latter a friend of Gorbachev, could be forgiven for believing in some small way that by their actions and sacrifices they may have influenced the Soviets in their adoption of *perestroika* and *glasnost*, and moved them just a little bit closer to peace with the West.

R.G.